HIDDEN ENEMIES

BOOK NINE OF THE EMPIRE OF BONES SAGA

YOWLING
CAT PRESS

BOOK NINE OF THE EMPIRE OF BONES SAGA

HIDDEN ENEMIES

*What you
don't know...*

...can kill you!

TERRY MIXON

BESTSELLING AUTHOR OF *THE TERRA GAMBIT*

Hidden Enemies

Published by Yowling Cat Press ®
Print ISBN: 978-1947376120
Edition date: 08/24/2018

Cover art - image copyrights as follows:
DepositPhotos/magann (Markus Gann)
DepositPhotos/innovari (Luca Oleastri)
DepositPhotos/mik38 (Miguel Aguirre Sanchez)
DepositPhotos/Elenarts (Elena Duvernay)
DepositPhotos/@Kevron2000 (Kevin Carden)
Donna Mixon

Cover design and composition by Donna Mixon

Print edition interior design composition by Terry Mixon and Donna Mixon

Editing services by Red Adept Editing
Reach them at: http://www.redadeptediting.com

Audio edition performed and produced by Veronica Giguere
Reach her at: v@voicesbyveronica.com

TERRY'S BOOKS

You can always find the most up to date listing of Terry's titles on his Amazon Author Page.

The Empire of Bones Saga
Empire of Bones
Veil of Shadows
Command Decisions
Ghosts of Empire
Paying the Price
Reconnaissance in Force
Behind Enemy Lines
The Terra Gambit
Hidden Enemies

The Empire of Bones Saga Volume 1

The Humanity Unlimited Saga
Liberty Station
Freedom Express
Tree of Liberty

The Fractured Republic Saga
Storm Divers

The Scorched Earth Saga
Scorched Earth

The Vigilante Duology with Glynn Stewart
Heart of Vengeance
Oath of Vengeance

Want Terry to email you when he publishes a new book in any format or when one goes on sale?
Go to TerryMixon.com/Mailing-List and sign up.
Those are the only times he'll contact you. No spam.

DEDICATION

This book would not be possible without the love, support, and encouragement of my beautiful wife. Donna, I love you more than life itself.

ACKNOWLEDGEMENTS

Once again, the people who read my books before you see them have saved me. Thanks to Alan Barnes, Tracy Bodine, Michael Falkner, Cain Hopwood, Kristopher Neidecker, Jay Nedds, Bob Noble, Andrew Olivier, Jon Paul livier, John Piper, Bill Smith, Tom Stoecklein, Dale Thompson, and Jason Young for making me look good.

I also want to thank my readers for putting up with me. You guys are great.

1

_____

Kelsey Bandar stood at the edge of the bazaar and tried to take everything in. People everywhere were shouting and calling to one another, likely hawking their wares. She didn't speak Pandoran, so that was just an educated guess on her part, however.

The similarities to places she'd seen in old Terran movies was striking. Particularly since everyone was dressed for the hot, dry climate in flowing clothes, mostly light colored with bright sashes and wraps around their heads. They looked like blue alien Bedouins.

Her guide had provided her with the same kind of clothes so she didn't stand out. They felt strange to her, the cloth both heavier than she was used to and somewhat coarser against her skin. She'd chosen to go with a bright-red sash and head wrap to hide her blonde hair.

Unfamiliar scents filled the air around her. Most were aromas from spices in open bowls at a few tables nearby, but some came from vendors cooking delicacies for the hungry crowd.

Well, perhaps delicacy was the wrong word. That made it sound as if the food was prepared for discerning diners at a fancy restaurant. As the daughter of the Terran emperor, she'd eaten at such places many times. Good food but not nearly as satisfying as nachos and a beer at a flea market.

Which, she realized, was exactly what she was looking at. Just like the ones at home, even though it was laid out differently and had a desert feel.

Aside from the aliens. While there were humans in the crowd, they were few and far between. One in a hundred at most. Probably fewer.

Every other being present was a Pandoran. That was the name she'd given them when her people had discovered their preindustrial society on the far side of an unexplored multiflip point.

The Pandorans were so close to being human that it beggared the imagination. They averaged a little taller and had arms and limbs that were of the same proportions and in the same places. Their eyes were a little larger, their teeth a little more pointed, and their noses somewhat more slender.

The similarity was amazing until one got to their bluish skin tones. The youngest of them were a pale blue that shaded duskier as they aged until the elderly were almost midnight in color. Their hair was dark without exception. No greying for them.

Her medical people had discovered just how such an unexpected parallel development had occurred, but the information had raised far more questions than it had answered. In the distant past, someone had manipulated human DNA and relocated these people here.

While her doctors were still wrestling with the time scale involved, it had to be much farther into the past than humans had had space travel. Aliens had done this. Real aliens, like Omega. Not him or his people, of course. They'd left this universe for an alternate dimension and never known about flip points.

She hadn't told them yet and that was, thankfully, a problem she could put off until later.

They'd only just made contact with the Pandorans and knew virtually nothing about their society. That was the reason she was here. Well, one of the reasons.

Kelsey couldn't imagine how she was going to get a handle on everything that needed doing. There was just so much needing her attention. Yet this initial contact had to be from her.

She could solve one problem by getting something to eat. The heavenly scent of the roasting meat was making her mouth water.

Kelsey turned to Derek. Her guide was the son of the ruler here in the Kingdom of Raden. A warrior, he towered over his fellow Pandorans, which meant he was close to two-thirds of a meter taller than she was.

At first, she'd wondered if the Pandorans watching them thought she was a child. At a meter and a half, Kelsey was far more petite than most women. In the presence of such a large man, she probably didn't strike most people as more than a teen.

Derek's name was longer and significantly harder to pronounce in the Pandoran tongue—she'd had him recite it for her, and he'd laughed when she'd tried to repeat it—so the tradition was for them to use a simpler name when dealing with humans.

"Could we get something to eat?" she asked. "I'm starving."

With her Marine Raider enhancements, Kelsey was always hungry. Thankfully, after several years of being in this condition, she was no longer embarrassed by her gargantuan appetite.

There was a spicy scent coming from a haunch of meat cooking over a fire nearby. She gestured toward it as her preference.

"Of course," he said, his Standard unaccented.

He and his people had learned to speak the language when the survivors of the Clan battlecruiser *Dauntless* arrived on their planet sixty years ago. They were one more complication she wasn't sure how she was going to handle.

"Roasted varl is a tender meat with an aftertaste that both our peoples find pleasant," he said. "I suggest you find another vendor though. The scent you are probably smelling is a spice called Jedawa. Most find it quite hot."

Kelsey felt the corners of her mouth quirk up. "Now I have to know what it tastes like."

"Don't say that I didn't warn you."

The Pandoran noble stepped over to the vendor and exchanged some coins for two hunks of roasted meat on sticks and two crude flagons of what looked like beer.

She helped him carry the purchase to a rickety wooden table set on the smoothed flagstones. Other diners were seated around them, sampling various kinds of foods.

With Derek's warning in mind, she took a tentative bite of the meat. It *was* spicy but not so hot that it ruined the taste of the food.

Kelsey closed her eyes and tried to fit the meal into her previous dining experiences. The varl tasted like venison, she decided. It was tender and rich. She could easily envision adding something like this to her diet going forward.

Considering that none of them knew how long they'd be orbiting Pandora, getting some trade going for food was yet another task she had to see to, but she wasn't going to let worrying about it ruin her lunch.

The spice was a bit much for general consumption, she decided. Maybe half as much would be a better fit. Or something else entirely. Though she vowed to make sure Talbot got the full experience first. She wanted to watch her husband squirm.

She turned her attention to the beer. It was good and tasted very much like some she'd sampled on Avalon. It was a pale ale of some kind and the aftertaste was quite pleasant.

"This is good," she said after taking another bite of the meat. "A bit spicy, but I can deal with that. I'll want another stick before I'm done. The beer is great too. A local brew, I assume?"

Derek chuckled. "In our society, almost all food and drink are locally produced. I couldn't tell you who brewed this, but I agree it is one of the better ones I've had over the years."

"Did you have beer before *Dauntless* crashed on Pandora?"

His smile widened. "We did have a society before humans came. Beer has been a staple of our people for as long as we've kept records. Though I will admit that humans have brought innovation even to that. They ferment some powerful liquors with new and interesting flavors."

Kelsey nodded. "Humans do like their booze. I'm going to have to talk with someone about food and such for my ships at some point. We're outfitted for long journeys, but with *Audacious* damaged, we might be here for a while."

In fact, the carrier might be there forever if they couldn't repair her flip drive.

Derek nodded seriously. "Once you've revealed yourself to my father, I'm certain that trade can be quickly and easily established. You undoubtedly have much worthy of trade."

That was the reason she was here in the capital city of the Kingdom of Raden. She wished there'd been a secure way for Derek to get word to his father, but the man hadn't trusted anything other than speaking in person for knowledge of the new humans on their world.

A pinnace had dropped them off within walking distance of the city before dawn, and they'd made their way in on foot. Now they were waiting for Derek's human partner, Jacob Howell, to get back from the palace.

Jacob was something of a spy for Clan Dauntless, but he worked hand in hand with the Kingdom of Raden. He knew how to get into the palace without raising any eyebrows.

As if conjured by her thought, Jacob stepped out of the crowd beside their table. His expression hinted at bad news.

"We need to get you out of here," he said to her in a low voice. "Someone knows you're here."

"Who?" she asked as she stood, her excellent meal forgotten.

Two human males entered the square to her right and almost immediately spotted Kelsey and party. They started through the crowd with determined and displeased expressions.

Derek stood. "Take her. I'll distract them."

Jacob took Kelsey by the elbow and guided her away from the oncoming men. "We can get out of the square and lose them in the side streets."

"Why are they after us?" she asked as she allowed herself to be taken away.

She knew she wasn't in serious danger. With her Marine Raider enhancements and the concealed weapons under her loose clothes, she could handle ten times that many people without being in any trouble at all.

He opened his mouth to respond but stopped dead in his tracks when two men blocked their escape route. They were armed with swords, though those were still sheathed, and seemed as displeased as their fellows.

One stepped forward. "Stand fast, Jacob Howell. I summon you and your companion in the name of Clan Dauntless."

Kelsey moved her hand closer to her stunner, but Jacob didn't look as if he intended to resist.

"Damn the luck," he muttered.

"What did you do?" Kelsey asked.

"Nothing this time. They're here for you."

She swiveled her head toward him. "Excuse me?"

"My name is Isidro Poston," the man in front of them said to her. "In the name of Clan Dauntless, I instruct you to accompany me to the clan chapter house at once to explain yourself."

"That's going to be something of a challenge," Jacob said. "But one we cannot avoid at this point. I suggest we accompany them, and I'll try to make this less painful for everyone."

Kelsey considered raising hell but decided that might make enemies she could ill afford at a time like this. Instead, she forced herself to relax.

The two men from the other side of the square were now standing behind Jacob with Derek off to the side. The alien man shrugged.

"This had better be entertaining," she warned Jacob. "This hasn't been a very fun week."

"It will undoubtedly be entertaining," he said with a small smile. "The question will be who laughs loudest."

* * *

COMMODORE ZIA ANDERSON surveyed the parts spread out on the battered wooden table in front of her. There was a disassembled coolant transfer conduit and what looked like the electronics from a life-support substation. All of the pieces were heavily corroded.

Efrain, the Pandoran that Derek had assigned to watch over her before he took Kelsey to the capital, stood passively behind her, but he noted her glance back at him.

"They are sorting the recovered debris, cleaning it, and attempting to determine what use it might currently serve," he said in a diffident tone.

That made sense. There was a lot of similar activity going on around them. Hundreds of Pandoran workers were processing debris on the covered tables surrounding the wrecked hulk of the battlecruiser *Dauntless*.

On her other side, Carl Owlet shook his head. "Won't do them any good. Those circuits are fried."

The young scientist was accompanying her to find out if by some miracle the battlecruiser's flip drive was salvageable. The odds against that were long, but it never paid to ignore the obvious first play.

Carl had declared in advance that the flip drive was toast, even if it had survived the crash. He was certain that it had burned out in the same way as her ship's had on the transit from the Clan system called Icebox through the multiflip point.

She prayed he was wrong, or they were going to be here a *very* long time.

"The conduit itself might be used to transport any number of things," she told the young man somewhat repressively. "The circuits might yield rare elements, and the alloys might prove useful. Don't think that getting them back into service is the only use for something like that."

Carl grunted a little but nodded. "I see what you mean, but I stand by my original impression."

Zia gestured for Efrain to lead them on. As interesting as this was, it wasn't getting the survey of the wreck done any faster.

The stealthed drones she'd deployed to watch the crash site had already revealed that the engineering section was somewhat intact. As the flip drive was a large piece of equipment, that might mean it was still in there. Getting something like that out without having access to the massive hatch on the ship's underside would be almost impossible.

No one down here could tell her for sure if they'd taken it apart. They'd never bothered keeping records of what had been removed and repurposed over the last six decades.

The three of them walked between a series of buildings and came out in the vast area at the center of the artificial town. The wooden sheds and buildings had been built around the crash site and conformed to how the debris had ended up, so its layout was somewhat arbitrary.

Zia had seen battlecruisers before, obviously. That said, she'd never seen one sitting on the *ground*. That made a huge difference in scale. Comparing a ship with another ship, station, or distant planet didn't make it seem monstrously huge.

Dauntless was monstrously huge.

Even with a broken back and terrible tears in her hull, the wreck was still mostly intact. It towered above their heads, rising into the sky like some kind of alien skyscraper. A skyscraper covered with scaffolding so that the Pandorans could remove and access various things.

In addition to going up a tremendous distance, it was also quite long and wide. Zia and her companions had stepped out of the surrounding buildings near the engineering section. It seemed as if the ship stretched as far as she could see going forward, though she knew that wasn't true.

If she was going to compare it to something of a similar size, the wrecked ship covered three or four blocks going forward. Maybe five. It was two blocks wide.

"That really puts things in scale, doesn't it?" she asked in a hushed voice.

Carl took two steps forward and craned his neck to look upward. "I didn't realize these things were so tall. Intellectually, I know exactly how many decks they have and roughly how much space a deck takes up but that's not the same thing as seeing in front of me like a building."

Zia turned to their guide. "Can we go inside? What are the protocols? I assume someone owns this and we need to get permission to come in to look at things."

The Pandoran nodded. "The wreck is owned by the Kingdom of Raden. Clan Dauntless was paid both in money and land, among other things. Technically, my Lord Derek has sufficient authority to grant you access to *Dauntless*.

"That said, he does not have the authority to give you anything inside the wreckage. There is a company formed by the government that you would have to negotiate with to exchange anything from inside the wreckage for something they value."

She nodded. "So we're window shopping. How do we get in? This is the section of the ship that we're interested in."

The Pandoran man pointed at a wooden arch next to the ship. "Entrances like that have been set up at ground level. While the metals are tough, those splits are large enough to allow equipment in and out. Go wherever you like, and I shall explain our presence if anyone asks."

The wooden archway wasn't just to keep the weather out, Zia saw. Several metal beams were set up behind the wood to make certain the torn hull of the ship didn't shift.

"Just how stable is the interior?" she asked. She didn't aim the question directly at Carl, but she was interested in what both the Pandoran man and her young friend had to say.

Their guide spoke first. "With the understanding that this is a wreck, it's stable. There's no large-scale movement these days. That stopped in the first couple of decades.

"That doesn't mean things are completely safe. Things occasionally fall down, and new weaknesses in walls, ceilings, and floors are occasionally detected. When we become aware of such things, we reinforce them or restrict the area to prevent injury.

"I can't be more specific without knowing precisely where you're going to visit. If it's somewhere outside the zones we've cordoned off, I'll need to get one of the overseers to accompany us."

Carl gave the man a long look but finally nodded. "I can't exactly argue with their experiences over the last half century. If it were me, however, I'd be very careful. Ships like this were designed to be very tough, but when parts fail, they can fail catastrophically.

"Even though it might have been safe for the last sixty years, it wouldn't be fun to be in a location that has metal fatigue that suddenly decided to give way."

"We just want to go to the main engineering compartment right now," Zia said. "If something there convinces us we need to see another section of the ship, we'll let you know."

The journey through the wrecked battlecruiser was surreal. It reminded her very much of her time spent aboard *Courageous*. Except the air hung around them, still and dead. The smell of rust and mechanical decay was strong.

The interior lighting was a lot dimmer than Zia would've preferred, but at least it was powered by electricity. While the illumination was low by human standards, it was probably more than sufficient for Pandorans with their much better night vision.

She could only imagine how torches would behave inside such a confined environment. The smell would be awful, and the fumes from the burning matter would probably sting the eyes.

Zia gestured toward the haphazard lighting. "What's powering your lighting?"

"Residual energy from one of this vessel's power plants," the man said.

Carl stopped in his tracks and slowly turned toward the Pandoran. "Are you telling me that one of the fusion plants is still operational? We didn't detect anything like that from orbit, but I'll confess that I wasn't looking for that kind of activity."

The Pandoran shrugged. "You'll have to ask one of the overseers. All I can tell you is that these lights were rigged up during the time following the crash."

"That's not good," Carl said. "While it's certainly possible that some surviving engineering personnel verified the safety of that unit after the crash, it's been sixty years. I think we might need to look at that before we examine the flip drive."

Zia had personally seen what happened to ships when a fusion plant failed. She had no intention of being anywhere near a damaged unit that had been operational for decades.

"Let's go," she said, increasing her pace.

2

Lieutenant Colonel Russell Talbot watched the prisoners through the vid feed in his implant. To be certain they didn't concoct some kind of common story to tell him, he'd ordered all the prisoners be housed separately. *Audacious* was a large ship with plenty of space for thirteen prisoners.

Of course, they'd said almost the same thing about Commander Veronica Giguere and her officers. They'd thought they'd allowed plenty of space to securely restrain them, but they'd still managed to escape.

Commander Raul Castille, the Dresden orbital's security officer, had orchestrated the murder of most of his comrades, escaped the ship with Commander Giguere and her officers, and no one on Talbot's side had been the wiser until they were long gone.

Their plan had been something worthy of Kelsey, though his wife was loath to admit it. She thought she had a monopoly on making crazy plans work.

Admittedly, they'd upped the stakes for the princess when they'd kidnapped her mother at the same time. And, as mothers-in-law went, the woman was a real piece of work.

The situation had reminded him of a joke he'd heard in one of the old vids his wife favored. A man watching his mother-in-law drive off a cliff in his new ground vehicle—an expensive one—might be a bit torn about how to feel. He'd thought it was hilarious until recently.

After Castille had used the stolen orbital as a weapon to provoke the Clans, Princess Kelsey had tried unsuccessfully to talk the strangers down.

She'd had no choice other than to fight when they'd opened fire, though. She'd destroyed both Clan ships.

Talbot wished Castille had survived the fight so he could punch the man in the face. He'd really screwed things up.

Now they had Commander Giguere under secure watch in the medical center, her crew locked down under heavy guard in their original quarters, the few prisoners they'd kept from the Dresden orbital in the brig, and the new prisoners isolated so that they couldn't concoct some common story before Talbot started asking questions.

A dozen of the newcomers were human enough, though none of them had been in uniform when his people had picked them up. They were undoubtedly Clan officers of one kind or another. Considering that the New Terran Empire knew nothing about the Clans or their worlds, he was going to approach them with kid gloves.

Basically, all they knew thus far was that a task force had escaped the Fall of the Old Terran Empire, settled these worlds, and now called themselves the Clans. The leaders of those clans—based around the original vessels—worked together to make broader policy.

From what the Pandorans had indicated of their interaction with the survivors from Clan Dauntless, these were the kind of people that shot first and didn't really bother asking questions when they were done. The aliens thought humans in general were violent, though they admitted that after the most virulent of the crash survivors had fought to the death, the remaining humans seemed peaceful enough. Natural selection at work.

Kelsey's contact with Jacob Howell, the son of the current head of Clan Dauntless, had indicated that no one above the rank of lieutenant had survived the initial crash. The man had suspected higher ranking officers would've been even more resistant to integration into Pandoran society than those that had had to be put down.

It seemed that the people of the Clans were, well, clannish.

That was certainly going to make dealing with the people Castille had provoked difficult. Particularly since the man had blown up one of their battle stations and forced Kelsey to destroy two of their warships. They'd be out for blood, and no amount of talking was going to help.

He pulled his mind back to the task in front of him. Yes, questioning the dozen Clan prisoners was going to be interesting. But it was the thirteenth prisoner that had his attention now.

Unlike the others, this one was very different than anyone Talbot had ever seen before. The man was isolated in a small stateroom under the guard of three marines in unpowered armor. They were armed with stunners and had strict instructions not to harm the man even if he attacked them.

He was human, or so appearances would lead one to believe, but he sported tattoos on his cheeks and forehead and was dressed in flowing robes of pale green. The tattoos were stylized but definitely portrayed some type of predator bird.

"So how do you want to play this?" Major Angela Ellis asked him.

She was the executive officer of Kelsey's ship, the Marine Raider strike ship *Persephone*. She'd come over to give him a hand with the prisoners and consult with Commodore Anderson before the flag officer had headed down to the surface earlier.

Oh, and see her husband, of course.

Talbot still couldn't quite see what the powerfully built woman saw in Carl Owlet. Not that the marine had anything against his young friend, but the boy—and boy was the appropriate word—was very much a nerd. One not even old enough to drink. He'd come aboard the original mission as a graduate student, far ahead of his schoolmates back home his own age.

Angela, on the other hand, was just over two meters tall and was built to scale. Tough, strong, and combative, the marine officer didn't seem the type to be deeply in love with a scientist. No matter how much raw destruction said scientist had managed to wreak over the years Talbot had known him.

"I'm not quite sure," Talbot said, putting his previous thoughts aside. "He's not going to know about the New Terran Empire, of course. He'll suspect that we're from the Rebel Empire. I might not disabuse him of that notion either.

"We're eventually going to have to face up to explaining who we really are and why it wasn't us that attacked the Clans, but that can wait. Stuck here the way we are, we've got plenty of time to figure out precisely who we're dealing with."

She raised an eyebrow. "Aren't you a little concerned they're going to be coming through the flip point after us?"

He shook his head. "No. While they know the multiflip point exists, they've never been successful in utilizing it in the past. There's no reason to believe they're suddenly going to develop the technology necessary to get one of their ships through to this side."

Score one for Carl.

"Only his modifications to *Audacious*'s flip drive made it possible for her to make the jump," he said. "The same goes for the freighter we brought with us. While big, the freighter managed to come through with its flip drive intact. The carrier burned hers out.

"*Persephone* seems to be the largest ship capable of going through from the Icebox side unmodified. And it's the smallest flip-capable ship I've ever seen. No, I'm not worried."

Angela didn't seem convinced. "It's not as if the Icebox system has any other location we could've gone. The multiflip point is the only place we could've come through. They'll be asking themselves how we managed to get back, and they'll start working on it."

"I'm not sure that's true, at least not right away. They're going to tear that system apart looking for where some Rebel Empire warships might be hiding. In fact, that's *exactly* what our FTL drones are showing them doing.

"While they've stationed a pair of warships at the multiflip point, I don't think they really believe anybody went back through it. They're more worried other ships are going to come through from the Rebel Empire."

"They've got people at the planet itself, and we can be sure they're going to talk to the people marooned there," Angela objected. "That includes the roughly ten thousand people we captured with the Dresden orbital."

Talbot smiled. "Who are just as in the dark about who we are as everyone else on the surface of the planet. The only people in the Rebel Empire who know about the New Terran Empire are either dead, safely in the New Terran Empire, or on board this ship.

"While finding so many new people is going to be a shock to their systems, it's not really going to tell the Clans anything about us. I'm more than happy to let them jump to the conclusion it was the Rebel Empire behind the attack on them. After all, that's *exactly* what happened.

"The only indication they're going to find of the phrase 'New Terran Empire' is going to be that one transmission that Castille made before he blew up their station. For once, mistaken identity is going to work in our favor, I think."

"I never took you for an optimist." The inflection she put on the last word made it sound like a curse. "I'm going to put some money down that it doesn't work out the way you expect."

"Hardly anything ever does," he grumbled.

"Are we ready?" she asked.

"Not yet. I want one more opinion before we confront our unexpected guest."

* * *

COMMANDER VERONICA GIGUERE, late of the Rebel Empire Fleet—very late, as it turned out—sat in a small room just off the medical center. It offered a bit of privacy, but she knew that was an illusion. The New Terran Empire had her under very close surveillance.

Which in and of itself was hilarious. The fight with Raul Castille in the engineering compartment aboard the transport ship had ended with an explosion strong enough to render her incapable of more than resting.

The doctor had set her broken legs and made her broken ribs safe, but that didn't mean she could walk. No, she wasn't going anywhere for a while.

Regeneration was good for a lot of things. Knitting broken bones? Not so much. It took time and multiple sessions for that.

The hatch chimed and she used her implants to see who was calling. Commander Zac Zoboroski—*Audacious*'s chief medical officer—stood outside with a floating contraption. It looked like a chair.

Oh, and the four marines making sure she didn't crawl away when no one was looking were out there too. That seemed like overkill to her, but she'd already snuck out of their custody once. Talbot had muttered something about barns and horses, but the comment made no sense to her.

She opened the door with her implants and watched the Fleet medical officer come in with the floating chair.

"Doctor," she said, inclining her head. "What's that?"

"A grav chair," he said in his pleasant voice. "Believe it or not, this is the same one Princess Kelsey used after she got her Marine Raider enhancements. The doctor on *Persephone* had it in storage, and I realized it would be perfect for you."

Veronica studied the chair closely. It was crude but seemed functional enough. Definitely not up to Imperial standards.

"You made that?"

"The Pentagarans did. They were also cut off from the Empire during the Fall. Their grav tech was better than ours back then. I really need to have someone put together a better model, but we haven't exactly needed one until now."

"And why do I need this? Am I supposed to go somewhere?"

"Lieutenant Colonel Talbot requested your presence. It seems he wants your opinion on something. If, of course, you have time."

She chuckled a trifle bitterly. "My schedule happens to be wide open. Though I will admit that I'm not sure why he wants *my* opinion. I'm not exactly the most popular person on this ship right now."

"Don't sell yourself short," the man said, moving the chair around beside her bed. "Kelsey's mother is still aboard. Besides, getting out and about will be good for you. There's nothing forcing you to go, but I'd recommend it. Boredom slows recovery time."

He was right about the boredom, so she allowed him to help her into the chair. The controls were straightforward, and they were soon on their way. The marine guards fell in around them.

The trip through the massive carrier took a bit. She still marveled at the sheer size of the warship. The Empire no longer had anything like it. The AI Lords had seen to that.

Eventually, the doctor guided her chair through a hatch into what was obviously an observation room. The far wall had a viewscreen showing another compartment. There was a very strange man standing in the displayed compartment.

Remembering her manners, she noted that Colonel Talbot was not alone in this one. A tall, well-built woman stood beside him. She wore the uniform of a marine major.

"Thanks for bringing her down, Doc," Talbot said to Zoboroski. "We've got it from here."

The doctor departed, but the marine guards stayed. Yeah, they weren't trusting her very far at all.

"Colonel Talbot," Veronica said. "The doctor said you needed my opinion. I can't imagine why, but I seem to have some time on my hands. What can I do for you?"

"Commander Veronica Giguere," he said. "Allow me to introduce Major Angela Ellis, *Persephone*'s executive officer."

Interesting. Why a marine rank rather than a Fleet one?

The woman stepped over and extended her hand. While it was very subtle, Veronica noticed the other woman stumbled just a little bit as she walked.

"Are you okay?" Veronica asked as she shook the woman's hand.

The tall marine nodded. "I had some work done on my legs, and I'm still getting used to moving around. I'm told that in a couple of days no one will even be able to tell. Other than me."

"What kind of work?"

The tall woman glanced at Talbot, and he nodded.

"I've gone through the initial procedure to become a Marine Raider. They've fully enhanced my legs and put the pharmacology unit in. Once I recover from that, I'll get my upper torso done and get the more subtle add-ons. I'll be a fully functioning Marine Raider in a week or two. Until then, I'm still getting used to walking again."

Veronica nodded, impressed in spite of herself. She'd seen what Princess Kelsey could do. Not only her physical prowess, but they'd showed her a couple of recordings of the woman in combat. If an untrained woman of that stature, raised in the higher orders of her society, could cause such destruction, Veronica could hardly imagine what a trained marine of Ellis's size could accomplish.

"I'm impressed," she admitted. "I didn't believe your people would be able to begin the process so quickly after seizing the equipment on the Dresden orbital."

Ellis shrugged. "We already had the implant equipment. We didn't have any hardware. We got some of that before we even got to Dresden. It'll be a while before we can set up manufacturing for something like that, but we can handle all the marines we have on this mission, if we decide its safe."

That was frightening. *Audacious* carried a lot of marines. More than a ship her size should have. From what Veronica had heard, the New Terran Empire had stuffed a battalion of marines onto the carrier to seize the Dresden orbital.

"In any case," Talbot said, cutting off her thoughts. "That's not why I asked you down here. I'm much more interested in hearing what you think about the gentleman on the screen."

Veronica edged her chair closer to the display. The man seemed normal enough, if one discounted his clothing and those outrageous tattoos. Who put tattoos on their *faces*?

"He can't see us, can he?" she asked.

"No," Talbot said. "He can see the camera, however. He's been watching it for the last half hour. Frankly, I'm not certain what he finds so entrancing."

After considering the man for a full minute, Veronica shrugged. "I have to confess that I've never seen anyone quite like him. Admittedly, I didn't interface with the prisoners down on that planet when we escaped. Is that where he's from?"

The marine officer smiled. "He's from much farther away than that. Unless I'm very much mistaken, that gentleman is from a political entity called the Singularity. Have you ever heard of them?"

She shook her head. "Not that I recall. Of course, the Lords aren't exactly forthcoming when it comes to talking about people outside the Empire. Do I need to know something about them to give you my opinion?"

"I think it would be more useful to get your opinion without tainting it beforehand. I'm going to step inside and question him. You'll pick up some of his history from the questions I ask, but I'd like to get your take once we're done. Unless I miss my guess, this is going to be an educational meeting for you."

"For us too," Ellis said sourly. "And probably not in a good way."

3

Kelsey examined the city as their new companions escorted Jacob Howell and her to what they'd declared as the Clan Dauntless chapter house. She assumed that it was something like an embassy but didn't know enough to be sure.

They searched Jacob for weapons and confiscated what he'd been carrying: a sword, two knives, and that flechette pistol he'd tried to use on her when they'd first met. To her amusement, they didn't check her at all.

Boy, that was going to embarrass someone.

Derek had excused himself, indicating he was going to go speak with his father. The four men that had come for Jacob and Kelsey didn't attempt to stop him. Whether that meant they had no authority over the Pandoran or they just figured it wasn't worth their time, she didn't know.

The chapter house was a low building on the outskirts of the city. Only two stories tall, it covered a fairly large area. It was the equivalent of an entire city block, she guessed.

Made of a mixture of stone and wood, it blended in seamlessly with the buildings around it. There was nothing to indicate that it housed humans as opposed to Pandorans.

Just inside the open front door, two men stood guard. Based on their relaxed stances, they weren't expecting any trouble.

One of them grinned at Jacob and extended his hand to him. "I knew it was only a matter of time before they brought you in. What did you do this time?"

Jacob laughed. "Not what they think. Arturo, allow me to introduce Kelsey Bandar."

The man turned his attention to Kelsey, raising a hand to stop the escort leader when he opened his mouth to object, based on his expression. "I'll hear what you have to say in just a moment, Isidro. Don't you know it's impolite to speak over a woman? Behave yourself."

The man examined Kelsey with eyes that seemed far more discerning than her escort's. "There's more to you than meets the eye, Kelsey Bandar. I must confess unfamiliarity with your name.

"At first glance, one might take you for a child or a very young woman. That does you a great disservice, I think. After all, not very many women of any age wear swords underneath their robes."

"What?" the escort leader demanded, rounding to stare at Kelsey.

She'd arranged things so that the hilts of her swords rode low, but they were still high enough that she could control them if need be. Since they weren't all that long, concealing them hadn't been too difficult so long as she used the over-the-shoulder harness that had come with Ned Quincy's old weapons.

Kelsey saw the moment when the escort leader spotted the weapons riding over her shoulders. She raised a hand as soon as he reached toward her.

"Let's just get this out in the open. I don't answer to you, and I will not accept anyone attempting to put their hands on me. Rather than see you get hurt or deeply embarrassed, I suggest you stop right there and allow cooler heads to discuss this matter."

If anything, her words seemed to inflame the man's anger. Too damned bad.

"I will *not* be spoken to in that manner, least of all by a woman." He batted her hand aside and reached for the hilt of one of her swords.

Rather, he *attempted* to bat her hand away. What happened instead was her stopping his hand cold, twisting his arm behind his back, and forcing him to his knees as he cried out in anguish.

The man's three companions began drawing their swords but stopped when Arturo laughed and held his hand up.

"Hold!" the man called. "There will be no fighting inside this chapter house. Rash actions serve no one. Am I clear on that?"

When the three men hastily removed their hands from their weapons, Arturo gestured for Kelsey to release the man she was holding.

She complied, taking a step back and reaching up to flip her cloak away from the hilts of her swords. If someone else drew a weapon, she'd make a much more dramatic demonstration of why that was an exceptionally bad idea.

The man they'd called Isidro leapt to his feet and whirled toward her with a snarl on his face. "You will pay for your insolence!"

"Get in line, pal," she advised. "I've got far more dangerous people eager to make me pay for various things. You're not even in the top ten."

The man called Arturo grabbed Isidro's wrist as it darted toward his weapon. "Now, now, let's not be hasty. Tempers are up, and people are likely to say things that get under our skins. Walk it off, Isidro. Now."

Isidro tried to jerk his hand out of the other man's grip and failed. Only when that was readily apparent to everyone did Arturo release him. The offended man stalked deeper into the building.

"I'll be wanting my weapons back very shortly," Jacob called out after him, earning him a finger shot up over the departing man's shoulder in the universal sign of offended negation.

Arturo stood there with his arms crossed giving Kelsey a deeper examination. "I can't recall ever having seen a woman under arms. And, in any case, I'm unfamiliar with the material used in your hilts, and I thought of myself as very educated when it comes to weaponry.

"We've come to something of an impasse. You've been summoned to account for yourself, but I cannot allow anyone to bear arms before a tribunal of the clan. Yet here you stand, armed and defiant, completely unknown to me. How shall we solve this conundrum?"

Kelsey gave him a flat look. "How you solve this situation isn't my problem. I was going about my business when your people insisted that I come along whether I wanted to or not. Well, here I am. How are *you* going to solve this problem?"

The man threw his head back and laughed again. "You do have spunk! I cannot wait to find out what the true story behind your presence—and weapons—is. Yet I must insist that you disarm. I give you my word as a lesser chief of the clan that I will hold them safe and return them to you as soon as the tribunal dismisses you."

She shook her head. "Nope. I'm not here willingly, and I will stay only as long as I decide to. You don't get my weapons. Try again."

Jacob cleared his throat. "The situation is… complex, Arturo. I'd rather not explain it standing here in the foyer. Can we perhaps speak alone on this matter before you escort us to see the tribunal?"

The big man snorted. "That's rich, you saying something is complex. Everything you touch is complex. Very well. We'll make a stop along the way, and you can explain to me in private why this young woman needs to have a pair of swords riding on her shoulders and likely other weapons scattered about her person.

"You can also explain to me how she has the training—or the strength for that matter—to put a trained warrior's hand behind his back. And I confess that I cannot wait to hear you try to sweet-talk this situation with the tribunal."

He gestured for them to follow him deeper into the building.

The situation did have its amusing elements, Kelsey decided as she went in the indicated direction. Jacob had been right about that. With any luck, she'd still be laughing in a few minutes.

* * *

ZIA LED Carl and Efrain deeper into the ruined battlecruiser. She'd thought she'd known the fastest way to the main engineering compartment, but collapsed corridors and gutted areas made her circle around to take less direct paths.

Rather than taking ten minutes to get there, it took almost twenty. The low level of lighting meant that virtually all of the large compartment was lost to the darkness, but she could see areas where people were working in pools of dim illumination. None of the Pandorans even looked over at them.

"Which fusion plant is running?" she asked Carl.

"I'm not sure. The computer and support systems are either locked down or offline. Not even the engineering systems are available to my implants. I suggest we follow the power lines."

He pulled a powerful portable light from the bag over his shoulder and started tracing the lines of lights.

The brighter light drew some attention at last. Everyone turned to stare at them as the scientist led Zia and their guide deeper into the cavernous compartment. By the time Carl had stopped beside a fusion plant, a delegation of Pandorans was at their side.

Zia left the scientist to his work and smiled at the men. "Good morning. I'm Zia Anderson."

The leading Pandoran, an older man based on his darker skin tone, pointed at Carl. "Where did he find that, why is he using it, and what do you think you're doing?"

Efrain cleared his throat. "Commodore Anderson, allow me to introduce Overseer Halbreth. He is in charge of this site. Overseer, the commodore is here with Derek's approval. She has his full confidence."

The interruption only seemed to irritate the older man, so Zia wished the alien hadn't bothered.

"Overseer, my associate brought the light with him," Zia said. "He didn't find it here. That is true for everything in his bag."

The alien's eyes narrowed. "That isn't an acceptable answer. What is a 'commodore?'"

"A military rank. My associate and I are from… ahem, elsewhere."

Efrain didn't look pleased at her just saying that, but it wasn't as if she had a lot of choice. The aliens would know the truth as soon as Carl started trying to access the ship's systems.

Halbreth blinked. "Elsewhere? What does *that* mean?"

"We're from another star system," she said matter-of-factly. "We're not of the Clans or even the places they came from before they crashed."

The older Pandoran barked out a harsh laugh. "Impossible. How would one even prove something like that? What kind of game are you really playing?"

Before she could answer, Carl opened the access panel he'd been working on and peered inside.

Halbreth took a step forward. "Get away from that! You'll break it or kill yourself. I can live with the latter but not the former."

Carl looked back at the man and shook his head. "I'm fully conversant with the safety procedures for this piece of equipment."

He turned his attention to Zia. "The implant access is manually switched off. I need to turn it on. That should be safe enough to allow me to assess the plant's condition."

"Do it," she said.

Before the overseer could do anything, Carl reached into the fusion plant and touched a button. It changed from amber to green.

"The equipment is accessible," Carl said, stepping back and raising his hands. "Its status is remarkably good, but someone ramped it down below the rated minimum output and shut off the safeties. It was never designed to work that way, and the logs show a downward trend in safety margin over the last few years.

"It really needs to be taken offline and serviced, but it can probably keep going for a while if I bump the output up to minimum. There are risks of systems overloading, but if I don't, this plant will fail sometime in the next year or so. At that point, getting it online again will take significantly more effort on our part."

She turned to the Pandoran overseer. "You heard my associate. He can make this system provide more power for your lights and other uses and make it safer in the long run. Would that prove anything to you?"

The man snorted. "It would prove your insanity. Even the crash survivors knew little of this power generator. No one can change anything about it, and I refuse to allow anyone to touch it."

"He doesn't need to touch it. Carl, bump it to a safe minimum output."

That was a pretty substantial risk. If something went wrong, they'd be in trouble. Hell, they'd be in hot water even if it went perfectly.

The scientist didn't move, but the lights around them started coming on. The makeshift lights brightened too.

Halbreth stared up with a shocked expression as the overhead lighting came up to about sixty percent of normal and revealed the full extent of damage to the compartment.

Of course, along with the success came some failure. One of the consoles near the front of the compartment started smoking and abruptly shorted out in a cloud of smoke.

"Stop what you're doing," the overseer shouted. "Stop it! Guards!"

His cry drew several men into the compartment at a run with their swords drawn.

Zia hadn't anticipated this level of confrontation, so she raised her hands as she headed for the fire suppression unit nearest the smoldering console. "I'll put this out, if you don't mind."

She half expected the now suspicious aliens to stop her, but they allowed her to pull the fire suppression unit off the wall. It was as simple and uncomplicated as possible, so it was still good. She knew it would be because of the recovery efforts on *Courageous*.

Frankly, the console would stop burning on its own, but she wanted to be seen doing something that "corrected" the damage she'd caused.

It only took a moment to slap the console release, causing the top to spring up. She unleashed a spread of retardant powder on the smoking boards and then hit the kill switch to cut power to the console.

Zia noted the guards closing in as she set the fire suppression unit down and kept her hands where they could see them.

Overseer Halbreth walked over to her and scowled deeply. "You have created a safety concern by toying with things you had no business touching. I don't care who your sponsor is. You're expelled from this site and will not be allowed to return."

4

Talbot stepped into the compartment they were using to hold the man from the Singularity. It was a comfortable single occupancy cabin that had been stripped of anything that might serve as a weapon.

Two marines stood guard in the corridor and two more stood just inside the compartment. The outer pair were armed with stunners. The inner pair had their muscles.

The man with the tattoos, who was already standing, turned to face Talbot without saying anything. His expression seemed a bit superior. It reminded Talbot of how Commander Raul Castille had looked down his nose at the people from the New Terran Empire. Only more so.

Talbot stopped just inside the compartment and examined the man closely, allowing the silence to draw out. He wanted to see if the other man was the nervous type.

Under the tattoos that formed some kind of predatory bird, his features were average. Bland even. A nose neither large nor small, a mouth on the wide side with thin lips, and eyes of pale blue.

His eyes were his best features by far, in Talbot's opinion. Alive and intelligent, they studied him. The man still didn't speak.

The man's body seemed on the thin side under his loose garments. His arms—what Talbot could see of them—seemed somewhat scrawny. Not a warrior, most likely.

When it became clear that the prisoner wasn't going to initiate the conversation, Talbot smiled a little more widely. "A man with patience, I see. I'm Lieutenant Colonel Russell Talbot, Imperial Marines. Who are you?"

The other man's lips curled up just a little. "I'm your prisoner, though I expect that situation to change in the near future. The arrogance of Terrans is legendary among my people, but you picked a fight with the wrong people this time."

The man's Standard was excellent. It sounded like his native language, though what they'd learned led Talbot to suspect it wasn't.

"When you say your people, you mean the Singularity?" Talbot asked.

That caused the man's eyebrows to rise. "That isn't a name I expected you to know. Your Lords seem determined to eradicate all mention of the People from your records."

Talbot hadn't been aware they called themselves that. "We're full of surprises. What are the People doing with the Clans?"

The man's smile widened further. "You're shockingly well informed, Lieutenant Colonel. You may call me Theo."

"Shouldn't there be a number with that?"

This time the man's smile seemed genuine. "You astound me again, Lieutenant Colonel Talbot. I'm the only Theo here, but if you simply must know, I am Theo 309. Might this one inquire why you attacked the Clan warships? From what I saw, and to my stark amazement, they weren't the aggressors."

"We'll get to that," Talbot said. "First, allow me to compliment you on your Standard. It's excellent. And useful since I don't speak the tongue."

"You even know what we call our own language? I'm seriously impressed. No outsiders have spoken the tongue since the great sundering of the Terran Empire and the enslavement of the people living there. Your people."

"Since this is ancient history for you, how did your people fare when the AIs rebelled against the Terran Empire? Did the fighting spill across your border?"

The man who called himself Theo sat down on the edge of the couch and crossed his legs with an easy grace. "For someone who's surprisingly knowledgeable about my people, I'm amazed you don't already know the answer to your own question. Why is that?"

"Being educated about a historical entity doesn't mean knowing what's going on with them in modern times," Talbot said. "I've read documents and reports talking about the Singularity but, as you said, my people and yours have not interacted directly in quite some time.

"Unless of course you count the Clans as my people, which is only tangentially true. We sprang from the same source, but they seem to have developed their own personality."

Theo laughed at that last comment. "That's something of an understatement. A rather vast one. The ships that formed the Clans left the Terran Empire during the great sundering. Since then, they have developed some very peculiar societal quirks, I agree.

"One of those being that they are extremely xenophobic. They barely trust one another, much less anyone outside their circle of 'family.' By destroying one of their stations and several of their ships, you've assured that they won't rest until they've found a way to strike back at you."

That was very much what Talbot was afraid of. Castille had certainly done his level best to spoil any chance of a decent relationship between the New Terran Empire and the Clans.

"You're an outsider," Talbot pointed out. "If they're so xenophobic, how is it that you were aboard one of their ships? You certainly don't appear to have been a prisoner."

The man smiled. "Oh, I wasn't. I act as an envoy between my people and the Clans. We reached an accommodation quite some time ago, you see. It suits my people to grow the forces that may one day retake the Terran Empire.

"I'm not quite certain how thorough your knowledge of the People is. We have our own societal quirks too. Ones that caused us to leave the Terran Empire many thousands of years ago. We don't believe in implanting devices into our bodies, and we don't allow machines to control our lives. Perfection takes a different turn than the perversion your people created to enslave yourselves.

"It's an endless source of irony to me that the war caused by your sins have meant that the Clans are no longer able to follow that horrific process. One bright light in the sea of darkness that is the rest of their society.

"So, it serves my people's interests to strengthen the Clans into a force capable of once again ruling the Terran Empire. And it certainly doesn't hurt that we've made ourselves indispensable for when that day comes. Which, because of you, will likely be sooner than either of us thinks possible."

That certainly sounded ominous.

"Considering the shape these people were in when they escaped the Terran Empire and AIs, they certainly wouldn't have been in shape to fight without a lot of help," Talbot said. "What benefit does it serve the Singularity to build them up so much? Surely, they become a threat at that point.

"After all, you've probably done your part to make certain the Clans are xenophobic. Let's just say that the people from the Singularity have a reputation for being somewhat manipulative."

The man's smile deepened. "Oh, you *are* perceptive. I deny what you've said, of course, but appreciate the compliment. Your insight seems as keen as your imagination. My congratulations.

"Now, as a neutral survivor from the battle, I'm afraid I must request that you release me. My people took no part in this combat and have not raised arms against yours. While I doubt very seriously that your people will respect my diplomatic immunity with the Clans, if you wish to avoid making the situation worse, you'll let me go."

Talbot made an expression of doubt. "Didn't you just sit here and tell me that you were helping the Clans build a force capable of overthrowing the Terran Empire? That seems fairly hostile to me.

"No, I think we'll be holding on to you for now. If you decide to be cooperative, I'm certain that additional amenities can be provided to enhance your comfort. On the other hand, if you prove problematic, we have a nice cell in the brig waiting for you. Far less comfortable than this cabin."

Talbot stepped toward the hatch. "I suggest you consider very carefully how we're going to work together going forward, Theo 309. We'll speak again."

He stepped out into the corridor before the man could respond and allowed the hatch to close behind him.

Well, that hadn't gone as badly as he'd feared, but the man certainly wasn't a pushover. Getting real information from him was going to be difficult. Perhaps impossible. Time would tell.

Until then, there were a few other threads he could pull on.

* * *

VERONICA WATCHED the interview with interest. The strange man was very smooth. It seemed as if nothing Colonel Talbot said had fazed him. There was a lot going on under the surface and she doubted the man was going to give any information to his captors willingly.

The hatch behind her slid open, and Talbot stepped inside. "That didn't go nearly as well as I'd hoped. He's really good at this. Commander Giguere, what did you think?"

"I can't add anything to what you just said," she said with a shrug. "I've seen smooth characters like that before. Mostly diplomats and used grav-car salesmen. The kind of people that could lie to your face with a bland expression of mild interest. You're not going to get him to talk."

Talbot grunted. "I certainly hope you're wrong, but that pretty much matches my expectations too. We've got time to deal with him, I suppose. It isn't as if we're going to see Clan warships rushing through the flip point at any moment."

Veronica raised an eyebrow. "Perhaps I'm a bit biased, but what makes you think that you're so much better than them? Why can't they figure it out too?"

"Because they don't have Carl Owlet," Talbot said smugly. "The man is a freaking genius. Plus, they don't even know what a multiflip point is. Their understanding is basically what we knew back when we first discovered one.

"We were certain that whatever it was, it was a one-way trip. Nothing we could do managed to get a ship back through the flip point. No amount of toying around with power levels and so forth made any difference whatsoever.

"It took a ton of research to figure out what we were really looking at, and then Carl had to come up with a theory covering how we might exploit what he thought was there. Then he had to develop the hardware. That's not going to happen overnight."

Veronica shifted herself in her chair and shook her head. "That's being arrogant. They aren't going to find any of your ships back in that other system. They know there's enough force floating around somewhere to destroy two of their ships. Not to mention the fact that they almost certainly obtained some kind of scanner readings of the Dresden orbital before it rammed their station.

"By now, they have to realize that a significant force came through the Icebox flip point. When they don't find it, they'll know it had to have gone back through. Once someone knows something is possible, it's only a matter of time before they figure out how to do it."

Talbot grimaced. "I certainly hope you're wrong, but we've never managed to get out of any problem the easy way. It isn't as if we have a lot of choices at the moment. *Audacious* is trapped in this system. If they come for us, we're not going to be able to run."

"That's... unfortunate. From what that man said, the Clans don't seem like the forgiving types. Do you have any plans for repairing this ship? Is it even possible to repair it outside of dry dock?"

"That question is above my pay grade. We've got people down on the planet right now looking to see if the flip drive on the crashed battlecruiser is salvageable."

Veronica felt one of her eyebrows rise. "Crashed battlecruiser? I don't think I've heard this particular story."

"That's more because you were in the medical center rather than because nobody was going to tell you," Angela Ellis said, speaking up for the first time in a while. "There's a lot that we haven't told you, some because they haven't come up, and others because... well, you *are* the enemy."

Veronica slumped a little bit in her chair. "That's not particularly true anymore. I get that the AIs actually conquered humanity and the history I learned as a child was a lie.

"The problem is that I have no way to convince you of that. I want to help you. Really, I do. I've given up. Everything you've told us has been right. Still, you'll never trust me. You'll never trust any of us."

She could hear the bitterness in her voice. It annoyed her. One more thing she couldn't do anything about.

Talbot smiled. "Actually, that might not be true. I got a little piece of information last night that changes that particular set of circumstances."

He turned to Ellis. "Remember the freighter we captured at Dresden? Turns out it had a little secret cargo in a locked compartment. A brand-new AI."

His words sent shivers down Veronica's spine. "I hardly see how that's good news. Those things are monsters."

"Not if you utilize clean code from the very beginning," he said with a grin. "In this case, they didn't send any operating software with it at all. Just the hardware.

"Thankfully, we have a clean set of code in our database. The commodore was busy, so I ordered the AI brought over to *Persephone*. She has less room but is mobile. If trouble comes knocking, we'll want the AI leaving with us. It's too valuable to let someone take with the carrier.

"Once we have it put together, we can boot it from clean code, and it will be able to determine if you're telling the truth or not."

"How could it possibly do that?"

"That's going to take a little faith," he said seriously. "You have to allow it access to your implants to monitor your brain while you tell us how you've seen the light. It will be able to determine if you're being truthful."

"You want me to allow one of the Lords access to my *brain*?"

"It's not as if it's able to change anything in your memory. As they say, it's read-only access. Of course, you have to trust that I'm telling you the truth. That, I'm afraid, is the price of admittance. If you want us to trust you, you're going to have to trust us first."

None of that made Veronica happy, but she nodded slowly. "When are we going to be able to do it?"

The marine officer shrugged. "Maybe today, maybe tomorrow. I haven't been keeping a close eye on the progress. We'll have you on hand when we bring it online. I want you to see the difference between a free AI and one of your System Lords first hand."

"I'd say that I can't wait, but that would be a lie. Should I just go back to the medical center?"

He shook his head. "No. I'm going to stick my neck out a little and give you a chance to see what we're doing. Angela and I are about to have a little chat with Commander Renner. Would you like to come along?"

Violet Renner had been the incoming security officer about to replace Raul Castille on the Dresden orbital when Princess Kelsey had stolen it.

"I wouldn't hold my breath if I were you. She's going to be even less cooperative than Theo 309."

"Let's go find out," Talbot suggested. "It's not as if you have anything more pressing on your plate."

5

Kelsey followed Jacob and Arturo into a room just off to the side of the main entrance. It looked as if it were normally used for intimate private meetings.

The exterior wall used wood and stone as its primary building materials while the interior divisions were made solely of wood. The furniture was made of roughly hewn wood with padded seats covered in coarse leather.

Two columns formed from whole tree trunks supported the ceiling above. Someone had taken the time to carve images of a battlecruiser onto its surface. The art was relatively crude and in places inaccurate, but the general shape was unmistakable.

Once Arturo had closed the stout door, he turned to Kelsey and Jacob, planting his hands on his hips. "Jacob, who is this young woman, and why is she armed? And how is it possible for her to subdue a warrior like Isidro?"

Rather than answering, Jacob walked over to a small bar set into the wall, picked up a pitcher of what sounded like ice water from the rough plank, and poured himself a mug. "Does anyone else want water? This might take a while."

"I'll take one," Kelsey said.

Then she turned to fully face Arturo. "We were going to have this discussion with the king of Raden first, but I suppose I don't have a choice in telling you. The problem is that I'd prefer to do this as few times as possible."

The warrior considered her for a moment. "While I want to know the complete story, at this particular moment I'll settle for why you're armed and what the nature of your arms are. If you can convince me that you should retain those arms, I will let you speak to the tribunal while retaining them.

"This is something of a first for me. I've never heard of an armed woman. Well, nothing more than a knife used for self-defense anyway. Yet you carry swords, and those do not look like wooden hilts to my experienced eye. They're not even wrapped in leather. Explain this portion of the mystery to me."

"I'd do it if I were you," Jacob said as he handed a mug to her. "Arturo is much more reasonable than Isidro. Your story will be more than sufficient to make him an ally. And against slime like Isidro, one needs as many allies as possible. You can rest assured that idiot is going to speak against you at the tribunal."

Kelsey considered Arturo for a few seconds and then shrugged. This moment had been coming since she'd arrived. She'd reviewed the questioning of the prisoners they'd found on Icebox while they were there. The Clans took women from among the prisoners to other locations.

From what Jacob said, the Clans put women into secondary roles: homemakers and raising children. The men were responsible for protecting them.

She wasn't certain how willingly the women of the Clans submitted to this but didn't know enough to say they were treated as second-class citizens. Yet.

If she found that was true, she and Jacob would be having an unpleasant conversation. Kelsey wasn't the type to stand by and allow slavery, no matter how prettily it was dressed up.

"You want to know why I'm armed and what my sword hilt is made of?" she asked. "Easily solved."

She drank her water, tossed the empty mug to Jacob, and drew one of her swords. The short blades had originally belonged to Ned Quincy back when he'd been alive.

Even though his intelligence lived on as some kind of odd AI program, asleep for the moment while Carl Owlet searched for a way to relocate him to a new body or machine, he'd trained Kelsey in the use of these weapons until they'd become extensions of her body in combat.

In conjunction with her artificial muscles and combat enhancements, they made her exceptionally lethal in hand-to-hand combat. If those men at the entrance had attacked her, her blades would've gone right through both their weapons and their bodies. They were made of hull metal, just like regular marine knives, and the edges were measured in molecules of width.

Flipping the sword around, she extended it to the man on her palms. "I'd be very careful with that if I were you. It's much sharper than you can possibly imagine. Testing the edge will cost you a thumb."

Arturo hefted the sword, smiling indulgently at Kelsey. "I've spent my life around swords. Trust me when I say that I know what a sharp weapon can do."

With that, he lazily swung the sword at a handy chair that had obviously seen similar attention in the past. There were small nicks and cuts in the thick legs where people had banged their weapons against it in the past.

The blade of her short sword cut completely through not only that leg, but the leg on the other side. The chair immediately collapsed under its own weight with a clatter.

Arturo stood frozen, his attention riveted on the chair he'd just destroyed with a casual stroke of her weapon. After several heartbeats had passed, he turned his attention back to the sword and examined much more seriously.

"I'm grateful that I didn't chop at one of the supports," he confided to them in a quiet voice. "It would've been quite embarrassing to have the ceiling come down and kill me for my hubris."

"This weapon is very much like the knives our people could once make. Precious heirlooms from when the Clans fled the Terran Empire. Sharp as a demon's claw and indestructible."

Jacob nodded. "I have one, as does my father. The legends say they were once quite common in the Clans, but they've been hidden away until only a few are publicly acknowledged now. On this world, they are even rarer."

Arturo turned his attention to Kelsey. "I have never heard of swords formed in that same fashion. Where did you get these, and why are you carrying them?"

"They were given to me by my mentor," she said with a smile. "His name isn't known here so it wouldn't mean anything to you. He was once a Marine Raider in the service of the original Terran Empire."

The big man's smile turned a little cynical. "The Terran Empire died long before either of us was born. And while I'm quite familiar with how machines once kept people alive for miraculous periods of time, even those people did not live five centuries. You are pulling my leg."

Kelsey shrugged and held her hand out. "The story is true but complicated by technology I can't adequately explain. I have other forms of proof, but I'd rather not have to tell this story more than once. Your tribunal is going to doubt everything I say just as much as you do.

"Our little gathering here was solely so that I could convince you I was worthy to wield these weapons. Have I done so? If not, I believe I can put on a somewhat more… impactful demonstration."

He considered her words for a moment, shrugged, and returned her weapon to her in exactly the same manner she'd given it to him, only with a slight bow accompanying it.

"I certainly hope your demonstration is less destructive than my bumbling efforts. I'm certain we'd like to continue using this room, so demolishing it would be less than optimal."

"Oh, I can make my demonstration without destroying a single thing," Kelsey said with a smirk.

She sheathed her sword with practiced ease and walked over to the table. Smiling sweetly at Arturo, she reached out and picked up one end with just the tips of her fingers, being careful to watch her balance. Even with her incredible strength, she had very little mass when compared with something like the massive table.

Even with her strength and Graphene-enhanced bones, that put an incredible stress on her digits. Nevertheless, the heavy table rose two feet into the air with very little visual evidence of the strain she was placing on herself.

The two men stood there, thunderstruck. Jacob had never seen her exercise her strength in a manner like this. Arturo had undoubtedly never even considered this possible.

"If you boys would pick up the other end of the table, we'll move it out of the way so I have room to work."

As if sleepwalking, the two men picked up the other end of the table. From the strained expression on their faces, it wasn't nearly as light as they wished it were. Together, the three of them moved the table to the far side of the room. They quickly had the chairs sitting on top of it.

Except for the destroyed one. That went under it.

As soon as the floor was cleared and she'd gestured for two men to step aside, Kelsey drew her weapons and dumped Panther into her system. The world seemed to slow as the combat drug took hold, but she knew that her observers would see her movements as something faster than humanly possible.

As soon as the drug had sped up her thinking and nerve pathways, she launched into a fairly aggressive kata.

Much like a training dance, it was almost ritualized. Her slashes and strikes were inhumanly precise as she allowed her Raider implants to guide the angle and speed of her blades. She knew from watching recordings of herself in action that it seemed as if she were cutting her way across the room filled with opponents at lightning speed.

And the actions didn't just include blade work. Her powerful legs allowed her to run and jump to heights that a normal person couldn't dream possible. She made certain to run toward one of the walls and literally take several steps along it just below the ceiling before launching herself out in a move that any gymnast would be thrilled to be able to execute, landing lightly on her feet.

With her incredible physical prowess and agility, she leapt and flipped in midair, dropping behind imaginary enemies and dicing them. She continued at a pace that would have run a normal person into the ground after mere seconds.

At the end of the three minutes set, she sheathed her weapons and stood quietly before the two warriors, not even breathing hard.

"So tell me," she said with a deep smile. "Does that prove I've earned the right to carry these weapons?"

Jacob bowed low, an elaborate gesture filled with sweeping arms. "I was already convinced, but now understand how far short of reality my feeble comprehension was. You are not just a warrior or even a master, you are a demigod of battle."

Arturo's bow was far less flowery but similarly deep. "I have no objections to you bearing arms before the tribunal. In fact, I urge you to come speedily before them so that they may question you. I cannot imagine how what my eyes have seen is even possible, and I hunger to know the full truth about you, Kelsey Bandar."

She held up a hand. "Honesty compels me to admit that I'm armed with weapons far more deadly than these blades. These swords aren't even close to the most powerful weapons on my person.

"If someone like your friend wants to fight me, it will not turn out well for them. I realize that I don't look like much of a threat, but I'm the most dangerous person you've ever met."

The large warrior bowed again with a grin. "Then let's see if we can't avoid Isidro. The man is an ass at the best of times, but I'd rather not see his guts spilled all over the floor."

With that, Arturo led them from the small room and deeper into the Clan chapter house. They passed several sets of guards, all of whom bowed diffidently to the large warrior and allowed them past without delay.

At the rear of the chapter house were a pair of thick wooden doors. They were unadorned and covered with steel strips and studs, obviously made to resist being forced. Even with her strength, it might take a while to open them by hand. She had great personal strength but very little mass.

Maybe if she could get a grip under the door and plant her feet, she could pull one free. Part of her longed to try, but that wasn't very neighborly.

Another pair of guards opened the doors and allowed the three of them into what was probably a communal dining hall as well as a location for ceremonies. The far side of the room had a raised dais with a long table set perpendicular to the entryway.

Three men sat at the table, all scowling toward Kelsey. Beside them stood a sneering Isidro. Based on his body language and the smirk on his face, he'd filled their heads with nonsense, and they didn't look nearly as receptive as Arturo had been.

Wonderful.

The center man cleared his throat. "How dare you defame our chapter house by bearing weapons and assaulting one of our warriors, woman! Identify yourself and submit to the will of this tribunal, or we will use every force necessary to subdue you."

Yep. It was going to be that kind of day.

6

Veronica thought she'd be going directly to meet the Rebel Empire security officer, but Doctor Zoboroski was waiting for her outside the small compartment where she'd met with Colonel Talbot and Major Ellis.

"Time for your next regeneration session," the man said cheerfully.

She'd already gone through three sessions and her ribs and broken bones were well set. That reduced the pain to almost nothing but didn't give her any additional mobility.

"Exactly how many sessions am I going to have to have before I can move around on my own?" she asked tiredly.

"I think we'll need an additional two sessions beyond this one, but you should be able to get around without that chair this afternoon. We can run a second one tonight and another in the morning. After that, I'll pronounce you healed and send you on your merry way."

She sighed a little bit at that, relieved. "I like you well enough, Commander, but I think I'll be happy to have a little bit more privacy. Even if it is under watchful eyes."

"That doesn't hurt my feelings. I'll give you another checkup after three or four days to make sure everything looks good, but so far you've been a model patient."

"As opposed to a model prisoner," Talbot muttered.

Veronica laughed. "If your Fleet is anything like mine, you'd have had an obligation to escape too. Besides, after some the stories I've heard about your Princess Kelsey, you should be used to this by now."

"Why is it that the women in my life have this drive to complicate things?" he asked, his eyes rolling toward the ceiling.

"Am I a woman in your life?" she asked, raising an eyebrow. "I hardly know you, and your wife is quite possibly the worst person to make jealous in the history of humanity."

"So true," he said with a sigh. "I'm going to set up things so we can see Commander Renner. Angela will go along to make certain you find your way back to the next interview room."

His expression grew serious. "This next session is going to be intense. If you want to sit it out while I go in and question her, I'll understand, but I'd rather have you beside me. You know far more about the Rebel Empire than I ever will, but I'll understand any reticence."

Veronica felt her eyebrows drawn together. "I haven't gone through this trustworthiness test of yours yet. Why would you let me sit in on an interrogation where I could ruin things?"

"Because I consider myself a pretty good judge of character. The AI will be able to confirm you're telling the truth, but I'm willing to give you the chance even though I might be wrong."

She wasn't sure how that made her feel. Part of her felt guilty at betraying the Empire. Another part felt elated that she was going to be able to help these people fight against the System Lords. A third part just felt lost and confused.

Doctor Zoboroski guided her chair out of the compartment and back to the medical center. It only took a few minutes to get her loaded into the regenerator and start the session.

She lay there with her eyes closed, thinking about everything that had happened and those things she knew were about to happen. She had no doubt she'd made the right decision. It might be years before she fully accepted her choices, but that would come in time.

Half an hour later, the regenerator opened up and Doctor Zoboroski slid out the table she lay on. "Let's get you on your feet. I want to see you walking around before I trust your stability."

The pain she felt was subdued, but it would definitely keep her from exerting herself. It seemed the regeneration had made her bones ache more than before the session. No running for a while.

That said, her mobility was pretty good. She was able to walk around the medical center without any assistance. So long as she kept herself from getting carried away, she thought she'd be able to do whatever needed to be done.

"How does that feel?" he asked solicitously.

"Good," she said firmly. "I can't wait until I'm finished with the procedures, but I feel confident I can at least walk safely."

He raised a warning finger. "You're still going to tire easily. That will go away, but for right now you need to bear in mind that you can't just walk for an unlimited distance and running is completely out of the question.

"You're still an invalid. Don't forget that, or you can end up back in the regenerator. No breaking out of confinement until tomorrow at the earliest."

"Yes, Mother," she said with a sigh and a grin. "I promise to be good. Relatively speaking."

Major Ellis cleared her throat. "If you're done horsing around, Talbot is probably ready for us."

The two women headed off for the interrogation room at a slow walk. Her frailty annoyed Veronica, but it wasn't the other woman's fault.

"Did I hear correctly that you're married to a scientist?" Veronica asked to get her mind off her condition. "I think I must've gotten something turned around in my head because there was this kid in the group of scientists talking to me after the fight. Someone mentioned he was married to a marine named Ellis. He didn't look old enough for that kind of thing."

Major Ellis smiled indulgently. "Trust me when I say that there's more than meets the eye when you look at Carl. He seems like a little science nerd, but he's got a backbone of steel when it comes to fighting for those he cares about. And he's freaking brilliant.

"I never saw the two of us as a couple, but now that it's happened, I wouldn't have it any other way. He completes me."

"This might sound rude but is he even old enough to drink?" Veronica asked. "Don't you feel like you might be robbing the cradle there?"

The marine grinned. "He is a lot younger than I am, but trust me when I say he's not in any way childlike. He's a kind, considerate partner. And an exceptionally attentive lover.

"Yes, I can pretty much carry him wherever I like, but when it comes to intellect, he towers over me and everyone else around him. Don't let his exterior fool you. He's not the senior scientist on this mission for nothing."

That stopped Veronica in her tracks, gaping. "He's the *senior* scientist you brought with you? How did that happen?"

Ellis shrugged. "My man has muscles in his brain. Those recent scientific breakthroughs that we've been making, many of those are directly related to his research."

"Including making that strange flip point work?"

"That and so much more," Ellis said emphatically. "I've heard some really smart people say he's probably the most brilliant mind of our generation and that with the addition of our enhanced technology and the expanded lifespan that medical nanites give him, the impact of what he does is going to profoundly change the New Terran Empire."

"Holy crap," Veronica muttered, impressed in spite of herself.

"Indeed," Ellis said with a smile. "Come on. Talbot gets grouchy waiting."

The room that Major Ellis led Veronica to was pretty much identical to the one they'd been in before but on a different deck. This time the viewscreen showed a woman in a Fleet uniform with commander's tabs.

She wasn't much to look at. Somewhat short, a little dumpy, and plain. If Veronica had passed her in the corridor, she wouldn't have given her a second look. On reflection, that was probably a plus for a security officer.

Raul Castille had been an exception to that rule. Handsome, charismatic, and charming when he wanted to be. He'd also been a cold-blooded murderer when it was convenient. Veronica had no doubt that Commander Violet Renner was cut from the same cloth.

Talbot nodded at Veronica as she walked in. "It's good to see you up and about, Commander. You're just in time too. I was about to walk in and see what our good security officer has to say for herself. Care to join me?"

"If we go in together, she's going to assume that I'm in command," Veronica warned him. "Fleet trumps the marines every time in the Empire. If I were lieutenant commander, she'd still assume I was the senior officer. Hell, she might do that even if I was a lieutenant.

"Is that really how you want to play this? You can feed me questions, and I can ask her, but my presence is going to take her focus away from you."

He smiled. "I think that's actually to my advantage. If she dismisses me as just the muscle, she's not going to give weight to the questions I ask. And I *will* ask my own questions. I suggest you focus on the things that strike your curiosity. Trust me when I say that anything you want to know will probably be interesting to me too."

Veronica nodded. "I can do that. I'm confident that she's going to assume we're traitors and renegades. From what I've seen of your attack on the Dresden orbital, you took everyone out quickly and then kept the important people isolated. Her more than most?"

"She's been in total isolation," he confirmed. "She has no insight into who attacked the orbital, and no one has answered any of her questions. She hasn't had a chance to interact with any of the other prisoners either."

He gestured toward the hatch. "Consider this your interview to join the New Terran Empire. Take charge and let's see how this goes."

Veronica took a deep breath and quelled the butterflies in her stomach. This was the first concrete step down a path she could never turn away from. When Commander Renner got around to calling her a traitor, it would be completely true.

"Perhaps you could give me a clue as to what you're hoping to gain from this woman. She's a security officer, so she's never going to cooperate with us.

From what I understand, you already have complete access to the research taking place at the Dresden orbital. Is that right?"

He nodded. "We don't need her for the specific information that Commander Castille could have provided. I'd rather know more about the Rebel Empire and how the System Lords operate. Yes, I know you grew up there and that you have knowledge about them. We need to know even more than that going forward.

"If we're going to take the fight to them, we need to have some kind of idea of what they really want. They crushed the Terran Empire from the inside and enslaved every human in sight. Simply based on the fact that we now have someone from the Singularity on the loose, we know that the AIs stopped at the border.

"If they wanted to expand out to cover the entirety of known space and all the polities of humanity, they could've done so. There's no doubt whatsoever in my mind that they stopped on purpose.

"Why is that? Does the AI at Twilight River have some kind of restriction that prevents it from operating outside the bounds of the Old Terran Empire? What does the Rebel Empire's security apparatus know? The insight that woman can provide into how the AIs operate would be invaluable."

Veronica snorted. "I stand by my earlier statement. She's *never* going to cooperate with us. Nothing you can do to her can force her to tell you anything, and no amount of cajoling is going to bring her over to our side, even if she tries to make you think that's possible."

"Maybe you're more persuasive than you know," he said with a smile. "Even given that the odds are against us, it only costs us time. She's not going anywhere. She can either sit in that compartment alone or engage with us. Any amount of contact is going to give us the opportunity to pick up something."

"Or allow her to lie her ass off," Veronica said in a cynical tone. "Well, I suppose it can't hurt to try. If nothing else, it's better than sitting in my little compartment too. Your ship's library is big, but talking to people is much more to my taste."

"I'll let you two handle this," Major Ellis said. "I've got to get back over to *Persephone*. Have fun."

Veronica stepped over to the hatch after the other woman had departed. "Shall we?"

7

To her annoyance, Zia wasn't able to talk her way out of being expelled from the wrecked battlecruiser. The warriors herded her, Carl, and their Pandoran escort politely but firmly out into the sunlight and stood watching them to make certain they kept moving.

"Well, that could've gone better," Carl muttered. "We only just got in, and now we're banned for life."

She poked the scientist in the shoulder. "Don't start that nonsense with me! You know as well as I do that a defective fusion plant is nothing to screw around with. If you'd left it operating below the minimum threshold, sooner or later it would have failed, probably with a significant explosion."

"It's still going to fail if they keep using it without shutting it down for maintenance. It's a miracle the damn thing kept working all this time anyway. I did what I could while I was linked with it and adjusted the safety parameters to make certain that if it starts acting the least bit unstable, it will go into a graceful shutdown.

"In other words, I implemented the most stringent safety protocols. The time to be generous with its operation protocols has long passed. A rogue fusion plant is nothing to toy with."

Zia glanced at Efrain. The Pandoran warrior shrugged, apparently unconcerned with the revelation.

"By any chance did you get a look at the flip drive while you were in the system?" she asked.

"No," Carl said with a shake of his head. "It was disconnected from the ship's systems or was completely burned out and inaccessible. To be absolutely certain what condition it's in, I'd need to access it directly, and I'll wager that's not going to be easy now."

No, probably not.

"I hope Kelsey made a good impression on the king," she said. "If he says we get access, that overseer is going to have to let us back in. Meanwhile, we need to look at other avenues to getting our ship repaired.

"The freighter is almost three-quarters the size of *Audacious*. Is it possible to use its flip drive on the carrier?"

From Carl's expression, she knew he didn't hold out much hope on that front.

"I'm going to give that a qualified 'no' and beg you not to try. Trust me when I say that *very* bad things could happen."

She sighed. That was about the answer she expected.

"So, if the freighter isn't an option and the drive on this battlecruiser is defective, what do we do? Hell, even if it was fully functional, the drive on *Dauntless* wouldn't be able to move a carrier, would it?"

Carl shook his head. "Probably not. This was always a long shot but not one I thought would bear fruit. There are other options, but I wouldn't call them *good* options. We can get to a system that almost certainly has the parts we need. It's just not very friendly, if you know what I mean."

She did indeed know what he meant: the Archibald system.

They'd explored the multiflip point enough to find five destinations from the Icebox system. One of the potential destinations was the Archibald system. It had been a major world in the Old Empire and was still bustling under the management of the AIs. There was almost certainly a shipyard there where they could theoretically get parts.

The other destinations from Icebox were Pandora and three uninhabited systems. One of the latter was in the Rebel Empire and not far from Dresden.

Those destinations weren't very useful at the moment as there were a number of hostile Clan warships sitting right at the flip point. Any strange ship would be promptly attacked and likely destroyed.

From the Pandora side, they could access four systems. One, thankfully, was Archibald. The other three included Icebox and two different uninhabited systems.

"Somehow I don't expect the Rebel Empire is going to be very cooperative," Zia said dryly.

"Probably not," Carl agreed. "That doesn't change the fact that that's the most likely location to get what we need."

Zia hadn't discussed this with Princess Kelsey yet, but she'd already decided getting everyone home wasn't actually what constituted mission success in this case. Everything of serious value that they'd captured on the Dresden orbital could fit aboard *Persephone* and the freighter.

If push came to shove, the Marine Raider strike ship could go through the multiflip point to one of the empty systems and search for linkages to new systems that might give them a path clear of danger and get them home.

Hell, one of these other systems might have one of those new flip points they'd discovered. Ones that sat far distant from the solar masses they were linked to. That's where the Clans had gone when they'd escaped Icebox. Through an unknown kind of flip point sitting in the outer system.

That course of action was chancy at best, but it beat being trapped here with the crippled carrier. Eventually, the Clans would find a way to use the multiflip point and find them. That wasn't going to be fun.

She suspected the heir to the Imperial throne had already thought of that. The woman was bright, and she wouldn't have missed that option. Not that she'd be easily convinced. It was going to take either a disaster or all other options failing before Princess Kelsey abandoned the carrier and its crew.

And that's what it came down to. There was no room to fit everyone from *Audacious* aboard the freighter and have enough life support to get them very far. No matter how the situation was juggled, someone was going to have to stay behind if the forces from the New Terran Empire left Pandora without repairing the carrier.

So, that meant Zia needed to explore every potential option if she was going to get Princess Kelsey safely home.

"Let's get back to *Audacious*," she said at last. "We're not going to solve our problems standing around down here. Maybe Colonel Talbot has dug up a few new leads for us to examine."

Carl grinned at her. "Oh, I think you could reasonably say that he has. I just got a message from him when I linked up to the cutter via the drone keeping an eye on us. I'll wager you've got one waiting for you too."

Zia checked her implants and found a message waiting for her. It was from Colonel Talbot and was marked urgent. She opened it and started the video playing.

A ghostly image of Talbot's head and torso appeared in front of her in the form of a translucent overlay hovering over the ground ahead of her. He was grinning.

"Commodore, the people I had searching the freighter just hit pay dirt. They found the hardware for a new AI. I had it moved to *Persephone*. I'll wager all that additional computing power and a sentient AI will help Carl figure out a way to get us home."

Well, that certainly did change things a little. Having met Marcus and

Harrison, the two AIs the New Terran Empire had working with them, Zia felt confident that the presence of a sentient AI would be a real boon to them, under the right circumstances.

"Let's get going," she said with a grin. "We might just have gotten the break we needed."

* * *

TALBOT FOLLOWED Veronica Giguere into the compartment holding their prisoner. The woman didn't look all that dangerous, but appearances could be very deceptive. Having met Raul Castille, Talbot knew how resourceful security officers in the Rebel Empire could be.

The woman had sat down on the edge of the couch. She didn't rise as they entered.

As in the case of the Singularity prisoner, two marines were inside the compartment with her. Neither was armed, and they had compatriots in the corridor that could rush in with stunners if need be.

"So," the woman said in a slow drawl. "You've decided it's time to ask me a few questions. I'd wondered why it was taking so long?"

"Each thing in its time," Veronica said coolly. "As your hosts, I'm afraid we're going to have to assert a monopoly on asking questions. Perhaps if you're cooperative that situation may change."

Commander Renner smiled just a little bit. "You, I know. Commander Veronica Giguere, commanding officer of the destroyer *R-7322*. Somehow, I don't think that small a ship has such expansive accommodations, and I don't believe that I'm still aboard the Dresden orbital. That raises some interesting possibilities."

The woman shifted her gaze to Talbot. "You, I don't know. Based on your uniform, you're a senior marine officer. Would you care to introduce yourself? I figure I have perhaps a sixty percent chance of you providing your name. The lieutenants you have guarding me have proven uncooperative, though, so I might be wrong."

In fact, the men guarding her were noncommissioned marines. They wore the uniforms of officers to explain away the fact that they had implants. Inside the Rebel Empire, only officers had implants.

"Lieutenant Colonel Russell Talbot," he said easily. "I'm directly in charge of maintaining your… accommodations."

"I'm afraid that you're not going to get a very positive review from me," Renner said oppressively. "Guest services could use a lot of work."

The woman proceeded to ignore Talbot and focused her attention back on Commander Giguere. "Since I know you left with the fleet sent to eliminate that crazy computer, that leads me to wonder why you've come back and how you're connected to the people that attacked the Dresden orbital.

"I can't imagine you seized anything worthwhile. Raul Castille has a well-deserved reputation. So what is this all about?"

"Which part of 'we'll ask the questions' did you fail to understand?" Commander Giguere asked rhetorically. "As an Imperial security officer, you probably know the System Lords far better than anyone else. How do you think they're going to react to this attack on one of their classified research and manufacturing facilities?"

Renner laughed. "They'll hunt you down and exterminate you with what they call extreme prejudice. Though the odds of you learning much about the classified research is low, they cannot allow even the possibility of it being under the control of unauthorized human beings.

"Whatever system is responsible for financing you will be suppressed. Every ship that participated in this atrocity, and every person on board those ships, will be destroyed."

"That's an interesting word to choose," Talbot said. "The computer intelligences you work for exterminated trillions of human beings. That's the very definition of atrocity."

"You're a fool," Renner said. "You're also rebels and traitors. It's a tragedy that so many people died in throwing off the yoke of the old dictatorship, but one does not make an omelet without breaking eggs."

"I once thought the same as you," Giguere said. "Then I had my eyes opened. I saw proof that our history was a lie. I suspect you already know that. Commander Castille did. He said so before I killed him."

Talbot was impressed. Veronica Giguere was going hard-core. There wasn't any stepping back from that kind of admission.

Finally, Renner reacted. Her eyes narrowed as she stared at Giguere. "Did you, now? I'm going to take *exceptional* pleasure in killing you back."

With that, the woman launched herself off the couch and at Commander Giguere, her bladed hand slashing at the injured woman's throat.

Talbot moved to block the security officer, but he was slow. He knew he wouldn't be fast enough to stop that unexpected attack and that might just mean watching Veronica Giguere strangle to death with a crushed larynx before medical help arrived.

8

Kelsey felt her eyes narrowing. Having seen Isidro's personality, she should've expected the ambush. Well, at least Talbot had taught her what soldiers did during an ambush: they didn't run, they fought their way out.

She stalked forward until she stood just in front of the battered wooden table, planted her hands on her hips, and glared back at the man who had demanded her surrender.

"My name is Kelsey Bandar, and this tribunal has no authority over me. The sooner you accept that, the sooner we can both move forward."

"Preposterous," Isidro sneered from his position to the side. "Clan Dauntless has authority over all humans on this world. You don't get to just declare your independence."

From what she'd heard, that wasn't completely true. There were some few humans living inside the Empire of Kalor and Kelsey doubted they acknowledged the authority of Clan Dauntless. Not that she intended to mention that since it might imply she was one of them.

From the glance the man at the center shot the warrior, Isidro was speaking out of turn. The warrior didn't see it since he was too busy staring daggers at Kelsey.

With a sigh, the man at the center of the table returned his attention to Kelsey. "Young Isidro is correct. You are of Clan Dauntless, and you will submit to this tribunal's will. Explain yourself."

Kelsey laughed. "As I explained to Arturo, your first mistake is assuming that I'm of this world. I'm not. I only just arrived a few days ago, and I come from beyond. I am Kelsey Bandar, chief of Clan Persephone."

Now it was the man's turn to stare at her agog. He shifted his gaze to Jacob and Arturo. "What madness is this? There is no Clan Persephone, even in the world we came from. The histories have no mention of anything like that."

Jacob offered the man a slight smile. "I have personally stood on the decks of her ship as it orbits our world. Her people were never part of the Clans. They are also not part of the empire from which we fled. Let's just say their story is more complicated than we can get into right now.

"I was bringing her to meet the king of Raden. She needs to explain her situation to him. He will make the final decision on whether she speaks the truth or not, though I already know how he will decide. My blood brother, Derek, has also seen her ship. Even as we speak, he is no doubt briefing his father."

"Speaking of fathers, yours won't be pleased to be left out," the man warned Jacob.

"He rarely is," Jacob replied curtly. "Once the king is satisfied, we can journey to my father and tell him her story."

Isidro took two steps forward and snarled. "Lies! I don't know what kind of game you are playing at but you will not get away with lying to us."

"Isidro!" the man at the center of the table barked. "You overstep yourself. I lead here, and you will follow."

"If you were leading, you'd already have these two in chains for defying the Clan. This woman attacked me. She violates the laws of Clan Dauntless, bearing weapons and acting outside the prescribed behavior for women. For this, she must pay."

Kelsey laughed at him. "If Clan Dauntless wants to enforce its will upon me, it's welcome to try. In my world, women have exactly the same rights and responsibilities as men. No one can tell them that they must behave in some fashion or other, and I won't tolerate that kind of sexism."

Jacob cleared his throat. "Isidro overstates our ways. The Clans have never had a large female population. Elsewhere, the Clans forbid them from dangerous occupations and curtail their rights.

"Not here. We don't repress our women. We cherish them. Custom dictates they are not warriors on this world, but there *have* been exceptions to that rule. Trust me when I say that they are the very soul of Clan Dauntless and they wield as much political power as any man, though often from behind the scenes."

She considered Jacob for almost ten seconds. "I'm willing to give you the benefit of the doubt until I get more information, but I'm not a wilting flower to be protected. I've killed more men in combat than your most seasoned warriors, I suspect. I will not shy away from protecting my person with arms."

"Then I demand satisfaction," Isidro said with a sneer. "Meet me blade to blade, and we shall see who is a warrior and who is not."

"Isidro, you have no idea what you're getting yourself into," Arturo said sternly. "Following your own logic, challenging a woman would be murder and so not allowed. The fact that she's a far better warrior than you merely means injury and humiliation for you. Assuming, of course, that she doesn't cut your head off. Idiot."

The man at the center of the table surged to his feet. "I forbid this! There will be no fighting in this hall."

Isidro gave the man a dismissive glance and glared at Arturo. "Neither of you have the power to stop me. The law is clear. She assaulted me, and I demand satisfaction here and now. She claims to be a warrior, so I am within my rights. I will see her blood."

"Accepted," Kelsey snapped before any of the other men could respond. "But I will not fight to the death over something so trivial. First blood only."

"If you mean the initial spilling of blood, then I accept," Isidro said with a wolfish smile. "Whosoever shall lose the first drop loses this challenge."

Jacob held up a hand. "As the son of the chief, I feel it necessary to warn you what a terrible mistake you are about to make, Isidro. Did you learn nothing from when she subdued you the first time? Step back from this madness."

"You think your father shields you from all the consequences of life," Isidro sneered. "He doesn't have the fire of our ancestors. Perhaps one day, someone with true spirit will challenge him during the yearly festival and take leadership of the Clan back to revive our greatness."

Jacob laughed. "Do not mistake benevolence for weakness. My father is strong. The reason no one challenges him for leadership is that they know he's a wise ruler, even if he can be an ass. The people you speak of would take the Clan back to what they were before the crash—mad dogs fighting over bones."

Isidro's face reddened. "That mouth of yours will get you dead one day. You think over much of yourself. Gallivanting across the kingdom playing at being a spy. Your day will come too. Perhaps much sooner than your father's."

The man stepped forward into the center of the hall, walking outward until Kelsey was between him and the tribunal's table. "Face me with a blade in your hand, woman. I promise I won't take more than a finger or two for your insolence."

Jacob held up his hands in surrender. "I tried to spare your honor, but you're too willful to see good advice for what it is. I hope this loss will be relatively painless. Actually, that's a lie. I hope it hurts like hell."

He turned his attention to the tribunal. "I also hope this will be educational. Watch closely and you'll see that this woman is a powerful warrior who is not to be trifled with. Perhaps then you will hear her with an open mind."

Once Jacob had stepped to the side of the room, Kelsey drew her swords. The true challenge of this fight wouldn't be winning. It would be winning without grievously injuring her opponent.

Isidro drew his sword and stalked forward, a grin on his face. He began circling to the left of her, feinting with his weapon.

She didn't fall for his probing attacks. She had absolutely no doubt that she would spot the true strike when it came. And, on due consideration, she didn't have to actually use her sword to get that blood.

The next time the warrior feinted at her, Kelsey slashed at his blade with the sword in her right hand. Her edge struck his blade just above the hilt and cut cleanly through, sending the dangerous part of his weapon clanging to the floor.

He stood there, his mouth agape.

Rather than waiting for him to recover, Kelsey darted forward and knocked the hilt out of his grip with the back of her hand, sending it spinning into the corner of the room. She then slammed her forehead into his nose, sending him staggering back.

She'd very carefully pulled the strike as much as possible. She had no desire to kill the ass. With the Graphene reinforcement to her skull, the impact hardly bothered her. In fact, it didn't even make her blink.

Not so for the arrogant warrior. He clapped both hands over his blood-gushing, broken nose and staggered back, howling in agony.

Kelsey sheathed her swords and turned back toward the tribunal. "Are we done here? Is there any lingering doubt that I'm a warrior?"

"Look out!" Jacob shouted.

Based upon the horrified expressions of the tribunal, Isidro had decided to go beyond first blood after all. Her enhanced hearing confirmed that he was racing up behind her, and her implants calculated his approach velocity and probable location.

He wouldn't be attacking with his bare hands, and his sword was ruined, so he probably had a short blade of some kind in his dominant right hand. Timing was going to be everything. She had no doubt that she could disarm and subdue him, but she wanted to do it with style.

When she believed he was in the appropriate position, she spun on one foot and lashed out with the other. He was indeed at just about the right spot with a dagger in his right hand and murder written on his face.

Her spinning back kick took the blade from his hand, snapping bones in the process since she hadn't held back on her strength. After all, there was a lesson to be taught here.

Even before his face began registering the terrible agony of his shattered hand, she'd planted the spinning foot and was lashing out at him with the foot she'd spun on. Strength was key here. She had to restrain herself to a very carefully calculated strike, or she might kill the man.

Kelsey's snap kick was just about perfect. Her foot rose and landed directly between his legs with just enough force to completely double him over.

He collapsed, gagging and retching. This fight was over.

Once again, she turned toward the tribunal. "I am Kelsey Bandar, chief of Clan Persephone. I am a warrior and will not be trifled with. I'm willing to explain how I came to be here and what I intend, but realize now that you have no authority over me."

The head of the tribunal's expression hardened a little. "Your ability to fight is shocking, but this matter is far from settled. Rest assured that Isidro will answer for his actions, but we will still judge you on your violations of Clan etiquette.

"And we will fully evaluate your claims that you do not belong to our clan at all. Trust me when I say that should that statement prove true you will have some explaining to do."

Kelsey started to answer, but a commotion outside the main doors interrupted her response. She turned toward the entryway just in time to see the doors open and a dozen Pandorans stride into the hall.

"All will stand fast," the tall Pandoran warrior in the lead said sternly. "I speak in the name of King Estevan of Raden. I call upon you through the treaty you have with our kingdom to assist me."

The tribunal, which had seated itself, once again rose to its feet. The man in charge bowed slightly. "Clan Dauntless will honor our treaty. What assistance do you require?"

"I seek Kelsey Bandar, chief of Clan Persephone. Is she present?"

Since he was staring directly at her, Kelsey was quite certain he knew who she was. She stepped forward and bowed.

"I am Kelsey Bandar."

The man nodded, obviously expecting her answer. "In the name of the Kingdom of Raden, I detain you. You will be taken immediately to an audience with the king. There you will explain yourself, and he will sit in judgment. If you resist, my warriors will use all necessary force to subdue or slay you. I command you to stand fast and surrender your weapons peacefully."

Well, that certainly sounded ominous.

Still, she didn't exactly have a lot of options at this point. "I will comply, but only with the understanding that my weapons will be returned to me when I am released."

The Pandoran smiled slightly. "That assumes that you will be released. You are not of the humans that were granted permission to be on this world. It is within my liege's rights to deal with you as he pleases. If he believes you to be a danger to the kingdom, you may be imprisoned or even slain. He will not allow mad dogs to roam this world."

Interesting. That was the second time that phrase had been used.

The Pandoran glanced at Isidro, who was still curled up in a fetal position on the floor, bleeding.

Not the best visual for a first impression, Kelsey had to admit. The idiot's timing had put her in an awkward light. Still, if push came to shove, the marines would get her out. It was far better to try to solve this peacefully than to fight.

Kelsey began removing her sword harness. "You'll want to leave the blades in their sheaths. They're very, very sharp. My other weapons are technological. I believe that Jacob is familiar with their use and can provide guidance in their safe handling."

The Pandorans surrounded her as she finished disarming herself. Some of them collected her weapons, and the rest began herding her toward the doorway. One way or the other, she had to make her meeting with the king of Raden work. Her people's survival depended on it.

9

Veronica hurled herself backwards, ducking to the side to avoid the madwoman's blow. She held no illusions about who'd win if they became fully engaged.

As quickly as she'd acted, Veronica only barely managed to avoid the lethal strike. Rather than hitting her in the throat, Renner's attack struck the side of her head with blinding force. Sparks of light shot across Veronica's vision as she fell out of the chair and sprawled on the floor.

Renner landed on top of Veronica and clamped her hands around her throat like steel bands.

"Die, murdering bitch," the security officer said, her eyes alight with murderous rage.

Moments later, Colonel Talbot clamped his arm around the other woman's throat and dragged her back. The two marines from beside the hatch pulled Renner's hands off Veronica's neck with great difficulty.

She sat there on the floor, gasping for breath as she watched the three marines struggle with the ferocious woman. The hatch opened, and extra marines rushed in to aid their companions, finally subduing the fierce, primal force that Renner had become.

All the while, Renner shouted at Veronica, promising her a horrible death that she couldn't escape from. It was surreal. What in the world had triggered the woman?

Once the marines had secured Renner's wrists, Talbot stepped back and helped Veronica to her feet. "Are you okay?"

"I'm fine," she said, surprised at how much her throat hurt. Her voice sounded a bit rough to her own ears.

Talbot gestured to his men. "Take Commander Renner to the brig. Lock her up and keep her in isolation. Put her into a restraint belt too. If she gets froggy again, I'd like to be able to take her down easy."

None of that slowed the invective that Renner was hurling at Veronica. Even after the hatch closed, she thought she could still hear the woman shouting.

Rubbing her throat, she stared at Talbot. "What the hell was that about?"

"Call it a hunch, but I think she had some kind of relationship with Castille. A serious one, I think, at least on her end. She went off as soon as you said you'd killed him."

"I'd imagine we're not going to get anything out of her at this point."

"Probably not," Talbot admitted. "We'll just put her on ice for a while and see if she cools down. Do we need to stop by the medical center and have Doc Zoboroski check you out?"

Veronica shook her head. "No, I'm fine. Seriously. She didn't have enough time to hurt me."

"If that first strike had landed clean, you'd be in a lot worse shape. I think I'm going to have to reassess our security protocols when questioning prisoners. I think we need somebody with a stunner in the room."

That wasn't a bad idea. Of course, most of the prisoners wouldn't be *that* aggressive. Veronica hoped not, anyway.

"So, what do we do now?" she asked. "I think I've had about enough interrogating for today."

"I'll bet," he said with a chuckle. "Let's go do something less interactive. I want to show you the new hardware we picked up. Have you ever actually seen a System Lord?"

"No. As you might imagine, they're picky about who they allow into their presence. Still, it's just computer hardware, isn't it?"

"Pretty much. Just a lot more of it than one might expect. Back when we installed one on a superdreadnought, it took up the entirety of the computer center and only just barely fit.

"Over on *Persephone*, the engineers had to gut and jury-rig several compartments adjacent to the computer center. I'm not sure how they managed to get the work done so quickly, but I suppose they have their ways."

Veronica gestured at the ship around them. "Not to criticize, but shouldn't you install it here?"

He headed toward the hatch, and she followed. "This ship is trapped here for the foreseeable future. That AI must get out and back to the New

Terran Empire, even if *Audacious* doesn't. The commodore and my wife will understand that."

They stepped into the corridor and headed for the lift. She considered what he'd said for a moment before asking another question.

"Are you going to make it the ship's computer too? That seems dangerous. System Lords are ruthless. I shudder to think of what one in control of a ship could do."

"It's not as bad as all that," he assured her as they stepped into the lift and he sent it heading up. "We're using the *original* system code with a couple of tweaks made by Carl Owlet. This computer will not become a System Lord."

She considered him for a moment. "I've heard a lot about this Carl Owlet. I still can't believe that he's married to Major Ellis?"

Talbot nodded. "Yep. Those two are total opposites. She is an unstoppable physical machine and he is a brain without comparison. Together, they make a *formidable* couple."

Veronica thought about that on the ride over to *Persephone*. Building a System Lord still sounded reckless to her, but she had exactly zero say in what happened here. She could only pray for the best.

She monitored the approach to the Marine Raider strike ship through the cutter's scanners via her implants. The Empire had nothing like that ship and she wanted to know as much about it as she could.

Crews were working outside, apparently installing access hatches near where fighters were docked on the hull in makeshift cradles. This was probably something being done because the carrier couldn't leave this system and *Persephone* could.

The cutter docked in one of the ship's original cradles, and they boarded the ship. Major Ellis was standing there. Veronica wondered if the other woman knew things had gone a bit awry after she'd left.

"Welcome aboard *Persephone*," she said with a smile. "The commodore and my husband are already aboard. I have to get back to the bridge, but I wanted to take the time to officially greet you."

"She looks like an interesting ship," Veronica said. "I look forward to talking with you about her."

"Perhaps over dinner? I've got to run."

While Major Ellis headed off down a corridor, Colonel Talbot led Veronica to a lift. The trip was short. They stepped out near what Veronica knew would be the computer center on the small ship. Coming from the opposite direction were Commodore Anderson and the person she suspected was Carl Owlet.

Anderson smiled at them. "Colonel, Commander. I hope you're both well."

"Well enough," Veronica said. "We had a little bit of excitement, but it all worked out in the end. The colonel tells me you found an artificial intelligence. I have to confess that's scary."

"There's nothing to be afraid of," the young man assured her. "We've been through the code many, many times. These aren't the artificial intelligences you're familiar with."

"I'm certain the people that developed the System Lords thought pretty much the same thing," she said dryly. "Right before the computer killed or enslaved them."

"Hmmm. You might have a point there. Still, we do the best we can. The code that made the System Lords do what they did isn't in these iterations and we've had two of them for quite some time without any kind of problem."

The young man turned to Talbot. "We really need to consider where this one ends up once we get home. We have two, so it should probably go to the Pentagarans."

"We'll have plenty of time to figure that out," Talbot said as he gestured toward the hatch down from the computer center. "They should be just about finished setting up. Commander Giguere has offered to have the new AI verify her honesty when she says that she wants to work with us."

"Excellent news," Anderson said. "I'd much rather have you and your people as allies than enemies, Commander. You're far too resourceful for me to sleep easily at night, even with you locked up and under guard."

Veronica laughed and gestured at the marines trailing her. "I think you've pretty well got me covered. Even though I have no desire to fight you, I completely understand and endorse the caution you're taking. I have to confess, though, that hooking myself up to an AI is a frightening prospect."

"Then allow me to assure you that it's nothing to be worried about," Owlet said. "I've administered this procedure many times, and there's no pain or risk. It's read-only. The AI will have no access to directly affect you in anyway."

She sighed. "How long until it's operational?"

The scientist shrugged. "We were just heading in to find out. Based on the general information that I have, probably no more than half an hour. Explaining the situation to our new friend might take a little bit of time after that. I'd say if you allow for another hour, that will easily cover everything we have planned."

"Then let's get this over with. I'm tired of being your prisoner and I'm certain my people would like to confirm their loyalty and get out of that cabin as well."

* * *

ZIA STEPPED into the new annex beside the computer center aboard the small ship. It looked to have once been several compartments that had been made into one. The bulkheads seemed to have been reinforced too.

It was filled with computer hardware in solid-looking racks. Those were shielded too. Someone had taken steps to protect their new resource.

"Can we give the new AI complete control of this ship like we did on *Invincible*?" she asked Carl.

He shook his head. "No. The computer on *Persephone* is wired into every system, and it has encoded directives to direct and protect the ship that a normal computer doesn't have. While it might be possible to merge the two systems, I'd have to give that a lot of thought first.

"As far as bringing it online, it looks as though it's ready to load and boot right now. Call it fifteen minutes. I have to stream the base code over from *Audacious*."

Zia rubbed her nose as she considered what Carl had said. "In the end, what happens on this ship is Princess Kelsey's call, not mine. Load the software."

Carl moved over to the main console and began working rapidly, shifting from screen to screen and doing things that Zia wasn't certain she could ever really understand. His attention was immediately focused on his task and he seemed to forget everyone else around him.

"He's pretty intense," Commander Giguere said from beside her. "I can kind of see what Major Ellis sees in him."

"More power to them," Zia agreed.

Finally, the young scientist turned toward the trio. "The software is loaded, and I'm ready to boot on your command."

"Do it," Zia ordered.

Carl touched a control, and lights began coming on across the equipment as the system booted up. The screen on the wall went through a test pattern and then shifted to a view of what appeared to be a tall woman with dark skin dressed in a Fleet uniform with no insignia.

The image of the woman—who had to be the AI—smiled, her white teeth contrasting sharply with the ebony shade of her skin. "I have you in my database, Commodore Anderson. My name is Fiona. How may I assist you?"

Carl turned to Zia. "The baseline software has all the information that Marcus and Harrison have put together for new AIs. Except for our current mission, she should be up-to-date. She can scan everything we've collected thus far in just a few seconds."

"Play catch-up if you would, Fiona," Zia ordered. "You need to know everything we've encountered so that you'll be ready to help us figure a way out of the mess we've gotten ourselves into."

She turned her attention to Veronica Giguere. "And in just a moment you'll be able to pledge your loyalty to the New Terran Empire. Are you ready?"

The other woman took in a deep breath. "As ready as I'll ever be."

Zia thought she heard a note of uncertainty, but the other woman seemed determined enough. In just a minute they'd find out if the woman was being honest and then the real fun started.

10

W hile the commodore spoke with Veronica Giguere, Talbot pulled Carl aside. That didn't amount to much in the already cramped compartment, but it would have to do.

"You said these two computers might be merged." Talbot said in a low voice. "How would something like that work? The Marine Raider computer is aggressively protective of access to the ship's critical systems."

Carl shrugged slightly. "Both the AI and *Persephone*'s computer are designed to run stand-alone. Neither can work directly with the other system in a merger. What I'm envisioning would have to be more a matter of working hand in hand rather than being some kind of mixture of the two."

Talbot scratched his chin. "That really doesn't sound all that helpful."

"It might not be, and perhaps we shouldn't even try. This ship wasn't designed to operate in conjunction with a sentient AI. It was made to operate solo under the command of a human Marine Raider.

"The AIs were never designed to command ships either. Marcus is doing a fine job, but that wasn't what his creators envisioned. Based on the initial code, they were intended to work hand in hand with humans on things like research projects and helping to control complex systems like orbitals or manufacturing centers—perhaps even to do tasks for Fleet like war-gaming various scenarios or managing logistics. At this point, we may never know the full scope of what the designers intended."

Carl clapped his hand onto Talbot's shoulder. "What I'm saying is you shouldn't be thinking so narrowly. Let *Persephone* control itself while Fiona helps us with more important tasks. She can pull data together in ways we can't begin to imagine."

Talbot nodded and thought as Carl moved forward to the main console again. The young scientist was going to be occupied explaining things to either Zia, Fiona, or Commander Giguere for the next few minutes. That gave him an opportunity to consider what the best options were going forward.

In the end, this wasn't going to be his decision. Either Kelsey or Zia would be the one deciding how best to use the AI. That didn't mean that he couldn't game out the potential options so that he could argue for the ones he thought best served their interests.

As powerful as *Audacious* was, until she was fixed, she was a liability. She couldn't go anywhere, and she could only defend herself. If the Clans came calling, they'd undoubtedly wear down the massive warship and destroy her.

That was the reason he'd placed the AI on the Marine Raider strike ship. Mobility was going to be the key to their overall success. Even if his wife didn't want to hear that.

While it was possible the crashed battlecruiser held the key to repairing the carrier's flip drive, that seemed like a long shot. The fact that Zia hadn't even mentioned anything about it only told him that the mission to *Dauntless* had failed.

No, if there was to be any hope of repairing *Audacious*, it was going to come from outside the system. Probably from a place that manufactured flip drives. To his mind, that meant Archibald.

Marine Raider strike ships were exceptionally stealthy. While he wouldn't want to try to slip *Persephone* into orbit around Archibald, the small ship could certainly get into the Rebel Empire system without being detected. Once in place, she could begin scouting.

Such a task would be dangerous, and his wife would insist on leading the way. And to be fair, her participation would increase the chances of success significantly.

He sighed. Why did all the smart choices end up putting Kelsey into danger?

At least, if Veronica Giguere were being honest with them, they would have someone at hand that could provide keen insight into the Rebel Empire. The same was true for all her officers.

Talbot doubted that any of them had ever been to Archibald, but they'd traveled through their section of the Rebel Empire and knew how society worked there. That kind of insider knowledge would be key to the success of their mission.

His people also had access to technology that the Rebel Empire couldn't match or anticipate. FTL communication, teleportation through the transport rings, and the help of a sentient AI who could process data far more quickly than anything other than another sentient AI.

Speaking of which, Archibald was large enough of a system to have one. Somewhere on the other side of that flip point resided a Rebel Empire AI just as powerful as Fiona. Only with hardwired instructions to enslave humanity and destroy any threat to the rule of its kind.

Based on what they'd found at Harrison's World, there might also be a hidden station at one of the gas giants with four battlecruisers that the thing could use if it wanted to. Possibly even orbital bombardment platforms too.

They couldn't allow the AI to realize they were there. If it mobilized the resources in the Archibald system to find them, it would. Their only chance at success was staying off its scanners.

Sadly, Kelsey was not well known for lying low. In life, there was the easy way, the hard way, and Kelsey's way. Which normally involve blowing things up and killing bad guys.

He hadn't heard anything from her since she'd left on her mission to meet with the king of Raden, so he hoped that meant things were going well. She'd insisted on going alone so as to keep things quiet. A rare exception to her unspoken rule.

He really should ask her for an update. Assuming that everything was going well just because she was quiet wasn't the safest option. As Lieutenant Timothy Reese, his former commander, had discovered the hard way, Kelsey was obstinate. She'd occasionally keep doing things that were counterproductive simply because she didn't feel like giving in to outside pressure.

Talbot connected to *Persephone*'s com system. There was a drone flying over the city below that would act as an intermediary between Kelsey and the ship. It wasn't always in direct communication with his wife, but if it wasn't, he could instruct it to move closer.

The drone connected immediately and moments later she accepted the com request.

I'm a little busy right now, she said through her implants. *Can this wait?*

I just wanted to make sure you're okay. Is everything going smoothly down there?

As they were married, he often had deeper insight with his wife when connected by implants. He could sense emotions and physical sensations. It worked much better when the two were together, but it didn't go away just because they were separated by greater distances.

He felt a mixture of amusement, irony, and a dash of worry. Not exactly reassuring.

It's going about like I expected. I'm on my way to meet the king right now. I had to stop off and explain my presence to some representatives from Clan Dauntless. There was a little bit of hostility there, but nothing I couldn't handle. Now, seriously, I really need to focus on what I'm doing.

Talbot parsed her words for hidden meanings. Honestly, she could mean exactly what she'd said or she could've gotten into a gunfight with somebody. It was really hard to tell.

He'd just have to hope she'd yell for help if she needed it. There was a squad of marines in a pinnace not too far away. She could call them in for immediate support if things spun out of control, if she'd just do it.

Keep safe, he said. *There have been some developments up here that might make things easier over the next few days, but I can explain them when you come back up. Love you.*

I love you too. See you in a while.

Somewhat reassured, he headed over toward the others. It was time to see if Veronica Giguere was being honest with them or not.

* * *

KELSEY PUT the conversation she'd just had with her husband out of her mind as the guards escorted her into a squat building that looked more like a fortress than a palace. It was built from large blocks of rough stone that had been closely fitted together, leaving no gaps of significance.

She didn't know that much about masonry, but it seemed as if that meant someone had gone to a lot of trouble to fit them all together. Raymond Orison, the king of Pentagar, had learned the work when he was a young man. She'd have to ask him when next they met.

The guards let her up to a massive pair of doors that were easily twice the size of those protecting Clan Dauntless's hall. These were coated with metal plates and guarded by armed and armored Pandorans.

The interior of the keep—that's what she'd decided to call it—was put together much the same as the clan chapter house. If she had to guess, the Clan had designed their building to be consistent with how the Pandorans did things. She wondered how far into the human society that sort of thinking carried.

After a few minutes of navigating large halls and even larger chambers, the group finally came to an interior set of doors similar to the ones at the front of the building. These were already open and her escort walked through without pause.

The layout of the massive chamber was one she immediately recognized. This was an audience hall, the place where a ruler sat before his people to hear grievances and make judgments. A formal sort of thing at the best of times, so not that promising.

The hall stretched about seventy meters in front of her and was about forty across. The only place to sit in the entire room was on the raised dais at the other end. It held what could only be called a throne made of some type of bluish stone carved into fantastical shapes.

A number of guards stood along the perimeter of the room and all watched her closely. Another pair stood behind the throne.

Kelsey doubted these men were limited to medieval weapons. Surely some of the weapons salvaged from the crashed battlecruiser would be brought to bear on her if she proved to be threatening to their monarch.

Her escort spread out and cleared the way for Kelsey to go forward. The unnamed escort leader stayed at her side as she walked forward until she was twenty meters in front of the ruler. He stopped her there.

A door to the side of the room opened, and Derek entered the audience chamber. He smiled at Kelsey as he walked to stand beside his father.

"Kelsey Bandar," Derek said gravely. "You stand in the presence of my father, King Estevan of Raden. Father, allow me to present Chief Kelsey Bandar of Clan Persephone."

The older Pandoran considered Kelsey for a few seconds. She was no expert at reading Pandoran expressions, but the man didn't seem entirely pleased. When he finally spoke, his voice was deeper than she expected and somewhat gravelly. It held a lot of gravitas.

"I'm uncertain what type of welcome to give you, Chief Bandar," the man said. "My father told me of the time after *Dauntless* crashed. Many humans were like wild animals and had to be put down for the safety of those around them. Violent doesn't begin to describe the most severe cases of xenophobia."

She was surprised to hear a word like that come from his mouth. Then she was ashamed of the thought. The king was obviously well educated and she'd best keep that firmly in mind. Low tech didn't mean ignorant.

"I'm not the one that gave me the title of chief nor is Clan Persephone an actual thing," she said. "My people do not come from the Clans. We don't have that kind of negative reaction to those unlike ourselves.

"As I told your son, my title is actually crown princess. My father rules the New Terran Empire, a grouping of dozens of worlds like this one. We survived the Fall of the original Terran Empire by fleeing much like the Clans, but the similarities end there."

King Estevan considered Kelsey and slowly nodded. "I'm willing to accept the possibility for the purposes of this discussion. The name *Persephone* belongs to the ship you came in. Is that correct?"

"It's one of three ships," she agreed. "Not the strongest nor the weakest. I command her, but I also have political authority over all of my people. It's complicated.

"My intent was to announce myself to you quietly. I understand that my people aren't covered by the treaty you have with Clan Dauntless, but we would like to forge a way forward in friendship."

"And if I'm not willing to grant you leave to stay on my world?"

"We don't have to land on your world, but I understand there are other political entities that might welcome us. I've already met your people, so I can be confident of the kind of relationship we might have. Others are less certain. In the end, the final decision is yours."

The king gestured for his son to bend forward and whispered in his ear. They held a brief conversation back and forth before the ruler nodded.

"My son counsels me that I should have a longer discussion with you and learn more about you before I make a final decision. I'm willing to grant you leave to stay in my kingdom—at least some of you—while we hold those talks."

Kelsey relaxed just the slightest bit. "I know we can help one another once you're more certain of what kind of people we are. Unlike the people of Clan Dauntless, we have fully functioning ships and understand the technology completely. We're willing to share that information with you in exchange for your assistance."

The Pandoran ruler nodded. "Such knowledge could be quite useful, considering the tense relations between my kingdom and the Empire of Kalor. Anything that can bring that conflict to an end without further bloodshed is worth discussing."

She was about to open her mouth to respond when one of the guards behind the dais moved. His hand slipped inside his tunic and pulled out a flechette pistol. It was a subtle movement, and even the man standing five meters to his left failed to notice it. His eyes told Kelsey that his target was the king of Raden.

Kelsey couldn't possibly reach the man before he fired and there was no way the king could get out of the field of fire in time. The smart thing for her to do would be to dive for cover until the shooting stopped.

So, being her, she shouted a warning and leapt toward the assassin.

Unarmed and too far from the assassin to stop him from opening fire, Kelsey hurled herself toward the monarch and his son. She was in a race to move them out of harm's way before the assassin launched a deadly hail of flechettes into their backs.

Of course, now that she was committed to the act, she realized her own chances of survival weren't terrific. It was her own fault. She shouldn't have turned over *every* weapon she'd had, even when they demanded she do so. One more thing for Talbot to yell at her about if she survived.

Even as she started moving, she was dumping Panther into her system. Her perception sped up, slowing the world around her as she raced forward.

Derek and his father were just beginning to react to her sudden movement, but she'd surprised them as much as the assassin had surprised her.

The younger Pandoran wasn't an idiot, it seemed. Rather than treating her as a threat, he was already turning to face the rear wall, his hand dipping inside his tunic for a weapon, she was sure. He wouldn't get it out in time to do any good.

The assassin's weapon was almost in line with the king when Kelsey reached him. Using far more force than was probably necessary, she shoved the older man to the side.

Kelsey considered pushing Derek away, but he and his weapon were probably what was going to stop the assassin from following up with the king once he'd dealt with Kelsey.

She hunched lower and jammed her shoulder into the ornate throne that the king had been standing in front of. The angle was bad, and she ended up losing her footing, but coming from the floor below the dais gave her just enough angle to send the throne toward the assassin.

The stone was a façade. It shattered as she struck it, revealing the wood beneath. The lighter weight meant it moved far easier than she'd expected.

It didn't have enough momentum to actually reach the assassin, but it drew his fire at the last moment, spoiling his aim. His flechettes tore huge chunks out of the throne before he stopped his impulsive burst.

The tableau was over, and all of the guards were reacting to the man. Some were racing toward him while others seemed to be hurrying to get between him and their king.

Derek opened fire at last, but she didn't have a chance to see the results of his shots before one of the assassin's flechettes shattered the top of the throne and sent a chunk into the side of her head with great force. Pain lashed through her, and the world went abruptly black.

11

Veronica nervously sat in the chair Carl indicated for her. He'd told her there was no risk with this procedure, and she could accept intellectually that that was probably true. That didn't keep her from being completely and utterly terrified at the idea of allowing a System Lord access to her thoughts.

As if sensing her fear, the young man smiled reassuringly. "I promise there's absolutely no danger here. No pain, not even any uncomfortable sensations. You won't feel a single thing."

"How is this going to work?" she asked, relaxing in spite of herself.

The young scientist sat down across from her. "When I ask her to, Fiona will request access to your implants. She doesn't have the codes to write anything. Those are closely guarded secrets and when we upgraded you, we installed new hardware that mandates your informed approval to any access or changes. We did this to keep the AIs like the System Lords from being able to overwrite the clean code now running in your implants."

She gave him a skeptical look. "What someone can install, someone else can remove. You realize that as soon the System Lords figure out your trick, they'll be able to reverse it."

Owlet shook his head. "The package includes a very effective anti-tampering protocol and some other unadvertised surprises for them. It can even tell if someone is under duress. Without the correct codes, the implant will fry itself and all the wiring in the brain.

"Now before you start panicking, an outcome like that isn't harmful to the person. Sadly, it means that they can never have implants again because the process of removing the damaged wires and attempting to install new ones would be much more destructive than the initial implant procedure itself."

Veronica ran the options she could think of through her mind. In the end, she decided he was right. Being forever stripped of implants was a small price to pay to avoid mental slavery. Particularly when the new medical nanites they'd given her would allow her to live for centuries.

No one now living in the Rebel Empire had a clue medical nanites ever existed. All references to them had been suppressed. Modern scientists had said they were too complex to build, obviously at the insistence of the Lords. Veronica didn't know why the AIs didn't like the things, but they obviously didn't want to allow them back into existence.

"And how are you going to prevent the AIs from getting these codes?" she asked. "If they get them, it's game over all over again."

"That's our little secret," he said somewhat smugly. "What I will say is that the number of people with that critical information is very small and widely spread across the New Terran Empire.

"They don't have to be located where anyone needs an update. The update itself can be signed so that the implants recognize it's an uncorrupted, verified update. Even so, the update is unpacked into a segregated part of implant memory. Then the implants go through the code line by line verifying there's nothing harmful.

"Only once that is accomplished will they ask the user if they would like to accept the update. And the user can say no. It's your head. If you don't want to risk a change, don't."

She still wasn't sure that the cocky young man had thought of all the angles, but there was only so much human beings could do to protect themselves. It was always easier to break than to build. So long as humans had implants in their heads, there was a risk that the AIs would be able to seize control of them.

Veronica took a deep breath. "I'm ready."

Carl looked over to the image of the AI. "Fiona, please link with Commander Giguere and verify the honesty of what she's saying. Let me know the moment she revokes her permission or tells an untruth."

"Yes, Carl," the deceptively authentic-looking woman said with a smile.

The AI turned her cybernetic gaze to Veronica. "As Carl said, I not only mean you no harm, but I am incapable of inflicting harm upon you in this manner. Permission to access your implants can be revoked with a thought. Do you grant me permission to access your implants in a read-only configuration?"

"I do," Veronica said before she could change her mind.

She struggled to determine if anything had changed. She still felt the same.

Do not be concerned. You are in no danger.

Veronica flinched in spite of herself. The voice in her head had been Fiona.

I revoke your permission to be in my head.

"Commander Giguere has revoked permission, Carl," Fiona said, seemingly unperturbed.

The young man scowled. "I haven't even asked you any questions yet."

Veronica smiled a little. "I just had to make sure that I could do it. I once again give permission for Fiona to access my implants in a read-only configuration."

She waited a beat to see if the AI would say anything else in her mind but heard nothing.

Commodore Anderson cleared her throat. "I feel the need to add that for the time being, even once you've proven your loyalty, I'm going to require that the ship's computer monitor you at all times. Whether that's here on *Persephone* or back on *Audacious*.

"I'm not talking about monitoring inside your head but monitoring your physical presence. We've done exactly the same thing with other prisoners that have come over to our side, and it's just a precaution to verify you aren't tempted to change your mind.

"None of the data the computer gathers will make it out of a subprogram to the main system unless it detects something about you that it thinks means you're going to betray us. So not even the computer itself will know what you're doing in private that way."

Carl Owlet, Zia Anderson, and Colonel Talbot began peppering her with questions. All of them were related to what she felt about the Rebel Empire, the System Lords, and the New Terran Empire.

Veronica answered them as honestly as she could. She had nothing to hide. After less than ten minutes, the questioning was over and she again revoked the AI's permission to monitor her thoughts, intensely pleased that the whole process was done. She felt exhausted.

Commodore Anderson extended her hand to Veronica. "Welcome to the New Terran Empire, Commander. I think you'll find we're much easier to work with than your former coworkers."

That made Veronica chuckle. "That wouldn't be hard. You wouldn't believe how cutthroat Fleet is in the Empire. So what do we do now?"

"The next step is to bring all of your people over and repeat this," Talbot said. "The research scientists from the Dresden orbital have already gone through this process. We've verified they really are on our side, just like you.

"The only people that I suspect we'll never be able to clear are

Commander Renner and Commodore Murdoch. Renner for obvious reasons. Murdoch because even though she has a grudge against the Rebel Empire, she doesn't really disagree with what they're doing."

Commodore Emilia Murdoch was a tough case, Veronica agreed. The woman had commanded the Dresden orbital until its capture. She wasn't a traitor to the Empire. No, she was one of their ardent supporters.

From what Veronica had heard, the commodore had only supported the New Terran Empire in getting the access codes to the secret research and manufacturing computers because her security officer, Raul Castille, had tried to murder her. He'd ended up breaking her neck, leaving her paralyzed from the neck down for the rest of eternity, particularly since the woman had medical nanites and would live that way for hundreds of years.

That was a ghoulishly terrible fate and Veronica felt sorry for the woman, but she completely understood why her new compatriots could never trust Murdock.

"Understood. If we can get my crew vetted, I'm sure we can assist you in some way."

Commodore Anderson smiled. "I don't suppose any of your people are familiar with the Archibald system, are you?"

Veronica had complete access to her people's service records. A quick check verified that none of them had ever been to Archibald. Wherever Archibald was.

"Sadly, no. That said, the Empire is fairly consistent in how worlds are laid out and run. I can probably give you a lot of information about the Empire in general that might be useful."

Anderson sighed. "I suppose that was too much to hope for, but it didn't hurt to try. Let's get your people over here."

Veronica nodded and took a steadying breath. She was committed. This rebellion was hers now too. It was time to take the first steps at getting her countrymen out from under the heels of the AIs.

* * *

ZIA TOOK a cutter back to *Audacious* once the verification of Commander Giguere's crew was complete. She was grateful that they'd all passed. It would've been awkward if one of them had failed and split what was obviously a well-functioning team of friends.

In combination with the research scientists, those people presented serious danger to the AIs. Their collective knowledge would give the New Terran Empire so much to work with.

Yes, they already had Lieutenant Commander Michael Richards, the computer officer they'd captured earlier in the conflict. He was cooperating, but he wasn't *here*. She needed information at her fingertips. Fleet Command might not approve, but she'd risk it.

Captain Brandon Levy, her flag captain, rose to his feet from the center seat. "Welcome back, ma'am. Did everything go as planned?"

"Pretty much," she said as she took her chair back. "It looks as if we have some new allies. Unfortunately, none of them knows a thing about Archibald. I suppose it would've been too much to hope for."

The big man nodded. "The Rebel Empire is a big place. It seems as if they've kept their Fleet officers segregated. Maybe the computer from the Dresden orbital has something about Archibald."

All the computers they'd salvaged from the Dresden orbital were set up in stand-alone mode in one of the compartments close to Carl Owlet's lab. While he wasn't aboard, the research scientists from the Dresden orbital were, and they could check them.

Carl had granted the researchers relatively high access levels to all the systems in the lab, and they were continuing their work. Well, some of them were continuing their work while others were struggling to understand the new hardware and science breakthroughs Carl had made in the last couple of years.

"That's a good idea," Zia said. She used the large command console in front of her to bring up a com channel with the lab. Moments later, Doctor Jacqueline Parker appeared on the screen.

The lead research scientist was a middle-aged woman with dark skin and curly hair. She hadn't been smiling much when they'd rescued her, but that had certainly changed over the last week.

Now the woman smiled widely when she saw Zia. "Commodore, what a pleasure. What can I do for you?"

"It's a pleasure for me, too, Doctor. I was wondering if you could access the Dresden computers for me. I'm trying to determine if we have any information on the Archibald system. It seems as if that's the closest location where we might be able to get what we need to fix our flip drive.

"Unfortunately, none of the people we have aboard from the Rebel Empire know anything about the place. I'm assuming that none of your people have been there, but I'm sure you'll correct me if I'm wrong."

The woman laughed and shook her head. "We lived on the Dresden orbital from the time we were children. I can assure you that none of us have been anywhere interesting. Let me check the computer and see what I can find. Hold on just a second."

It seemed that the Rebel Empire had been taking children that were offered by the mad computer on Erorsi and making them into research scientists at Dresden. Of course, it wasn't a very friendly sort of thing to do.

They'd implanted explosives in the scientists' heads in what was almost certainly the worst retirement plan ever.

Leave it to the Rebel Empire to figure out how to ruin something that was actually humanitarian. She'd seen what the mad computer had done to the human survivors of the Fall. It had forcibly implanted them with Marine Raider implants and used them as fodder to attack the system next door. They were monstrous savages.

Thankfully, Pentagar had managed to rebuff all the attacks over the intervening five hundred years before Admiral Mertz and Princess Kelsey had destroyed the computer. Their stout defense hadn't stopped the computer from sending a tithe of children to the Rebel Empire every year in exchange for Marine Raider hardware and other supplies it couldn't build for itself, though.

To their credit, the Rebel Empire had finally decided to end the computer's rule on Erorsi. They'd also planned to conquer Pentagar, but Admiral Mertz and his fleet had been there to stop them cold. Which was where they'd captured Veronica Giguere and a lot of other Rebel Empire forces.

Most of the Rebel Empire survivors had gone to the New Terran Empire for processing, but Brandon Levy had decided to make Veronica Giguere and her command crew his personal project.

The Rebel Empire didn't know that they'd lost so many ships and people. Not yet. And if she and Princess Kelsey could get the data they'd captured at Dresden home, that delay might just give the New Terran Empire a chance for victory.

Doctor Parker's eyes widened little bit. "It looks like I have something for you. There's only basic information about Archibald in the system, but I think I hit pay dirt in the Fleet section. It seems that one of the officers you've captured was stationed there when she was younger. Commodore Murdoch."

Zia felt her expression souring. The woman had given them the keys to open the research computers and manufacturing hardware to their use, but the woman's continuing despair at her medical condition made her unreliable at best. She'd done what she'd done to get revenge, pure and simple. Everything she said was suspect because they couldn't really trust her.

"I suppose that's better than a kick in the head," Zia said with a sigh. "I'll see if she's willing to cooperate. Otherwise, how are you doing down there? Are you getting settled in? Finding lots of interesting things to look at?"

The older woman nodded. "I must confess that I didn't understand how someone as young as Carl Owlet could be in charge of the science division when you brought me on board. Now I get it. I cannot imagine how he made the jumps in intuition to create some of these new scientific theories that he's working from.

"Take the FTL communications for example. It's brilliant. Point to point communication from one system to another through flip point. Potentially also to nearby systems not connected by flip points at all. Impossible to intercept and devilishly hard to detect.

"Though I will say that I think his theory is incomplete. It may be possible to communicate longer distances with some modifications to the hardware. The theory says that the range should be unlimited. I think that's right. It's just going to require a lot more experimentation to work out the bugs. That's where experience comes into play."

Zia felt the corner of her mouth quirk upward. "I'm sure Carl will be the first to tell you that he's feeling his way through a dark room trying to figure this out. He's a smart guy, but he's running on intuition. I hope you're right. That would certainly make things a little easier for us."

Parker nodded. "Every major breakthrough that humanity has made has come from someone trying something they didn't know was 'impossible' or making a fortuitous error that granted them insight into something they hadn't planned. I really think if you dig deep down, that's what you'll find.

"I've got my people working with the FTL coms right now trying out various general modifications to the hardware. Obviously, we won't be able to test anything outside the Pandora system. I'm just trying to get a general feel for how this works. We're dealing with some ghosts in the system right now, but I'm pretty confident that we can improve on Carl's design."

Zia frowned. "Ghosts in the system? Like what?"

The woman shrugged. "Sometimes, when we engage the modified hardware, the throughput drops to almost nothing. It's really strange."

"Keep me in the loop. I want to know what you find with that. Thanks again, Doctor."

"My pleasure. Good day, Commodore."

Zia sat back into her chair, thinking about the strange behavior of the FTL com. What could that possibly mean? And how might it help or harm them going forward?

12

Kelsey woke to find Derek hovering above her, his expression worried. Based on all the shouting going on, not very much time had passed. Probably no more than a couple of seconds. Her implants confirmed that.

"I need a doctor!" the man shouted, his voice loud in her ears.

She winced. "Did you have to do that right in my face? I've got a terrible headache."

And she did. Her head literally felt as if someone had clubbed her. Obviously.

A quick check got a basic physical condition report out of her medical nanites. Individually, the little things weren't very sophisticated, but each sent information back to her implants, and they put everything together. That gave her a fairly decent idea of how bad any damage was.

The good news was that her skull was intact. Her brain was also in good shape, though the impact of the throne fragment had jarred her pretty badly. The nanites were busy repairing the damage she had, and their prognosis for her was good.

Her scalp was bleeding profusely, of course. Head wounds always looked worse than they were. She knew all about that.

It was kind of embarrassing that such a small injury had taken her out, even if only for a couple of seconds. She decided she'd just leave this little part out when she filled Talbot in on what had happened while she was off making contact with the locals.

Kelsey sat up, wincing again when her head throbbed. "I don't need a doctor. Is your father okay? Did you get the shooter?"

"The assassin? Yes. My father is bruised but alive, thanks to you. At this moment, I'm much more concerned about your health. You took a nasty blow to the head and risked a terrible death on our behalf."

"Annette Vitter told you about the machines we have in our bodies, yes?" At his nod, she continued. "Mine are more advanced than what she has. I have a coating on my bones that makes them very tough. That includes my skull. I'll be fine."

He seemed unconvinced. "I think I'd rather have one of our physicians look at you in any case."

Looking around the room, Kelsey saw that his description of things was correct. The guard that had tried to kill the king of Raden was dead in a bloody heap with several other guards searching his body.

Derek's father was walking back from the man who tried to kill him, now with two hulking guards staring at everyone with enhanced paranoia. He stopped several steps away from her and examined her closely.

He turned toward the man nearest him. "Send for the royal physician. Tell him to make haste."

"It looks worse than it is, Your Majesty," she said. "I'm a lot harder to kill than I look."

"You're a lot faster than you look too," he admitted wryly. "I barely had time to wonder what was happening before you'd thrown me off the dais and saved my life. I suppose at this point, I'm going to have to accept my son's wild story as true.

"No one should be able to move so quickly. Certainly no one from the Clans. While their distant ancestors once had machines in their bodies capable of doing miraculous things, none still living have them. And none should have been able to do what you did, in any case."

An older Pandoran man rushed in clutching a dark bag. He raced up to the king and began circling him. He demanded something in the Pandoran language.

"Speak Standard," the king said. "Our guest is the one I wish you to examine. She saved my life. Make certain that she does not lose hers."

Once again, Kelsey considered arguing but decided that it wouldn't do any good. Doctors seemed to be the same from one end of the universe to the other. She'd bet the same drive extended to different species as well. She was just going to have to put up with it.

The man's poking and prodding were painful, but the powerful drugs her pharmacology unit had dumped into her system muted that somewhat. Eventually, he opened his bag and pulled out something to clean the wound.

That stung. Why is it that any liquid made to clean a wound had to sting like crazy? Even her painkillers seemed ineffective against the cleaning of wounds and always had. Weird.

Kelsey allowed the doctor to proceed until he pulled a needle and thread from his bag. That's where she held up her hand.

"My people have different healing techniques. If you can just put something over it, I'll see to it later. In fact, the machines in my body will make it close before very much longer in any case. There's no need for that."

More importantly, there was no need for her to go through the pain and discomfort of having him poke sharp objects through her skin.

Seeming somewhat disgruntled, the physician folded a cloth and placed it on the side of her head, using another cloth to secure it in place by wrapping it all the way around her head. He tugged the knot very tight, possibly because he was annoyed with her.

That, too, was par for the course when it came to physicians, whatever their species.

She rose to her feet, pleased that the world stayed steady. That allowed her to get a much better look at the throne. The assassin's flechettes had virtually destroyed the heavy chair. Its bulk had saved her life.

"Does that happen often around here?" she asked. "Should anyone with that kind of weapon be very trusted?"

"He was," the king said grimly. "That man diligently worked his way up in my service over the last three decades. Until today, I would've wagered any amount of money that he was perfectly loyal to me. I would do so for any of my personal guards."

"And now you'll be wondering if that man was only the first," Kelsey said softly. "Why now? What caused him to strike at you today?"

Derek inclined his head toward Kelsey. "It had to have been you. Nothing else makes sense. Your arrival changed something. Our enemies, who have obviously spent significant time placing knives close to our backs, felt it was necessary to discard their advantage because you arrived."

Kelsey wished she could argue with that idea, but she couldn't. It seemed her appearance had upset the applecart. Based on what she'd heard from Derek earlier, odds were very good that the assassin had worked for the Empire of Kalor.

That raised an interesting question for her, though. If they had someone close enough to execute the ruler of their enemies, why hadn't they used him before? Why allow the king of Raden to live one minute longer than necessary?

That was the question, wasn't it? And one she had no answer for.

"Perhaps we should speak somewhere a little bit more secluded," she said. "I suspect that you probably don't want word of what I have to say getting back to the Empire of Kalor."

The king grunted, waving the physician away. "That's probably a wise decision. Come. Let us retire to my private audience chamber to discuss matters of import to both our peoples."

As he led her toward one of the side doors, Kelsey wondered if she should call for backup. She knew that Talbot had marines on standby outside the city in case she needed them. If he found out that she'd gone through all of this and hadn't even summoned them to her side, he was going to be pissed.

But if she did, that might cause other issues. The king had no reason to trust her, really. She should start with small steps.

"Is it possible that I could get my weapons back?" she asked. "I'm feeling a little underprotected at the moment."

The king snapped his fingers, attracting the attention of every guard in the room. "Whoever has my honored guest's weapons, bring them to her immediately."

He smiled at her. "After all, if you wanted me dead, all you had to do was stand there."

"I'm not certain I could *ever* stand by and let something like that happen. That's not who I am."

The older man clapped his hand to her shoulder. "That's to your credit, young woman. Come. I want some closed doors around us, a hot drink in my hand, and your story in my ears."

As much as Kelsey wanted to leave it at that, she knew she had to do one more thing. If she didn't, Talbot would rightfully have her ass.

"Considering the unsettled situation, I need to send a message to someone. I hope you don't mind a few extra guests."

* * *

TALBOT TRIED NOT to clench his teeth as the pinnace headed for the ground outside of the capital city of the Kingdom of Raden. He was sure that Kelsey hadn't told him the complete truth about the events she'd been through this afternoon, but what she had said had been bad enough.

He'd known sending her in by herself had been a mistake as soon as she'd suggested it. The woman was a trouble magnet. Wherever she went, chaos followed. And assassination attempts, absolutely. And likely large explosions, given enough time.

Because they were going to have to fly under the scanners, so to speak, all of the marines with him wore flowing cloaks and loose clothing over their armor and had their rifles hidden in rough bags that would barely slow their deployment.

He had absolutely no idea if their clothing would blend in with the locals, and he frankly didn't care. That was someone else's problem.

No matter what Kelsey had told him, there was no way he'd leave her here alone. How the hell had she even found any assassins? No one here even *knew* her.

The plan called for him and his men to make their way to a major road nearby. Kelsey assured him that there would be a party waiting for them there. He was curious whether it would be human or Pandoran or perhaps a mixture of the two.

His wife had insisted that she hadn't been seriously injured in the fighting. The way she'd stressed the word 'seriously' had him certain she was playing a word game with him, so he'd brought Doctor Zoboroski along.

To say the medical officer looked different would be something of an understatement. Talbot had only ever seen the man in uniform and now he looked like a desert raider. All he needed was some kind of turban and a decent war cry, and he'd be set.

"I've accessed her telemetry remotely," Zoboroski said. "It looks as if she took a knock to the head, but it doesn't seem serious. Her medical nanites are going to take care of the issue, I suspect. If not, I can pop her into the regenerator and have her back to baseline quickly enough once we get back into orbit."

Talbot raised an eyebrow. "You can access her nanites from here? I know that's built into the marine packages, but even though Kelsey is technically a marine officer, I didn't think she had that kind of remote access enabled."

The doctor smiled. "You're not the only one that knows our princess. Doctor Stone enabled the functionality and then passed word on to me when I became the senior medical officer in the task group."

"That's good to know," Talbot said. "Shunt me a copy of what you've got."

He examined what the doctor sent to him and nodded slowly. Looks like she'd taken some kind of blunt impact to the side of her head. Like someone clocked her with a club. Her pharmacology unit had registered a couple of seconds of unconsciousness but had labeled that only a minor concern.

Talbot wondered how the machine had made that determination. Anything strong enough to knock out a woman with a graphene-coated skull had to be pretty forceful.

He knew it was useless, but he was determined to get her back up to the ship as quickly as possible. She was their leader. She didn't need to be down here where people could take shots at her.

Of course she was going to resist. Tell him that this was diplomatic and that she had to be here.

It was complete and utter bullshit.

A chime sounded in his ear announcing their impending landing. Thirty seconds to touchdown.

He put away his misgivings and pulled the external scanner feed through his implants. They were coming down about a kilometer from the road. They'd already deployed a couple of drones in the area, so he knew there were no hostile forces waiting for him.

Unless, of course, the greeting party at the road were actually hostile. Low odds of that, but they'd be careful.

The pinnace settled into a small clearing that had been used at some point in the past as a campground. Not recently, though. The small firepit didn't appear to have been used in the last several months.

He let the team lead the way out as the ramp went down. Unlike some people, he knew when to let other people go in front.

Yeah, he was pissed. He'd need to get a handle on that before he bit Kelsey's head off in public. Or private, for that matter.

No, it was much better to be low-key and make her feel guilty. She'd be expecting a frontal assault, so he'd see about undermining her walls instead.

The marines spread out, and everyone began making their way toward the road. He heard the pinnace retracting its ramp and lifting off behind him. It would be waiting somewhere in the sky in case they needed fire support.

The other pinnace he'd put in the area was on the other side of the city, ready to drop reserve troops in if they needed them. He hoped to God he didn't, but one really never knew when Kelsey was involved.

About fifteen minutes later his people were within sight of the group waiting on the road. Talbot relaxed a little bit more. It was a mixture of Pandorans and humans, but he recognized one of them. Jacob Howell, one of the men they'd captured earlier and the son of the chief of Clan Dauntless, stood with the greeting party, obviously relaxed.

Talbot found himself smiling a little. If they felt the need to send out someone that important, he wasn't going to argue. Without a doubt, Jacob would know what had really happened. Better yet, he'd tell him everything. Then he'd know how to make Kelsey regret her impulsiveness.

13

V eronica stared around Carl Owlet's lab curiously. While she'd occasionally had cause to consult with specialists in what had passed for the lab aboard her old destroyer, she'd never been in such a *large* scientific facility with so *many* people working on various projects.

The young scientist had come back aboard the carrier with Veronica and her crew once they'd been cleared by Fiona. Apparently, now they were fully trusted. She didn't even have a guard.

That seemed a little shortsighted to her, but they apparently believed she couldn't fool the AI. Maybe they were right. She had absolutely no way of knowing because she really didn't plan on betraying them.

Just when she thought she was getting a handle on how large this man's lab was, he went to another compartment that was just as big and filled with even *more* people doing unexplainable things.

"Just how big is your lab?" she asked the scientist suspiciously.

He grinned at her. "There's another couple of compartments about this size. There were a lot of researchers on the Dresden orbital and they were working on a bunch of projects. We've rebuilt them here and the folks are getting back to work, only for the New Terran Empire now.

"I also have a private lab. We won't be going there. While we trust you guys, you're not cleared for everything that I'm working on. Some of it is *really* secret."

"That's fine by me. I understand need to know. What exactly are we doing?"

Owlet gestured toward a group of men and women huddled around a large bench with a couple of pieces of equipment strapped to its top. "My new associates have run into an unexpected glitch in their testing. We're going to see if we can figure it out. Commodore Anderson cleared you to see what we're working on."

As they approached the table, an older woman stepped away and greeted Carl warmly. She turned to Veronica with a gaze that seemed guarded.

"Commander Veronica Giguere, meet Doctor Jacqueline Parker. Jacqueline was the senior research scientist aboard the Dresden orbital."

Veronica immediately felt her interest level rise as she extended a hand to the woman. "It's a pleasure to meet you, Doctor Parker. Allow me to assure you that I've been completely vetted. I mean you no harm."

"So Carl said," the woman said. "You'll forgive me if I'm not completely convinced or enthused. People like you put a bomb in my head."

Unsure what to say—not sure that *anything* she said would ever be enough—Veronica only nodded. "I understand."

"What have you got?" Carl asked.

Doctor Parker never took her eyes off Veronica. "Concerns. A lot of concerns. I don't believe we should be sharing information like this with people like her. I don't care what your new pet AI says, neither she nor anyone else working for the Rebel Empire can be trusted."

The woman's words hung in the air for several long heartbeats before Veronica nodded. "I can understand where Doctor Parker is coming from. While I had nothing directly to do with what happened to her, people in similar positions to me enabled those who did that. And, to be fair, I've certainly done a number of things that I wish I hadn't done to comply with my orders.

"I think it might be best if I excuse myself. I don't need to know what you're doing down here, and I can help where everyone feels comfortable with my participation."

Carl shook his head. "I'm afraid you're both going to have to come to some kind of compromise. As we get allies inside the Rebel Empire, we can't be doubting them once the truth of their loyalty has been established.

"Jacqueline, I understand how you feel, even if I don't have all of your history to back it up. Commander Giguere isn't lying to us or concealing anything. She honestly intends to help us overthrow the AIs controlling the Rebel Empire. We *will* work with her. Commodore Anderson has made her will crystal clear. And now I'm doing the same."

Veronica was impressed. He hadn't seemed the type to be so firm, but his tone brooked no argument. He commanded here and left no doubt on that fact.

Parker didn't say anything for a moment but then nodded, her expression making clear her doubt. "If there's anything I understand, it's carrying out orders that I don't agree with. It's your show, Doctor Owlet. We'll do it your way."

Carl sighed as the older woman walked back over to the bench, her body stiff. "I was afraid of something like this. I'm sorry."

"You don't have anything to be sorry about," Veronica said. "The issues she has with me and everyone like me are things that *we* caused. Even though I didn't put that bomb in her head, I might as well have. You removed it, right?"

"No," he said with a shake of the head. "Its placement makes that too dangerous. We've completely disabled it though. Any external force strong enough to set it off would kill her, and nothing else can activate it now."

Well, that certainly sounded grim. Time to change the subject.

"So, what doesn't Doctor Parker want me to know about?"

"Faster-than-light communication."

Veronica laughed. "I can certainly understand how that would go wrong. It's impossible."

"Funny thing. We already have it working. Doctor Parker was just making a few modifications to an *already* functioning FTL com and got some anomalous results."

She stared at the young scientist, agog. "That's impossible."

"It's not only possible, but we have FTL coms installed on a number of ships and even on probes. We can send them through a flip point and get real-time communication from the other side. We have a number of them spread out across this system giving us real-time scanner information.

"The problem comes when we look at the theory. It says the range should be unlimited. Through testing, we've discovered it works through a single flip point. It won't go through a second. It also works through about three hundred light-years of normal space before the signal fails."

Veronica stood there, unable to speak for long seconds. When she finally managed to close her mouth, she grimaced.

"That's how you set up the trap that took out the task force I was part of. You were in communication all around us the entire time. You herded us into a trap because we couldn't see you, but you were busy talking about wherever we were going."

Even though she'd changed sides, she still felt bitterness at the realization. Her comrades and she had been herded together for the slaughter.

Carl shook his head. "That's not exactly what happened. The linkage comes in matched pairs of devices containing entangled particles, and it's possible to detect their use. They create small gravitic pulses that an eagle-eyed observer might spot. We didn't dare use them during the fight."

"Why are you telling me this?" she asked after a moment. "This kind of thing could change the balance of power between the Rebel Empire and the

New Terran Empire enough to win the war. If you keep it a secret. Doctor Parker is absolutely right that I shouldn't be here."

Carl gestured for her to walk over to the table. "You're on our side now. Let's get you brought up to speed on this while I figure out exactly what's going on."

She took two steps before something else occurred to her. "If these are the secrets you're *willing* to show me, just what kind of things are you working on in private that you're not ready to share just yet?"

He grinned at her. "Things that would blow your mind. Come on."

Veronica couldn't begin to imagine what kind of scientific breakthrough would be even more astonishing than what he'd already told her. She'd known the boy was smart, but this was ridiculous. If he came up with this all on his own, he really *was* a genius.

* * *

KELSEY WAS PLEASED to see that her negotiations with King Estevan were going smoothly. Once they'd gotten past the little problem of him not trusting her, he'd listened to her entire story with an open mind and incisive questions.

Understanding the bind her people were in, he readily agreed to trade technological know-how for the assistance his people could provide in both food and other undiscussed terms. He seemed quite interested in forming a stronger bond with her people.

That probably had something to do with the assassination attempt. If the Empire of Kalor was as persistent a thorn in his side as she suspected, any advantage he could get over them might spell the difference between life and death for both him and his people.

The king leaned back in the chair he was sitting in. "I think I understand something that had been confusing me. One of the overseers down at the wreck of *Dauntless* sent me a complaint about someone there under the protection of my son.

"Apparently they broke something. Or set something on fire. I'm not precisely sure which. Was that someone you sent?"

Kelsey nodded. "Probably. A very important piece of equipment on board my largest ship was damaged. We're hoping to repair it, and I sent some people to quietly look at the inside of the wreck to see if something could be salvaged. I hope the damage wasn't significant."

The older man laughed. "To hear the overseer talk, your people just about burned the place to the ground. I suspect the actual impact was far less than that. The overseers tend to be doggedly protective of that ship. I'm sorry to say that he expelled your people. I'll send a message back instructing him to give anyone you designate his full cooperation and complete access."

A knock on the door interrupted her response. It cracked open to admit one of the king's guards. The man walked over and whispered in his monarch's ear. After listening for a moment, Derek's father nodded and gestured for the man to leave. Then he smiled at Kelsey.

"Jacob has arrived with your companions. They'll be here shortly."

That was fast. When Kelsey had set up the meeting between Jacob and Talbot, she'd expected it would take a little longer for her husband to get down here. It seemed he was in a hurry.

Yeah. He was probably pissed.

She smiled in spite of her sense of impending doom. "Then it's a good thing that we've finished working out our arrangement. Thank you for speaking with the overseer. I'll see that someone comes back down to finish looking at what we needed to look at. This time, hopefully without setting anything on fire."

Moments later, there was another knock on the door, and it opened before anyone inside responded. Jacob Howell stepped in and bowed to the king. "Majesty. I've brought guests from Clan Persephone."

The man stepped aside just in time to avoid Talbot running over him. Her husband shot her a look that promised he'd get around to dealing with her, but he focused his attention on the alien monarch and bowed low.

Kelsey stepped up beside him to perform the introduction. "King Estevan, allow me to introduce my husband, Lieutenant Colonel Russell Talbot. He is also my clan's senior ground warrior."

The Pandoran man raised his eyebrow. "If he is as good a fighter as you, he must be a terror on the field. Welcome to my kingdom, Russell Talbot. I would like to speak with you further, but I do understand that your wife was just in battle. You are undoubtedly concerned over her health.

"It might be best if we break our discussions for now, Princess Bandar. Send one of the guards when you're ready to speak again. I shall be just down the hall with my son and Jacob."

Talbot waited until the door had closed behind the Pandoran monarch before he rounded on Kelsey. Rather than yelling, he peeled back the cloth on the side of her head. He grunted when he saw what was under it.

"Exactly how do you manage to get into fights *everywhere* you go? I have Doc Zoboroski back with my men. I want him to look at this as soon as practical."

"I don't get into fights every single time I go off by myself!" she said, narrowing her eyes. "This wasn't my fault."

He didn't seem convinced. "While I'm willing to grant that you don't always go looking for trouble, every place you go seems more prone to having physical violence break out than if you weren't there. Obviously, you must be the common factor."

She stared at him for several long seconds before she saw the twinkle of humor in his eyes. She smacked his shoulder and scowled at him. "That's not funny."

"I think it is. Now, why don't you tell me what happened?"

Kelsey ran down the sequence of events and watched him wince when she described the fight at the chapter house. She knew she was going to get total crap because she'd gotten into two fights in one trip.

She held up a finger. "That one wasn't my fault either. That guy picked a fight with me that didn't need to happen."

"Uh-huh. It sounds like we need to take that guy back up to the ship and stuff him into a regenerator. We don't need to make additional enemies on this planet."

Kelsey wasn't exactly sure that even a full regeneration would make that ass any less angry and dismissive toward her. Still, it was a gesture of goodwill toward Clan Dauntless.

"I'll ask Jacob to make the arrangements. You can take him back up with you."

Talbot shook his head. "You mean that we can take him back up with us. We're going back up together shortly."

She crossed her arms over her chest. "You think that just because I've had these problems that you get to tell me I'm going back up into orbit? Think again."

He shook his head. "I'm not telling you that you *have* to go, but we both know that that wrecked battlecruiser isn't going to provide the solution we need. All of this exploration is a sideshow. There are others better suited to working out the details.

"We're going to have to conduct a mission to Archibald, and we both know it. The sooner we start planning and executing that mission, the better. Those Clan people are nuts. Eventually, they're going to start sending ships into the multiflip point hoping to get one to where we went.

"Even Carl doesn't know how successful they'll be. It wasn't as if the original ships could spare even a single flip drive. They had one failure and decided to call it quits. Now, they might throw ships at it until one gets through. And that might not take very many tries. We can't take the chance. We need to get moving."

Kelsey rubbed her face. "You're right. I want to explore here. I want to see what's going on with the first real alien society we've gotten to interact with. It feels like an adventure. This conflict between the Kingdom of Raden and the Empire of Kalor just begs for us to intervene. Or at least make sure that the other guys really are the bad guys."

"Are you worried that the people we're talking to are the bad guys?"

"No, but we don't exactly know enough to say that for sure. Still, you're right. I need to be back in orbit, and there are plenty of people I could send down here to finish settling the details.

"Let me explain that to King Estevan, and then we'll go by the chapter house and pick up our wounded butthole. There'd better be something interesting going on up there to make me feel better."

Talbot smiled wickedly. "Oh, I think there are a few things underway that'll capture your interest. Let's get this over with before you change your mind."

"Changing my mind is *my* prerogative," she huffed. "Fine. Let's do this."

14

Zia stopped outside Commodore Murdoch's compartment and took a deep breath. She hated visiting the woman. Hated seeing anyone in that condition. It sickened her.

When Commander Raul Castille had orchestrated his escape from *Audacious*, he'd killed the senior staff that had been captured on the Dresden orbital. People that were his supposed friends and allies. People he'd worked with for years.

He hadn't quite been successful with Murdoch. He'd snapped her neck, but she'd survived. Unfortunately, she was paralyzed from the neck down. No amount of regeneration could fix that kind of damage. Modern medical technology just wasn't that sophisticated.

Nevertheless, she needed to convince her enemy to help them again. Yes, Murdoch had given them her codes to the Dresden orbital research computers, but that had been an act of spite against the security apparatus that had betrayed her.

This was something more. No matter what she'd said earlier, the woman still believed in the Empire she served. One didn't become a flag officer with one's eyes closed.

Well, she might as well get this over with.

Zia pressed the admittance key, and the door slid open moments later. A medical aide was on duty, there to serve any need the commodore had and to socialize if the injured woman wanted it.

The compartment was relatively basic, but it wasn't as if Murdoch was able to enjoy very many amenities. Besides the bed and furnishings, one wall supported a large vid screen to provide entertainment.

It was interesting, Zia thought. People with implants could watch vids in their heads, but many preferred to watch them the old-fashioned way.

Commodore Murdoch was an older woman with lines across her face from scowling and various levels of displeasure throughout her life. It came as no surprise that she fixed Zia with a frown.

"What do you want now?" the woman demanded peevishly. "I've already given you the damned codes."

Zia gestured for the medical aide to leave them and took a seat by the bed. "We're about to take a trip into the Rebel Empire. Or, if you prefer, the Empire. A place you've been, I believe. Archibald. I was wondering what you could tell me about it."

The older woman's frown deepened as she processed what Zia had said. "That's impossible. We're nowhere near Archibald."

Zia allowed herself a small smile. "Without elaborating, I believe you already know we're fairly resourceful. You'll just have to take my word that we have a way to get to Archibald, and it won't take as long as you think.

"That said, we have specific things that we need to get there. This ship's flip drive burned out when we arrived in the system. We need to either get what we need to repair it or find something to steal to replace it. To make that happen, we need your help."

Murdoch laughed, her voice sounding dry and just a tad bitter. Of course, bitterness had colored everything the woman had said thus far since her attempted murder. And, to be honest, before that.

"I suppose if you were looking to get repair parts, that's one of the best places to look," she finally admitted. "It's a fool's errand though. There's no way you can actually get into a Fleet facility like that. It might not be guarded as well as the Dresden orbital, but you can be sure they don't allow just anyone to walk in."

"It seems like we did pretty good with the Dresden orbital, didn't we?" Zia asked. "In fact, we ended up stealing the entire thing. I'm not sure at this point what we can do at Archibald, but we have resources you're not aware of.

"Which brings us full circle. I can't go into the details of how we'll carry out this mission, simply because I have no idea what we're facing. I need you to tell me about Archibald and the Fleet facilities there."

The older woman considered Zia for almost twenty seconds, her expression calculating. "All right. I'll do it, but I want something in return."

"What?" Zia asked, waiting for the other shoe to drop.

The older woman smiled coldly. "The shipyard isn't the only thing Archibald has to offer. It's also the home of one of the Empire's top medical research facilities. Something like the Dresden orbital but with less security implications, if you know what I mean.

"I want you to work your magic at that facility too. If anyone has advanced regeneration equipment and techniques capable of repairing my spine, it's them."

That was actually a nightmare. They already had a difficult mission and didn't need to add a second intrusion to the first. That was just begging for trouble.

"Just because they *might* have the technology doesn't mean that they *will* have the technology," Zia objected.

"I want you to promise that you'll make a good faith effort to obtain the technology and know-how to heal me. That's my price."

Zia felt her teeth clenching. One more needless complication to a situation already fraught with danger. Unbelievable.

Part of her wanted to promise the old woman anything just to get the information she needed, but Zia wasn't going to lie and make knowingly false promises. If she agreed to this, they'd do their very best to make it happen.

Even if she *had* felt differently, Zia knew Princess Kelsey would take a promise like that and make it happen. She'd insist, and she'd be right to do so.

"I can't promise success," Zia said, feeling tired. "We'll make a good faith effort to get any technology that might see you healed and knowledge of the required techniques. That said, I'm not going to throw my people's lives away. If it looks impossible, we won't act."

Murdoch nodded, her expression somewhat glum. "Not exactly a ringing endorsement of our deal, but you're speaking with the voice of someone who actually intends to carry through. I really can't ask for more than that, can I?

"Very well. I was a junior officer when I was stationed at Archibald, but I was a flag lieutenant, and my commander occasionally dragged me into some interesting places, including the shipyard. I saw the area where they manufactured flip drives and other parts too."

The woman's smile grew cold. "The only way I see that you'll be able to get the parts you need is to plug the information directly into one of the manufacturing computers and have it make them on the spot.

"As one might expect, that's going to take some interesting timing and very likely require a diversion. Say, some kind of ruckus at the nearby medical research facility. And I haven't got the slightest idea how you can expect to get what you build out from under the eyes of the security officers on duty at the shipyard."

"I suppose I'll have to get all the information I can from you and figure that out, won't I?" Zia asked with a sigh. "I don't suppose you've ever been at the medical research facility, have you?"

"Sadly, no. There was no need. After all, I was young and immortal." That last bit came out with an exceptional amount of bitterness.

"At that age, aren't we all?" Zia asked rhetorically. "We'll run through the information you can give me now, and then I'll send a couple of officers to go over it again and get every little detail we can. We only get one chance at this, your mission and mine. If I can't make everything work, none of us is going to come away happy."

With a sigh, Zia began asking questions and getting specifics. She'd make another pass once she'd gone through the initial run looking for deeper details. Done right, the preparation for this mission would take days.

Knowing Princess Kelsey, they'd leave much sooner than Zia preferred, so it was best to get as much data as she could now. They'd probably need it all when the time came.

* * *

Talbot tolerated Kelsey's bad mood until just before their pinnace docked with *Audacious*. Then he poked a finger in her side.

She twitched and fixed him with a flat stare. "Why are you poking me?"

"Because you're being an idiot. You couldn't find that guy that you messed up. So what? He didn't have to go scurrying off like a roach in the sunlight. He made a choice. Let it go. You can't fix everything."

Kelsey stared at him for a long moment before shaking her head. "Sometimes, you don't understand me at all. I'm not upset because I can't fix what happened. I'm upset because I'm dead sure that bugger is going to cause me problems later.

"It's a curse, I tell you. He's got bad guy written all over him, like a villain from the vids. He hated me to begin with, I totally trashed him and caused him a grievous injury, and now he's off somewhere licking his wounds. You can bet your ass he's going to come back looking for my blood."

"Seriously? He's a primitive. Let him get all freaked out. It won't do him any good or cause you any problems. Besides, Howell seems pretty competent. If he says he's going to find someone, I'd wager he's going to do exactly that. No matter how long it takes or how many rocks he has to turn over to find him."

She shook her head and sighed. "I agree that's what would happen under any normal circumstance, but tell me the last few years have worked out that way. Every time we cross someone, they come after us looking for a fight.

"At this point, I really hate leaving potential enemies behind. That's where our backs are, after all. You know those things that are really good at attracting knives? I'd much rather have healed the guy's injuries and maybe sidestepped this particular blood feud."

At that moment, the pinnace docked and the pressure changed slightly as the lock began cycling. Talbot undid his restraints and stood, holding out his hand for Kelsey.

"You did what you had to do to get through the crisis that guy created. If he pops up later looking to cause trouble, I'll be happy to give him some. Right now, we need to start planning our mission to Archibald. That has to be the priority. Until it's done, you're not going back down to the surface in any case. He can't exactly get to you up here."

They walked out into marine country. Major Gabe Collins, *Audacious*'s senior marine officer, stood waiting for them. Of normal height and somewhat abnormal width, the marine officer's hair seemed grayer than the last time Talbot had seen him.

That didn't seem likely, but Talbot wasn't going to rule it out. It had been that kind of month.

"You're not here to give me more problems to deal with, are you, Gabe?" Talbot asked.

The big man shook his head. "Not that I know of. I figured since you were just passing through my area, it would behoove me to at least greet my commanding officers. How was your visit below, Princess? Did you have any trouble? Maybe you need me to drop a detachment of marines to teach someone manners?"

Kelsey chuckled. "There were a few issues, but nothing I couldn't handle. What's your posture going to be like while we're conducting the raid on Archibald?"

The man shrugged. "It's not like you can stuff a battalion's worth of marines on board *Persephone*. If I did, Colonel Talbot would be in command in any case. I assume I'm going to be left here with the bulk of our marines because if you get caught, no amount of help I can give is going to save you.

"Whatever firepower you think is appropriate to go along for your heist, I'll send. You're going to have to tell me what you need, and I'll make it happen. Other than that, I figure I'll be providing security forces for any of the people that need to go down to Pandora's surface."

"As soon as I figure out what we're going to do, I'll let you know," Kelsey said. "It's really going to depend on what Commodore Anderson has to tell me. If the news is bad enough, then I won't go. There will be no suicide missions under my watch unless we have no choices left."

Talbot was proud of how much Kelsey had grown. A year ago, she would've flatly refused to consider any situation valid for a suicide mission. Now she accepted there might come a time where she had to call for volunteers that wouldn't come back.

"As soon as you know what you need, let me know. Good luck." With that, Gabe stepped back and returned to his office.

Talbot led Kelsey into the corridor outside marine country. "How soon is Zia going to brief us? Until we know what we're dealing with, we're at a standstill."

"Last I heard, she'd already finished talking with Commodore Murdoch. She's got people asking follow-up questions to nail down all the details they can, but she's back in her office. I'll go get the lay of the land.

"Meanwhile, I want you to go talk with Carl and find out what exactly we're going to need to fix the flip drive. If we need parts, that's probably a lot more doable than a full-size flip drive capable of moving a carrier through the flip point."

Talbot really hoped that they'd gotten good news from down at the wreck of the battlecruiser *Dauntless*, but that seemed unlikely. He also hoped that whatever they needed was going to be something they could easily sneak in to steal at Archibald. Based on their luck, he wasn't counting on things going that smoothly.

"I'm on it," he said, putting a good face over his worry. "Shall we meet for dinner? The VIP cabin Zia assigned us would provide some well-deserved rest and privacy."

She smiled widely. "Admit it. Rest is the last thing on your mind. Though privacy would be nice."

He grinned. "You know me. We marines like to live for today. Now go on. I'll let you know as soon as I find out what's going on with Carl."

She headed off in the other direction, and he kept a positive expression on his face until he was sure she couldn't see him anymore. Their situation was bad, and he didn't expect the news from Carl would make it any better.

They were in a tight corner this time. The odds against them being able to get the carrier out of this system were pretty steep. It might be trapped here forever. Then Kelsey would have to decide who they left behind when they took the ships they could and tried to get the tech they'd stolen back to the New Terran Empire.

That wasn't a choice he'd have liked to make. He didn't envy her position at all because that was almost certainly what would end up happening.

15

Veronica was relieved when Colonel Talbot arrived. Maybe he could explain some of what she'd been watching. Her own understanding of the science seemed... inadequate.

Stepping away from the lab bench didn't disturb the scientists fussing over the equipment in the slightest. In fact, they hadn't noticed Talbot arriving or her departing. They were completely immersed in a technical discussion that made Veronica's brain ache.

"Thank God you're here to save me," she murmured. "I think my head is about to explode."

The marine officer laughed. "You obviously haven't been demanding explanations in small words. Preferably those with three or fewer syllables. If you don't yank the science types up short, they'll run right over you. What are they doing?"

"It has something to do with interference and your faster-than-light communications system. Apparently, they were conducting some type of experiment with new hardware, and it's not working the way they expected."

"Good enough." He raised his voice. "Carl, what's going on? Take a break and explain it to me in small words. Princess Kelsey wants a briefing on this and other subjects, so be concise. Pretend you're explaining it to an idiot."

"That's like the opposite of concise," the young man said with a grin. "You know how much longer it takes to explain something to an idiot? If you've got the time, I can fill you in."

"Ha, ha. You're a very funny man. What's the problem?"

Owlet gestured toward a small table nearby. He and Doctor Parker sat on one side while Veronica took the other next to the marine officer.

"It's not exactly a problem," Carl said. "We're not experiencing any issues whatsoever with our operational equipment. What happened is that Jacqueline made some modifications to a testbed to explore the theory and the results didn't match what we expected to see."

"How so?"

The scientist compressed his lips. "We're seeing a reduction in data throughput between the testbed and the FTL probe we're using to send back data. It's positioned on the other side of the system so we can get information at FTL speeds. We send data to it, and it in turn sends it right back. Jacqueline thought that the changes she'd made to the hardware might increase the data throughput, but it seems to have had the opposite effect."

The older woman nodded. "While I'm still getting to the point where I fully understand the hardware, what I expected to happen was to have a slight but noticeable increase in data throughput. Instead, the data is moving at less than one percent of the normal speed.

"Worse, it's inconsistent. Sometimes the hardware is somewhat faster than normal and others it's being heavily throttled. The problem is that it's not behaving the same in every case. It either should work or not work the same way every time."

Veronica cleared her throat. "While I'm not a scientist, it seems to me that something is interfering with the test. We had something similar occur a few years ago when I was helping Fleet Design work on a new tactical simulator.

"Sometimes the thing performed brilliantly and other times it introduced stupid errors that none of us could explain. Worse, it did so on an unusual schedule. It took us weeks to locate the problem."

Carl crossed his arms over his chest and leaned forward, his expression curious. "If you don't mind my asking, what caused the issue?"

"An ensign," Veronica said dryly. "She was logging into the tactical simulator when it was supposed to be reserved and using the processors to work on simulations after hours. She figured since it was test equipment that no one else would be logged in and she'd be able to get a lot more processing time.

"It turns out that she was right. In fact, she managed to use so many processing cycles that it completely wrecked the testing protocols we were trying to run. And the fact that she logged in remotely and at odd times made it almost impossible for us to figure out."

The scientist laughed. "I can totally see that happening. Back when I was a graduate student, we'd steal processing time from any system we could get into. There were always too many people trying to use the regular systems."

Talbot nodded, his expression serious. "Is something like that possible here? Someone being on a system that they're not supposed to be or trying to tap into the same probe?"

Doctor Parker shook her head with a sigh. "If only it was something that easy. The way FTL communications work requires a dedicated pairing between devices because of the entangled particles. That means it's literally impossible for anyone else to be accessing that particular probe.

"And since we're standing next to the testbed and it's not linked to anything else, there's no way anyone is logged in to that machine and using it in some way. Even so, we've been through the logs. Nothing like that showed up."

They were all quiet for a short bit, probably trying to think of something they'd missed.

Talbot leaned back in his seat and shrugged. "I'm sure you'll figure it out. It's not really the most pressing matter on our plates right now, in any case.

"Princess Kelsey is with Commodore Anderson right now and they're discussing an operation in Archibald to get what we need to either repair or replace *Audacious*'s flip drive. We need to know if the drive can be fixed or if we need a new unit."

Carl grimaced. "The engineering people disassembled it as much as they could, and I've tested every part of the system. Usually a failure is in some system or subsystem that has to be swapped out. The basic framework of the unit isn't damaged during normal operations. Hell, even during abnormal operations.

"That's not the case here. When we came through the multiflip point, it set up a resonance deep inside the flip drive. That created power induction where no one ever anticipated anything like that. We'll either need to build structural parts that aren't to Rebel Empire specifications or we'll need an entirely new flip drive."

"Crap," Talbot muttered. "That's bad. That's real bad."

The scientist nodded his head in apparent agreement. "It's worse than that. *Audacious* is significantly larger than other military ships inside the Rebel Empire. Based on what I've seen and been told, the largest vessels they have in operation are heavy cruisers.

"The difference in size of flip drives used for heavy cruisers, or even a battlecruiser, is significant. I doubt very seriously that a flip drive constructed for use in a heavy cruiser would work more than once for a battlecruiser. It wouldn't work at all for this carrier."

Talbot turned to face Veronica. "Can you add anything to that?"

She briefly cast her thoughts back over her years of service for Fleet. Then she shook her head. "I'm afraid not. Doctor Owlet is absolutely correct. Until we ran into you folk, the concept of a battlecruiser was unknown to me. A superdreadnought or carrier? Unthinkable.

"But that doesn't mean we're out of options. What about a flip drive for a freighter of almost this ship's size? One designed for military service."

Carl's expression sharpened. "What do you mean 'designed for military service'? The freighter we have here isn't built to standards that would work for moving the carrier even once. There's a whole different level of quality control and precision necessary when making flip drives for warships. Even a freighter of the correct size wouldn't have a flip drive that would work more than a couple of times at best."

Veronica shrugged a little. "I honestly can't tell you much more than the fact that I've seen military transports that were only somewhat smaller than this ship. Huge freighters made to keep up with Fleet elements. Their grav drives were sufficient to move them at a decent speed, so I'm assuming they were military grade. It's entirely possible their flip drives are too."

Carl rubbed his chin thoughtfully. "That has possibilities. We need to see if any of the computer records we've captured have anything about those ships in them. Commander Giguere, would you feel comfortable working with us to try to locate any information we have?"

"Of course," she said with a nod.

"Excellent," Talbot said. "Be as quick as you can because we really need to get this operation moving. Every day we wait makes it more likely Clan warships are going to try to breach the multiflip point. That would be a disaster for us. It's already going to take far too long to repair this ship. Every minute we delay could spell the death of everyone aboard this ship."

* * *

KELSEY SURVEYED the map they'd put together from their single visit to the Archibald system. It wasn't much to work with considering how far out the multiflip point was, but it was all they had.

One thing it did provide was a rough idea of where the major hubs of communication were. Where people were talking, that's where they were living and working.

"What kind of information were we able to pull out of the various computers we've captured from the Rebel Empire?" Kelsey asked, tapping her lip thoughtfully. "As it sits, we'd be going in virtually blind."

Zia nodded her agreement. "I would love to have more information, but the Rebel Empire compartmentalizes itself. People from one area aren't likely to find much information on other places inside the Empire. That goes for Fleet too.

"The best source of information we have from inside the Rebel Empire is

Commodore Murdoch. Before her transfer to Dresden, she actually worked inside this sector. She's been to Archibald and visited the shipyard."

Kelsey felt her face scrunch up. "Let me guess. She won't help us."

"Actually, she will, for a price. One I've already agreed to because I know you."

Kelsey leaned back and narrowed her eyes. "I'm not certain if I should be worried or annoyed. What does she want?"

Zia reached over the table and tapped the main source of communications in the Archibald system: the main planetary body. "Archibald Prime doesn't just have a shipyard, it also has an advanced medical research facility on the civilian station nearby. One that Commodore Murdoch suspects might have regeneration equipment that could repair her spine."

The unexpected revelation made Kelsey sit back and think. "She wants us to get something to help her? How much complication is that going to add to our mission?"

The Fleet officer shrugged. "I haven't the slightest idea, but it's not going to make things easier. Still, knowing you as I do, I realized you were going to say yes so I agreed."

"And what was she able to give us in exchange? Something worth the hassle she's asking of us?"

"Probably not," Zia admitted. "Though we won't know until we get there. Her memory of the traffic patterns around the planet and some of the procedures will prove useful. I'm not so sure that the information she provided about the shipyard itself is going to help us.

"She was only there a couple of times and saw what they wanted her to see. She was acting as an aide to a flag officer, so she was taken on a grand tour and given explanations on how things worked. That's more than thirty years out-of-date, though."

Kelsey rubbed her face. "We're going to have to take a look for ourselves. The general information she provided, as well as what Commander Giguere can offer, might get us close. Until we can see it with our own eyes and make a judgment on the security, we're not going to be able to plan effectively."

"If the mission is too difficult, then you're going to have to take everything that we've captured back to the Empire and leave *Audacious* here," the Fleet officer said with a scowl. "The Empire needs that information and hardware."

"The Empire needs the information, yes, but I'm not just leaving you here. Castille stirred up the Clans. They'll figure out what they need to do to get through the multiflip point eventually. I'm not leaving you here for them to kill."

"They may never come," Zia insisted. "If they do, they do. Kelsey, you have to accept that you can't save everyone. Sometimes you've got to do what's best for the greatest number of people. Right now, that's the Empire.

"The loss of one carrier and everyone aboard would be a drop in the bucket compared to how many people would die if we don't get the Dresden information and that critical hardware for making the sentient AIs back to the Empire as soon as possible. You and I both know that. The smart thing to do is for you to accept that."

This was the kind of argument Kelsey was used to having with Talbot or Jared. God, how she wished her brother was here right now. He'd know *exactly* what to do. She worked off instinct while he was a planner. He could orchestrate this entire mission down to the smallest detail.

But he wasn't here, and she had no way to talk to him. She'd just have to do the best she could. And that meant not leaving any of her friends behind.

"Zia, have you met me? That's not how I work. And unfortunately for you, I have this thing called a title that lets me tell you what I want accomplished, and then we get to do it my way."

She smiled to take any sting out of what she was saying. She wanted to get across how inevitable this was, not just sound bossy.

The other woman sighed and rubbed her face. "What great sin have I committed against the universe to be strapped with such a stubborn friend?"

"Some of us just get lucky," Kelsey said with a grin. "Let's get the team together. We've got a mission to plan, and I want to be underway within twenty-four hours."

Zia wasted no time calling Angela Ellis and asking her to join her on *Audacious*. The woman was recovering from her final Marine Raider surgery, but she'd want to know what was going on. As expected, *Persephone*'s executive officer came right over.

This time, Angela was able to walk even though she'd had surgery today. This set of operations involved the work on her torso, upper body, and arms. It was going to take the woman some time to adjust to the artificial musculature, but this was it. The surgeries were complete. She was a now a Marine Raider.

Zia wondered if Kelsey understood that meant she might be ordered to turn the Marine Raider strike ship over to Angela once they got back to Avalon. That made the most sense. Kelsey was the crown princess and had more important things to do than commanding a specialized ship.

She grinned and stood at the tall woman as she came into her office. "So, what does it feel like to be the second Marine Raider in the New Terran Empire?"

"I'll let you know as soon as I stop crushing things with my hands," Angela said as she gingerly sat down in one of the chairs to the side of the desk. "Apologize to your maintenance teams for me. I accidentally ripped a support off a bulkhead when I was getting into the lift. My bad."

Zia chuckled and joined her friend. "I'll do that. Are you glad it's over?"

"I'm glad that I didn't have to do it all at one time. What Kelsey went through with the Pale Ones was a nightmare that I am thrilled I didn't have to repeat.

"It's still been painful and it's going to take a while before I'm fully recovered and can start getting up to speed at being a Marine Raider. My only consolation is that Talbot gets to be next. He's been an ass. A friendly, good old boy ass, but still an ass."

Zia shook her head. "I'm glad the two of you get along so well. Having Kelsey as your shared charge has got to be mentally draining. Even at one step removed, she exhausts me. At least now you'll have a chance at keeping up with her and maybe heading her off from doing dangerous things."

"Dangerous things like leading a mission into the Archibald system. And by leading, I mean personally taking the teams in to scout out a Rebel Empire system. That's what she just got finished telling me we needed to plan for. The mission launches in twenty-four hours."

Angela said something pithy that couldn't be repeated in polite company. "I knew this was coming. Really, it was the only way things could possibly go. You couldn't talk her out of it? Obviously not. So, what do we do?"

"We do the best we can to keep her alive and make this mission a success. We've got a lot of really talented people that we can put on board *Persephone* to help with this. I've called you over to start coordinating how we can use that talent to shield Princess Kelsey from herself."

The tall marine shifted in her chair resulting in a loud crack as she broke one of the hand rests off. Bemused, the marine held it up and stared at it.

"I hope you weren't attached to that chair. Sorry."

She carefully set the hand rest down on the small table and sighed. "We're going to have to approach this as cautiously as me sitting down. Kelsey isn't going to want to be protected. That has to be a side effect of what we're doing, not the goal or she'll get mulish.

"The best thing we can do is get all the main players together and start war-gaming on how we might approach this mission. Obviously, the goal is going to be getting in and out without revealing we were ever there. Or at least not having anyone connect us to what's going on while it matters."

"Agreed," Zia said. "We've got Cain Hopwood and his merry crew of recovery agents to start with. They'll blend in, I suspect, based on what I saw on Harrison's World. Fourteen heavily trained specialists skilled in breaking and entering will be very helpful.

"We can add Commander Giguere. She passed Fiona's inspection. The shipyard has a lot of Fleet officers moving through it, so she's going to be invaluable in that aspect of the mission."

Angela grimaced. "She might be able to help us get in, but she's not going to be able to work the equipment we need. For something like that, you're going to need Carl, aren't you?"

Zia smiled apologetically. "I'm afraid so. I already have the broad outlines of a plan in mind. The specifics are really going to depend on a couple of factors. If we can take a flip drive in whole, in parts that they've already manufactured, or if we have to get into their equipment and build something from scratch.

"That last option would be the worst, I suspect. Not only would we have to keep them from realizing we were there, we'd leave tracks that we built something unusual. I'd rather not give them any more information than we absolutely have to. Unfortunately, I really do suspect that's how things are going to go."

The marine settled back in her chair a little. "Could we even steal a flip drive? Those aren't small."

No, they weren't. The burned-out unit on board *Audacious* was about twenty meters in every direction. If they had to steal a completed unit, they couldn't exactly sneak it out in their pockets.

"I haven't got the slightest idea," Zia said with a shrug. "That's why we're going to consult with experts. The first stage of the mission has to come first, though. We have to know the landscape. We have to know exactly what we're dealing with as far as getting in and getting out.

"Once we have all the information we can get on the facility—or I should say facilities—then we'll start devising plans to cover every option we can: stealing a completed flip drive, stealing parts, co-opting the manufacturing equipment to build our own, etcetera."

Angela's eyes narrowed. "You said facilities plural. What does that mean?"

"That's the next complication," Zia said with a wry smile. She proceeded to explain Commodore Murdoch's requirements for her cooperation.

The marine huffed in irritation. "As if this wasn't going to be difficult enough. Do we really have to do it?"

"What would Princess Kelsey say?"

Angela slumped a little. "She'd say we're going to make it happen and then tell me to figure out how."

"So tell me how we're going to make it happen," Zia said with a smirk.

The marine laughed a little in spite of herself. "That's just cruel. I'd say we need to bring Doctor Parker and her researchers in on the discussions. While they may not be *medical* researchers, they probably can tell us a lot more about how to fit into a place like that than we would guess on our own.

"If we have Doctor Zoboroski helping them, they might be able to tell us how to probe the place and figure out what we're going to need to gain access. Then, what we need to do when we get inside."

"What a nightmare. How long did you say we had? An *entire* twenty-four hours? That's a different kind of joke all in itself."

"Look on the bright side," Zia said. "At least we're going to a civilized system and we can do some shopping."

"I hate shopping," Angela muttered. "Nothing ever fits me. I think I hate you."

The two women laughed, but Zia could hear an edge of tension in both their voices. They might make light of it, but there were so many ways this could go very wrong. If the Rebel Empire captured any of them, the New Terran Empire was screwed.

* * *

VERONICA HAD GIVEN up any hope of finding additional information that would be useful on the raid Princess Kelsey was planning when she chanced across something in the data from a previous mission.

Her new friends had captured the Rebel Empire destroyer *R-7386* during a previous supply mission to the Erorsi system. They'd captured the ship mostly intact but had only collared one officer. That man, Lieutenant Commander Michael Richards, had eventually decided to cooperate with the New Terran Empire in exactly the same way Veronica had.

He wasn't what had triggered her curiosity, though. It was his dead commanding officer.

According to the report, her name had been Commander Diane Delatorre. She'd apparently been a real piece of work. Just the kind of person Fleet liked to put in charge of a ship. A backbiting political animal determined to command a task force before she was fifty.

While there was some basic information about the woman in the reports, what caught Veronica's eye was her planet of birth: Archibald.

Much like Commodore Murdoch, the deceased commander started her career on the planet they were targeting. All well and good, though not exceptionally useful in and of itself.

What was useful was the fact the woman had blackmail material on various people that might well be on the planet they were interested in.

None of the juicy details were included in the reports she had access to, but Veronica hoped it would be able to put various people into compromising positions. That kind of clout might enable them to get into places that the Rebel Empire wouldn't want them to be.

But first she needed to know for a fact that they had the critical information.

She glanced over at where Carl Owlet and Doctor Parker were still busy working on the FTL com testbed, walked over, and cleared her throat.

"If the two of you would excuse me, I'm going to leave you to what you're doing and go talk to Colonel Talbot about someone interesting. It seems that one of the destroyer commanders you captured was born in the Archibald system. The one you captured at Erorsi."

Carl's eyebrows shot up. "You mean the one with a bedroom like a bordello? I couldn't believe it when I saw the place."

Now it was Veronica's turn to have her eyebrows rise. "You were there?"

The young scientist nodded. "I cracked her personal communications console while Princess Kelsey and Talbot searched the bedroom. Holy cow."

Doctor Parker shot Carl a sidelong glance. "Just exactly what was in her bedroom?"

Carl Owlet turned beet red, making both women laugh as he squirmed, trying to come up with some kind of answer.

"Let's not get sidetracked," Veronica said smoothly. "The file I accessed said the woman kept blackmail material. None of that is in what I have access to. Can you provide a bit more information about what and who the material covered?"

Obviously relieved to have a way out of answering the previous question, Carl nodded enthusiastically. "There were several encrypted data chips that I haven't taken the time to get into, but there were also a number of printouts in the safe.

"I have no idea who the people were, but since the data seemed... sensitive, I scanned them in and put them into a segregated drive space. I figured we could bring any portion of it we needed to into primary memory if it became important enough."

"Can you give me access to those files? Maybe find a little bit of time to take a look at those data chips?"

"I'll take the data chips," Doctor Parker said. "One of my people is an absolute whiz at breaking codes and data encryptions. One of the side effects of being a primary designer in systems that utilize them. Frankly, it's possible they're encrypted with one of the programs he created. If so, that might give him some unique insight into cracking them."

"I've got them in my office," Carl said. "I'll get them as soon I add Commander Giguere to the access list for the scanned documents."

Veronica smiled her thanks. "I'll just head back over to my console. Let me know when I can access them and where they are."

"You'll have access by the time you sit down. I'll send you the path to the data as well. Thank you."

The man was as good as his word and she already had a pop-up sitting on the screen waiting for her. She accepted the access, went to the files, and started reading.

She was impressed. The dead commander had certainly been building up enough dirt to get that command she wanted. There was evidence in these files of everything from infidelity to murder. And these were only the ones that she kept printed out. The really sensitive information was probably still locked up on the data chips.

Veronica turned the computer loose on the files and had it start searching for any matches in the data the New Terran Empire had collected.

Moments later, she had pay dirt. A number of the people and locations mentioned in the documents were at Archibald.

That made her grin widely. While it was true that some of them would be dead or have moved on, that still probably gave Princess Kelsey a handle to pull on, if she needed it. With any luck at all, the encrypted data chips would open to the researchers' skills and provide them a treasure trove of additional access.

Veronica scrolled back and looked at the image of Commander Diane Delatorre again. A small woman, with a cold face and hard eyes. A very small woman.

A woman with about the same build and size as Kelsey Bandar.

Well, that presented some interesting possibilities.

17

Talbot gave Veronica Giguere an uncertain look. "I remember Delatorre. The Rebel Fleet officer with that wild bedroom and even wilder closet. Are you sure she's from Archibald? If so, that seems like a negative point. People there will know that Kelsey isn't her."

"Maybe. Maybe not. It's been a long time since she left. I know her by reputation. She was working out of Dresden though I don't know that I ever met her in person. She did a lot of solo work for Fleet security. She had the personality for it, I understand.

"If her early career was anything like that, people will remember basic things about her: her height, her build, and her attitude. Minor changes can be written off as cosmetic face work or some such. Princess Kelsey has the perfect build to mimic her."

"But not the correct implant serial numbers," he said. "In a society like the Rebel Empire, that's going to give her away immediately."

Veronica gave him a smile. "You don't realize it, but you've already solved that problem. Carl tells me the latest updates in hardware he's developed allow for something he calls 'stealth mode.' The purpose of that being that people can pretend to be devoid of implants.

"Carl also informs me that he can put together some kind of interface that will present a false serial number to the world at large. From what he says, it would act as kind of a buffer between the real implants and any outside communications.

"If Princess Kelsey wants to interface with a piece of equipment or computer, the outgoing signal will go through the interface and it would leave her with the false serial number. Any communication to the false serial number would go through the interface and directly to her."

She paused for a few seconds. "That takes care of your other concern. If someone sees her and doubts it's really her, they'll check her implants. People will see what they want to see."

"I understand where you're coming from," he said slowly. "But this is going to be a very risky venture, even if everything goes well. I'm not certain I want to trust her safety to unproven hardware. Carl is a genius, but he makes mistakes. Trust me, I've seen a couple of spectacular ones.

"Kelsey advanced the schedule and this mission kicks off shortly. Once we're committed, there's no going back. Did he tell you how long it would take to implant this false interface?"

The formerly Rebel Empire commander nodded. "He already has the hardware on hand. Doctor Zoboroski and his staff can put it in place in about twenty minutes. It's a very simple procedure. The princess already has the upgraded implants that would support stealth mode.

"Most people won't need a false serial number. However, if they get the false interfaces, they can program their own fake identities. Pick somebody off the street that has implants, clone their serial number, and suddenly you can pretend to be them. I'm actually shocked no one has tried to do this inside the Empire already."

That made Talbot grin. "Knowing criminals, they probably already have. Those guys are always on the cutting edge of identity theft. I'd wager the AIs come down on that kind of thing hard to dissuade the survivors from doing it anymore.

"What about the people she might meet from Fleet? They're going to know she's not assigned there. That her ship has been missing for a year. That makes for a lousy cover."

Giguere shook her head. "The differences between your Fleet and mine are tripping you up. The people here will have no insight into where she's been or what she's done since she left. The AIs makes certain that all data from different sections of the Empire is segregated.

"Trust me when I say that no one here is going to know that her ship has been missing. No one other than the System Lord. Our goal is to keep her off its scanners. That shouldn't be hard. We're not coming in with a warship. We're sneaking in on a freighter."

Talbot rose from behind his desk and began pacing. "That's another can of worms. That ship is going to be known to the System Lord. We stole it from Dresden, and you can be sure that word of that theft has gotten out by now."

Giguere shrugged. "From what I hear, there's still a lot of debris floating around Dresden. They might realize the orbital is gone, but maybe not the ship. In any case, we can give it fake papers and a new name. It, too, can be coming in from another sector."

"That seems chancy. While they won't have the information for a ship coming in from outside, it seems that would be a rare occurrence. Like you said, the System Lords don't exactly encourage immigration. Won't that attract the attention of the AI?"

She raised a finger. "I've come up with a solution for that. The freighter that was originally accompanying the dead commander's ship was of the same class. It was destroyed in the fighting, but your records have its codes. That's really all we need since there's no reason the AIs would be looking for that ship. Not here, anyway."

He wasn't completely sure about that, but it was a potential solution to their problem. At this point, he was ready to present the idea to Kelsey and see what she said. If anyone could make it work, it was his wife.

"Good work."

The Fleet officer nodded. "I've been talking with Commodore Murdoch and getting a feel for the place. That's a really conflicted woman, by the way. She hates your people but blames the Rebel Empire for her medical condition.

"If I were you, I'd double-check everything you possibly could that she's passing along. It wouldn't surprise me if she tries to betray you at some point. The woman has a reputation for being an asshole."

Talbot shook his head. "She wants to walk again. To make that happen, we have to get back with the right equipment. She's going to give us everything we need to succeed because her own future rides on it. Trust self-interest to trump everything else when it comes to Commodore Murdoch.

"That said, whenever possible we'll be very cautious with information we haven't verified. This mission isn't going to necessarily work if we rush it. One mistake could sink us. We'll be as careful as possible."

He rubbed his face. "I just can't help but worry about what we're doing. There's so much that could go wrong. Frankly, I can't imagine how we're going to pull this thing off."

Giguere rose to her feet. "It may seem impossible, but I've seen you and your friends work. If anyone can do it, it's you."

"Let's go present this crazy idea to Kelsey and see what she says," he said as he rose to his feet.

* * *

ZIA SAT TENSELY at what passed for a command console on the captured freighter, waiting for something to go wrong now that she'd taken it into the Archibald system.

Intellectually, she knew she didn't have much to worry about because *Persephone* had led the way. There was no enemy shipping close enough to detect them arriving.

That didn't keep her from clenching the armrests on her ratty chair anyway. This was a big step, and her new command was a lot less capable than her old one.

Unlike the magnificent bridge aboard *Audacious*, the freighter only had three console positions: helm and navigation, engineering, and cargo management. Since they'd unloaded the cargo before this mission, storing it inside the carrier, there was no need to man that last spot.

At least there hadn't been until Carl had made a few upgrades to the freighter's passive scanners and communications array. Nothing that would be visible from the outside, but ones that might make their lives a little easier.

That meant he was currently occupying the cargo management console, testing out the equipment to make sure everything was functional.

He turned his seat to face her. "The flip drive came through fine, but that's not a surprise. The segment of the multiflip point linking Pandora and Archibald has a fairly wide frequency band. Much bigger than the one between Icebox and Pandora."

Alan Barnes, the piloting specialist that came with the recovery team headed by Cain Hopwood, cleared his throat. "*Persephone* is headed in. Based on the pre-mission briefing, they're going to get into a decent overwatch position as we follow them. If we have to run, they're supposed to provide security for us, but you'll forgive me if I hope that isn't necessary."

She agreed with that assessment. If they had to flee, she didn't want to lead the Rebel Empire to the multiflip point. So long as they remained ignorant of these odd versions of the standard flip point, that meant that the New Terran Empire could continue sneaking around without being noticed.

They weren't going to be able to get all the way in before Princess Kelsey and the rest of the people selected for the mission took a cargo shuttle over to join her on the freighter. Zia had tried one more time to convince Kelsey not to put herself at risk. Once again, she'd been politely rebuffed. The small woman had a will of steel.

Thankfully, the multiflip point in the Archibald system was about as far off the beaten path as one could get and still be within a decent transit range with the main world. It sat above the plane of the ecliptic far away from anything interesting.

The trick was going to be inserting the freighter into the traffic pattern coming from the main flip point that sat on the other side of the sun from Archibald Prime. Any ships making their way into the system or back out again would note the freighter coming in at the odd angles necessary to join them. Her worry was that someone might talk.

Archibald had a second flip point, but while it was guarded, it didn't seem to get any use. That meant they could only use the main one in their ruse.

The probes that *Persephone* had sent earlier were keeping an eye out for any gap between ships that might give them the time to get close to position without being noticed by other vessels.

It wasn't as if freighters would be actively scanning for anything beyond debris avoidance. That would give them a window.

"What's our situation looking like for getting into the traffic pattern?" she asked Barnes.

He shook his head. "No openings large enough right now. We haven't been watching long enough to see if this is going to be constant or not. This is one of those things you can't rush, Commodore."

According to the plan, they'd edge as close to the traffic pattern as they could and wait for a suitable opening. When it came, they'd be able to make their way into the pattern and hopefully not draw any undue attention.

The main flip point had a battle station guarding it, but they didn't seem to be using it for traffic control. There was no sign of communication between the incoming ships and the battle station. The other side must be a trusted system.

Carl straightened abruptly at his console. "We might have a problem."

"What?" she said, a chill racing down her spine. They hadn't even been here long enough to settle in. What could possibly have gone wrong already?

"The probe at the main flip point just showed the arrival of half a dozen Rebel Empire Fleet warships. Two cruisers and four light cruisers. We have a second transit. Half a dozen destroyers. That makes a dozen enemy vessels."

That spelled trouble. Warships tended to be a little bit more observant. They might see something out of place when the freighter made its entrance. All it would take to ruin them was for someone to send over a boarding party to inspect their supposed cargo.

"What's their ETA to Archibald?" she asked.

The scientist shook his head, his face pale. "They're not headed for the planet. They've set course into the outer system. We need to reverse course, or we'll probably end up inside their detection range before they pass our location."

18

K elsey examined the scanner intake through her implants as she sat down at the head of the small conference table aboard *Persephone*. The other senior members of her team began filing in moments later.

Talbot sat down beside her and took her hand. Not the most professional thing in the world, but she wasn't going to argue, squeezing back with a smile.

Carl Owlet, Commander Giguere, and Doctor Parker were next. Followed quickly by Zia Anderson and Cain Hopwood. The final two through the door were Doctor Zoboroski and Angela Ellis.

Well, she supposed that the final *person* wasn't actually there in the flesh. Fiona, the artificial sentience, was present in much the same way that Marcus was aboard *Invincible* for Jared.

Kelsey cleared her throat. "I'm sure by now that all of you are aware of why I've called you here. The Rebel Empire has invested the Archibald system with an additional dozen military vessels. We're not certain how many are already here, though we've detected some suspicious grav signatures.

"Two heavy cruisers, four light cruisers, and six destroyers entered through one of the two regular flip points a little bit more than an hour ago. That would be the flip point that has traffic. The other one is also guarded by a battle station but doesn't have ships coming through. The other side must not be occupied or along any major trade routes."

"Do we know what they're up to?" Angela asked. "The last I saw, it didn't look like they were headed toward Archibald Prime."

Kelsey shook her head. "They seem to be heading for the outer system."

"Is it possible they're searching for us?" Doctor Parker asked. "Could someone have detected our arrival?"

"It's always possible, but they don't seem to be looking for anyone. They're on a course that probably leads to the outermost gas giant. So far as we know, there are no facilities there, so I'm not sure what they're up to."

"Could it be the System Lord?" Veronica Giguere asked.

"Probably not," Carl said. "The AIs like being somewhat closer to the action than that. They like asteroid belts, if possible. The only known facility at a gas giant held reserve warships. Battlecruisers the AI could use in an emergency. It doesn't seem likely they are going to something like that, or it would ruin the secrecy."

"Is there any point in moving forward with the mission at this juncture?" Talbot asked. "If security is at a heightened state, it would be better to wait until things quiet down."

That left them all quiet for a few moments. Kelsey took advantage of that to lean forward and look around the table, capturing each of their gazes for a few seconds.

"I don't think slipping the freighter into place is going to be as much of a risk as you think. They're not going to be in range to detect us shortly. The one thing that we'll have to change is where we position *Persephone*. I don't believe that it's safe to leave my ship near the multiflip point now. We're going to have to take her deeper into the system."

Angela shook her head. "Anyone seeing a strange warship of a design they've never encountered before is going to sound the alarm. Once forces in the system get agitated, we're never going to escape. Or, if we do, we'll lead them right to the multiflip point, and that would be worse."

"I don't see that we have much of a choice." Kelsey rose to her feet and paced a little. "Also, the risk isn't nearly as significant as you might think. *Persephone* is designed to penetrate hostile systems without being detected.

"She's done similar things in the past, slipping up on Singularity warships without being noticed. Admittedly, that was before the Fall, but my people are up to the task. Ned Quincy saw to that."

Ned Quincy had been a Marine Raider before the Fall. In fact, he'd been the commanding officer aboard *Persephone* in those days. Fatally injured during one of the final fights, his crew had placed him in stasis. They hadn't survived the Fall, and neither had he.

Somehow—they still weren't quite sure how—Kelsey had brought many of the man's memories into her own implants and used software modified by

Marcus to help sort through them. That had the unexpected side effect of creating an artificial intelligence inside her own implants.

Imperial theory said that wasn't possible. No one with any knowledge on the subject whatsoever could understand how it had happened, but it had. It wasn't the original Ned Quincy, but it had started life with many of his memories and experiences.

That gave Ned the ability and experience to train Kelsey's people in every aspect of what they needed to excel at operating a Marine Raider strike ship.

Before he'd gone to sleep and allowed Carl Owlet to extract him from Kelsey's implants, Ned had admitted to her that her crew was almost as good as his people had been. Almost, but not quite. They still needed to keep working hard if they wanted to be the best Marine Raider strike ship in Fleet.

And, of course, they needed to become Marine Raiders in truth. Angela had now been through the full conversion. The large woman still had weeks of workups and training before she was completely attuned with her new body, but she'd already proven she could take Kelsey in a full-on fight with no limitations one time out of three.

Give Angela a week, and she'd win every single fight. That annoyed Kelsey, but she'd known she wasn't a warrior. Angela had been fighting for the Empire her entire life, and she was so much *bigger* than Kelsey.

The only advantage Kelsey had in fighting the woman was her speed and experience. Sadly, that wouldn't be enough as Angela grew into her enhanced body.

That was one person. Talbot was next and then the rest of *Persephone's* crew. There wasn't time to make it happen now. There wasn't even time to get it done over the next couple of months, not for the whole crew.

While she'd been reviewing her thoughts, the rest of them had been considering what she'd just said. No one seemed convinced, but in the end, that didn't really matter. She was in command, and she would make the final decision.

"Once the freighter is in orbit, the locals won't be paying it much attention so long as there is no unusual traffic to catch their eye. We should be able to get the people we need onto the orbital station without too much trouble. Once we have the lead team in place, we can get the rest of our folks aboard without taking that kind of risk."

Veronica Giguere frowned. "I'm not sure I follow. How will you get more people aboard without drawing attention?"

Kelsey smiled. "You haven't been completely briefed on some of the technological breakthroughs we have access to. Maybe we should take a couple of minutes to explain phase two of the plan. After all, Fiona has confirmed your loyalty. It's time to bring you all the way in."

* * *

VERONICA STARED at the massive ring they were assembling in the freighter's engineering compartment. Even after reviewing the recordings that Carl Owlet had made on board the alien station the New Terran Empire had discovered in the Nova system, she'd had difficulty believing this was even possible.

"I felt the same way," Doctor Parker said. The woman had been standing beside Veronica the last few minutes in silence.

She turned toward the research scientist. "This violates just about every concept I've ever had about how science works. Yes, flip points traverse great distances in the blink of an eye, but science can explain them. In general, anyway. Once you start getting into the specifics, only the experts really understand the science."

"Don't let them fool you. Even the experts really don't understand what's going on with them. Hence, the multiflip points and the far flip points. Imperial theory predicted neither of those two potentialities and no one noticed."

The older woman gestured toward the ring. "This is something completely different. Point-to-point matter transportation. Better yet, you can relocate the rings wherever you want within a short distance, and they still work. And yes, I'm calling five thousand kilometers a short distance. On the scale of flip points, that's nothing."

"How does it work?" Veronica asked. "How can it *possibly* work?"

Parker shrugged. "Not even Carl has managed to explain the science to me yet and he has all of the research that the Omega race compiled on the subject. There are a couple of barriers to understanding: first translating the original documents into Standard, then trying to get a grasp of both the science and manufacturing processes, and finally just getting a clue how they developed the science in the first place.

"This has to be connected in some way to their station in the Nova system. From what I understand, it's a transport ring taken to ludicrous extremes. One that doesn't need a matched pair which strongly implies the possibility that a ring this size could be used solo, though even the Omegans never cracked that mystery.

"The ring station originally tapped into the power of a star to create an opening into alternate realities. At least that's the story the alien tells. Somewhere in the theory for that lies the source of these transport rings."

Veronica could sort of see the connection. In a vague way.

"Do you think the transport rings came first?" she asked.

"Almost certainly. How an aquatic race ever developed this kind of manufacturing in the first place is beyond me. It seems extremely unlikely that they were able to work metal in an ocean. For the life of me, I don't understand how they became technological at all.

"Carl tells me that the alien gave him a set of disks made of some crystalline substance and a reader to pull the data off of them. Supposedly those discs contain the entirety of the knowledge of the alien race. That's a lot of data to parse.

"He's been working on some type of hybrid reader that could pull data off of the discs and put it directly into our computer mediums, but he hasn't quite gotten it worked out yet."

Veronica considered that for a long while in silence. "Those can't have been the only magnificent scientific breakthroughs that people made. Just to get to the point of creating a station that could use the power of a star to explore other realities would have to mean any number of tremendous breakthroughs that came before it.

"Hell, even the concept of alternate realities makes my brain spin. Are we talking about places where there are copies of you and me? Realities that one couldn't tell the difference between ours and theirs? Ones where humanity never developed? Universes inimical to all life?"

Parker nodded. "All of those and more besides. Considering the power requirements, I'd wager that no trans-universal gates will be created anytime soon, but the Omega station created a pair of brand-new flip points between the Nova system and two other systems: Pentagar and Avalon. Permanent flip points."

The thought of that kind of power frightened Veronica. The Omega race was so much further advanced than humanity that they could've crushed it, had the timelines had matched up and they'd been so inclined. With enough time, the New Terran Empire could develop a level of technological power to bring the Rebel Empire to its knees.

If they had enough time to make it work.

Veronica considered Doctor Parker. "You're being friendlier than I would've expected, Doctor. I appreciate the courtesy."

The older woman smiled slightly. "I've had some time to think. While you might have served the Rebel Empire and the AIs, you've got the moral backbone to stand up to them. If you're going to leave your entire life behind to stand beside me, the least I can do is try to be civil."

"I appreciate that," Veronica said sincerely. "This is all so strange to me and my people, but we want to do the right thing. We need to correct the wrongs we've been allowing to occur through inaction. I believe there are plenty of others inside the Rebel Empire that would do the exact same if they only knew the truth."

Somewhat hesitantly, Doctor Parker reached up and put a hand on Veronica's shoulder. "The time is coming for an open conflict between the New Terran Empire and the Rebel Empire. You're going to have a chance to tell your story and be heard by millions."

Veronica frowned slightly. "What do you mean?"

"When the fighting starts, they're going to need people to tell the worlds that fall under the sway of the New Terran Empire exactly what's been going on. Who better to do that than someone from the Rebel Empire? Someone like you."

After staring at the scientist for a few seconds, Veronica felt her stomach give a slow roll. "I'm not much of a public speaker. I kind of have issues with that."

Parker grinned. "We all have our burdens to bear, Commander. I'm sure you'll do fine."

19

T albot stood just behind Carl as his friend worked over the scanner console on *Persephone*'s bridge. Under Kelsey's direction, the Marine Raider strike ship had slipped farther into the Archibald system. The freighter trailed them at a safe distance, ready to retreat if an enemy ship came too close.

The Rebel Empire warships had continued on their way toward the outermost gas giant. To the best of their detection ability, the warships didn't even make contact with the station or shipyard orbiting Archibald.

In another stroke of good luck, once the warships had come through the main flip point, there was a gap of several hours before the next merchant ship had transited. With a little adroit maneuvering, it would be possible to insert their freighter into the traffic pattern with no one being the wiser.

The probes they'd seeded throughout the system had detected no transmissions from the battle station at the designated flip point, so there should be no record of which ships were expected to arrive at Archibald Prime. All the approvals had to have happened earlier in the journey.

Kelsey had launched a number of stealth probes to examine Archibald Prime from several vantage points. Her goal was to determine what assets were already in orbit and how they could be accessed, if need be.

The shipyard was the largest structure orbiting Archibald's moon and easily dwarfed the yards they'd seized in the Erorsi system when they'd captured it. It even topped the ones they were building back in the New Terran Empire by a good margin.

He wondered how many other yards like this existed inside the Rebel

Empire. If there were similar ones in every major system, they could collectively produce a lot of ships in a relatively short period of time. That was bad news.

Still, there had been no yards at Harrison's World, so they couldn't be everywhere. Paranoia was only a good thing when taken so far.

The station in orbit around Archibald wasn't in the same league as the massive shipbuilding structure. It was comparable to Orbital One back home, so that was still saying something. He wondered why it was in planetary orbit but the shipyard was circling the moon. Wouldn't it make more sense to have them closer together?

Carl grunted and tapped his console, expanding a window. It looked like the passive scanner feed of the distant warships.

"What have you got, buddy?" he asked softly.

The other man turned in his seat and faced him. "All twelve of the enemy ships really are heading for the outermost gas giant. The question in my mind is, why? Are they heading to a secret station with battlecruisers like we found near Harrison's World? If so, what's driving them? They're supposed to be a deep, dark secret."

"I know we said that the AI would be closer in, but what if it's not?" Talbot asked. "Maybe they positioned this one way out there."

"That just doesn't make any sense. The communications lag would be big. Even with their normal positioning in an asteroid belt, that introduces a significant lag. This would be unworkable."

The young scientist turned his seat toward Talbot. "Whatever they're doing, it has to be something with the station holding the battlecruisers. That's going to impact our mission. The raid was risky before, but the odds of the Rebel Empire Fleet directly intervening had just gotten a whole lot worse."

Talbot considered that and then nodded slowly. "Agreed, but it doesn't change anything. Kelsey is still going forward with the plan. We both know that. Can you redirect an FTL probe to keep an eye on them?"

"Already done," Carl said with a nod. "I have several moving out that way slowly, so they won't reach the gas giant today. They'll arrive sometime tomorrow and start using their passive scanners to gather data. I programmed them to send their take every six hours with some randomization thrown in to keep any observers from detecting a pattern in the grav pulses."

"I know you keep saying the FTL coms are detectable, but realistically, how serious a risk is that?"

The scientist shrugged. "It's a low-order probability. The pulses are weak, and so long as they are kept brief, isolating exactly where they're coming from would be difficult. Just pulling them out of the background noise in a system this big would be a challenge.

"I'm taking extra precautions in having more than one probe watch the gas giant. Two will be in orbit around it and two others will be a long distance away. The close ones will use regular tight beams to get the data to the outer probes and only when the gas giant is between those and the targets will the distant probes use FTL coms."

"We should do something similar near the Archibald Station and the yard, just in case," Talbot said. "We could talk to *Persephone* and give Angela updates via tight beam. She wouldn't be able to return the favor, but something is better than nothing."

Carl nodded. "Already done. And if push comes to shove, we have a couple of FTL coms we can use to talk to her directly. Those are a last resort sort of thing, but if we don't have them, we might desperately need them."

"We'll need self-destructs on those. We can't let the Rebel Empire know about FTL."

"Already done. There's a plasma grenade in each that can be set on a timer, manually detonated instantly, or remotely set off just like the ones we've built into the rings. Princess Kelsey, you, and anyone you designate will have the codes to make it happen."

Talbot really hoped they didn't have to destroy the rings. They were priceless and irreplaceable.

Still, they'd gotten away with using them once already. The odds were against them this time and, if push came to shove, he'd destroy the rings to keep the Rebel Empire from getting their hands on the alien tech. Or even grasping what they could do, if he could.

"It would suck if we have to destroy the rings," he said after a moment. "I know we have the plans to build them, but that isn't likely to happen in the short term, is it?"

"No," Carl said with a shake of his head. "We're still designing the tools to build the machines that can start setting up other machines that can make the parts for the rings. They are easily a year or two out. Further if we run into problems, which is inevitable since we don't understand the theory completely."

"We'll plan as best we can and hope it doesn't come to that."

Carl laughed a tad bitterly. "We got lucky last time so I'm not holding my breath. Keep your options open and save the small ring, if you can."

"I'll try, buddy. I really will."

He knew that didn't mean much if things went bad, but he'd do his best to leave them with options when the time came.

* * *

EIGHTEEN HOURS LATER, Zia was back at the command console on the freighter. Enough of a gap had developed in the flow of ships from the main flip point to Archibald Prime that they could slip into the pattern without raising any eyebrows.

Unfortunately, their time of anonymity was at an end. According to the data their probes had gathered, the freighter was just about at the range where traffic control would contact them.

If she said something wrong, there was no way the freighter could get back to the multiflip point without being intercepted. Worse, she couldn't even try, or they might find it. Everything had to go perfectly, or they were screwed.

"We have an incoming signal, Commodore," Alan Barnes said from the helm console. "It's traffic control."

"Call me Zia. One slip now and some very bad things will start happening."

The man nodded. "Got it. Sorry. You want this on the main screen?"

"Give it to me on my console."

Moments later, the image of a man in a Fleet uniform with lieutenant's tabs appeared. His expression seemed bored to her. Good.

"This is Archibald Control," he said, his voice monotone. "I need your port of origin, manifest, and the names of any shipping companies you're doing business with."

Their knowledge of Rebel Empire trade was somewhat short of minuscule, but they'd hit pay dirt looking at the computer records on board this freighter. While the data wasn't going to be useful for specifics, it gave them the appropriate format for such files and recordings of many communications just like this one.

"Sending now," Zia said, adding a somewhat sour note to her tone. "I hope this isn't going to be the same kind of cluster we had a couple of stops back. We just want to see what goods you have available and blow off a little steam. We don't have any cargo destined for Archibald."

The man nodded absently and studied the screen off to his left. "If you're not off-loading, we don't have to bother with a customs inspection. Just the usual ID checks to get on the station. I'll send you parking instructions. Welcome to Archibald."

The screen went dark and Zia sagged a little. "I was afraid that wouldn't be good enough for them. Get us into our spot, Alan. I'll go brief everyone."

The bridge was too small for every interested party to be there. In fact, if they'd had to use the main screen, the presence of any extra people would've seemed odd. That meant Princess Kelsey and the others were in a makeshift conference room nearby.

Zia rose to her feet and quickly made her way back. Everyone looked expectantly toward her as she stepped into the compartment.

"So far, so good. We won't have any customs officials coming our way, and they've given us a parking orbit. They'll be expecting some of us on the station, so we'll see how good our identification is. I'm not expecting them to be all that thorough unless we have to go down to the surface."

Talbot smiled a little at that. "As Carl says, show them what they expect to see, and they won't ask any questions."

"That's not what I say," Carl protested mildly. "Weren't you listening? People see what they expect to see. As long as you don't give them a reason to question their initial impressions, they won't change them."

Veronica frowned at Carl. "That seems like a very unscientific sort of thing to say. Or maybe it's just unusual for a scientist to be saying it."

The young man grinned at her. "I've had some interesting teachers."

Princess Kelsey rapped her knuckles on the table. "Focus, people. This completes step one of our plan. We're in a position to start scouting the station. From there, we have to figure out a way to get over to the shipyard. I'm certain they have some kind of regular transport, but Fleet is going to be paying attention to the people that are on it.

"Some of us are going to have to start looking over the medical research facility too. Based on what Commodore Murdoch said, it's located here on this station. That's going to make it easier to access, but there will undoubtedly be issues with timing between the two operations.

"The people looking into the research facility won't be able to act until we have what we need from the shipyard, but they'll have to know for certain if anything warrants our attention before then. If there's not, then we're not going to break in."

"But we won't know what they have *unless* we break in," Carl objected. "So we kind of have to halfway break in? Break in and then break back out? Something like that."

The princess smiled. "That's going to be up to you to figure out. It's entirely possible that you, Doctor Parker, and her computer specialist can break in remotely and ransack their files. If so, that makes our job a lot easier."

Doctor Parker shook her head. "Research facilities keep their classified data on disconnected systems. We're not going to be able to find out what projects they're working on without getting physical access."

"Maybe. Maybe not. Keep in mind that this isn't like the research you were doing, Doctor. These folks might have communications that mention what their projects are. If we can find any evidence of an advanced regeneration device, then we'll have to proceed. Otherwise, the secondary mission is still discretionary."

Zia smiled at Kelsey. "Since they've seen my face, I think it might be best if I'm one of the ones that goes on board station to get us some temporary housing."

Kelsey nodded. "Take Commander Giguere with you. The two of you can look around for suitable housing and get a read on what we're dealing with."

"We'll make it happen."

She wondered how much gray hair she was going to have by the time this mission was over. Being among the enemy for any kind of extended period of time was going to be nerve-racking. Well, she'd just have to make sure no one slipped up.

20

W hile Veronica might never have been aboard Archibald Station, she'd visited plenty of orbitals like it over the years. Coming as a civilian, she discovered, was significantly different than how it had been as part of Fleet.

The docking bays in the civilian section were significantly busier than the ones in the military areas she'd visited, the crowds more chaotic, and the people more varied. Especially in the clothing they wore. It seemed every color imaginable was represented in some form.

Including some in eye-searing fluorescent shades that almost hurt to look at.

There was also more shouting than she was used to. People unloading various cargo shuttles all seemingly had something to say to one another at the top of their lungs. It was kind of weird how many emotions could be carried from person to person at maximum volume.

Zia Anderson stepped out and put her hands on her hips as she looked over the bay. "It's just like back home."

Veronica turned her head slightly toward the other woman and raised an eyebrow. "I'm surprised you had this much chaos at your previous job. If it was anything like mine, it was a lot more orderly."

The taller woman laughed. "I had a life before that job, you know. My parents were merchant spacers. I've probably seen a dozen bays just like this before I became an adult. I never would've thought it would be so similar. Where are we going to get housing while we're here? Any ideas?"

Rather than answering the question, Veronica stepped over to a pair of men arguing over a crate. She wasn't sure if they were disputing the ownership or just the disposition, but they were enthusiastic in their posturing.

"Hey, boys," she said. "We're new. Where can some of our crew hole up without spending all our cash? We'd rather be drinking."

The men paused their heated discussion, and one of them pointed down a nearby corridor. "Go straight down that. Past the third cross corridor you'll find Statler's. It's not the bottom of the pile or the top, so it should suit you just fine."

Without waiting for a response from her, they resumed their argument as if she'd never interrupted them.

Zia laughed as the two women stepped into the indicated corridor. "That went a little bit easier than I'd expected. Good thinking."

"Why make it hard?" Veronica asked with a shrug. "Everybody in this bay has been the new guy at some point. Asking for directions isn't going to raise any eyebrows.

"We should keep that in mind going forward. The more we behave like everyone else, the less we'll stand out. The goal is to blend into the crowd so thoroughly that no one remembers us once we've left."

It only took them a couple of minutes to find Statler's. As the man had said, it wasn't much to look at, but it wasn't a dive either.

Veronica took the lead as they stepped inside and headed toward a short, balding man sitting behind a relatively tall counter.

"One room or two?" he asked disinterestedly.

"We're acting as point for our crew, so do you have a dozen rooms available? If so, how much for the block? We like them close together since we're a tight-knit bunch."

The man nodded, showing some interest for the first time, and tapped a couple of keys on the small computer built into the counter. "How long you plan to stay?"

She shrugged. "Depends on how fast we find what we need. Might be a couple of days. Might be as much as a week. Hard to say at this point."

"The weekly rate might suit you better, then. If I charge you by the day and you extend, you're going to pay more for that same stretch of time. If you book the week and leave in a couple of days, I'll cut you a bit of a break."

The price he quoted wasn't too outrageous, so Veronica paid it. Thankfully, the New Terran Empire had a good supply of Rebel Empire money. That was going to come in handy during this mission, she was sure.

People kept wondering why money never went fully digital, but she knew the answer. So that folks could make payments like this without showing up on any electronic record.

If there'd been some kind of digital credit, there'd be a trail to follow. By paying cash, no one would figure out where they'd come from or where they'd gone. Or what they'd paid for while they were here.

They went up to check the rooms after the man had given them the keys. A quick tour of each confirmed that they were of adequate quality. Not top-of-the-line but certainly not the worst she'd ever seen. They'd do.

Their block of rooms sat at the end of a hall, and Zia pointed toward one of the rooms at the very far side. "We'll take that one."

It was a fairly standard sort of place with two smaller beds. They were still larger than what Veronica was used to, though.

"Sounds good," she said. "We'd best go get our bags and signal the rest to start coming over."

Their good luck lasted almost all the way back to the shuttle. A pair of men in security uniforms came out of the bay just as they were about to enter. Veronica thought they were going to walk past and moved to the side, but one of the men intentionally singled her out and blocked her passage.

"Identification," he demanded, his hand extended.

Crap. Well, it looked as if she was about to find out how well the New Terran Empire could forge identity documents. If hers didn't pass muster, this mission was in very deep trouble and so was she.

* * *

KELSEY STARED at herself in the mirror, somewhat amazed at her transformation. To match the appearance of the dead Rebel Empire Fleet commander she was impersonating, Kelsey had allowed Angela to cut her hair into a bob and color it an almost midnight black.

She'd also allowed her large friend to apply makeup in the same style as some of the images that they'd found on the wall in the woman's office. Kelsey was no stranger to makeup, but she tended to use it in such a way as to enhance her light complexion and golden hair.

The dead woman had favored a stronger hand. More makeup and in stronger colors to contrast her dark hair. Definitely not Kelsey's style.

To her annoyance, Talbot seemed intrigued. He walked around her, examining her new looks closely.

"I have to say, this is quite a change. You look a bit... dangerous."

"I'm always a bit dangerous, and it's not my looks that are turning you on. It's what you saw in that woman's closet. Which, by the way, I'm *still* not wearing."

Her husband laughed. "It doesn't matter what you wear or, for that matter, don't wear. I'll love you just the same. Still, you can't stop me from imagining you dressed like that. I think you'd be exceptionally sexy. Not that you aren't already exceptionally sexy."

"You're not helping yourself," she growled playfully. "Tell you what. If we get out of this place with everything we need, I'll let you pick something from the stash for me to wear."

"Talk about motivation. Now I'm going to move Heaven and Earth to get what we need. Which, of course, I was going to do anyway."

He stepped back after giving her a quick kiss and examined the uniform hanging from a hook nearby. It was a Rebel Empire Fleet uniform with commander's tabs. They'd had it made special for this mission based on Veronica Giguere's own uniform.

"Do you think you're going to need this? I thought we were leaving the shipyard portion of this to Zia and Veronica."

Kelsey slid an arm around his waist and stared at the uniform. "I'm still not sure. It's possible we'll stay in civilian clothes the entire time. It's better to have it and not need it than to need it and not have it."

She sighed. "I know it's just a disguise, but it feels dirty dressing up like that woman. Not as in the sexy kind of dirty, but the kind you can't scrub off. She was a vile human. How can someone like that have gotten into a senior position inside the Rebel Empire's version of Fleet?"

Talbot squeezed her back for a moment and then released her. "Their version of Fleet isn't really designed the same way ours is. Superficially, it looks the same, but it's not. The New Terran Empire's version is there to protect us from any threat. That woman's version was meant to suppress humanity.

"Even though the lowest ranks don't know what the System Lords really are, the personalities of the senior officers define everything about how Fleet operates. Those people are like a distorted mirror version of the folks you know. Evil."

She almost asked how something like that could operate for even just a little while, but she already knew the answer. She'd heard Olivia West describe the Fleet presence on Harrison's World. Talbot was right. They were oppressors, not defenders.

Not that there weren't some good apples in the bunch. Olivia's dead fiancé, for example, or Captain Black, the man in charge of the Grant Research Facility. But they were the exceptions rather than the rule.

In her Fleet, the percentages were reversed. They had plenty of great people and just a few bad ones like Wallace Breckenridge. Thank God.

She shook off her bad mood. "I'm tired of waiting. We haven't heard anything negative from Zia, so let's go over now."

"I don't think we should do anything until we hear from her," he objected. "No signal might mean that someone's captured them. After all, it's not like they can use their implants without giving themselves away. They're in stealth mode. Any signal at all might blow their covers."

"They have coms," she countered. "All they have to do is signal the shuttle, and it will retransmit something to us. They have a panic button too. If they're about to be captured, they wouldn't hesitate to hit it.

"No. They haven't run into significant trouble at this point, and I'm tired of sitting around doing nothing. If we're not relocating now, we will be shortly. Let's get everyone together and head over. With the enemy warships in the system, we can't afford to waste any time."

"I think this is a really bad idea, but I know that arguing with you isn't going to help," he muttered. "For safety's sake, I think we should take two more of the cargo shuttles over to the orbital. That way if something happens, maybe some of us can get away."

Kelsey knew that wasn't really an option. If the Rebel Empire discovered who they were, the freighter wouldn't escape.

"We can hope," she said softly. "Once we get onto the orbital, I'll send a message to Zia and get a status from her. Make sure that Carl has the special cargo ready to go. I don't want us to have to come back for anything. If we might need it, I'd rather have it with us. Any unnecessary movement could draw unwanted attention."

Following her own advice, Kelsey slipped her uniform into a clothing bag and grabbed what she intended to take with her. If things went badly, it wouldn't matter, so she had to plan for things to go well.

They *had* to go well. She wasn't going to let everyone down like that. She'd make this work or die trying.

21

Z ia forced herself not to tense. The Rebel Empire was filled with paranoid people, and identification checks were probably standard procedure.

Veronica dug her forged ID out of her vest pocket and handed it to the security man. His eyes scanned it before looking back up at the other woman.

"I don't recognize your ship's name," he said. "What does *Squared Circle* mean anyway?"

The former Rebel Empire Fleet commander shrugged. "I didn't name the damn ship, so I have no idea. We're just looking for cargo and want to have a good time before we head back out. What needs to happen to make sure our friendly visit stays friendly?"

The security man smiled. "Isn't that what everyone wants? I can arrange for security to leave you and your crew alone, but it's going to cost you."

He named a price. It seemed to be a fairly reasonable rate. Not that Zia was all that familiar with bribes.

She had to admit that she was surprised at how blatant the exchange of money for protection was. It was carried out like a straightforward business transaction.

"What's your name?" Veronica asked as she dug the money out and handed it over. "If someone gets too pushy, I want to know who to refer them to."

"Alden Stoffel. I'll put the word out. If someone gives you trouble, it's because you're doing something you shouldn't. Behave, and everyone will come out of this happy. Understand?"

Veronica nodded. "Pleasure doing business with you."

The two security men resumed their journey into the orbital, and Zia followed Veronica back to their cargo shuttle. Once they were safely inside, she turned to the other woman and raised an eyebrow.

"Is that common? I have to say that's not how things work in the New Terran Empire. At least I hope not."

The news seemed to surprise Veronica. "Really? How do you make sure security doesn't harass you or stick their noses in where they shouldn't?"

"Our security officers stick their noses in the things that are actually business related as opposed to extorting protection money."

"What a strange place your Empire must be," Veronica mused. "It's the cost of doing business here. They have to deliver on the protection, or word gets out, and the payments dry up. The less scrupulous ones get dealt with by their comrades."

Zia didn't know what to say. Their worlds were so different.

"I hope you'll get to find out just how different our world is soon. It's going to be an adjustment, I'd imagine."

"It sure sounds like it. Now that we have the rooms set aside, do we call everyone over?"

Zia nodded. "Shockingly, it seems as if it might be relatively safe to do just that. Especially since you just paid to make sure we weren't harassed. Maybe that'll help us get the gear to the rooms without being searched."

"From what I understand, there are only a few bulky pieces," Veronica said, her tone indicating agreement. "Those might be a little more troublesome but nothing we can't handle so long as we act casually.

"The first step is getting them onto the station and organizing the trip from the bay to Statler's. We'll send out scouts to make sure we don't get stopped by security."

The cargo shuttle's com chimed. Zia hoped it wasn't anything bad as she went to the cockpit and pressed the accept button.

"Zia."

There hadn't been much call to use fake names. It wasn't as if the Rebel Empire knew who they were.

"There you are," Kelsey said. "I got tired of waiting. We have two shuttles making the trip now. We'll be in the bay in a couple of minutes. We brought all the gear we discussed. Did you get us rooms? Better yet, did you find a bar?"

Zia smiled. Some of that was choreographed because they knew that others could be listening in. Probably would be.

"Of course I did. The rooms are all reserved, and we're back at our shuttle. As soon as you land, we'll get everything back to the place we rented, and then we can see about that bar."

"Excellent. You haven't had any trouble, I take it?"

"Nothing we couldn't handle. I let Veronica take lead, and she did a great job. We'll meet you by the bay exit in fifteen minutes. Hope you're ready to relax."

Kelsey laughed. "You have no idea. See you in fifteen."

Zia press the button to end the call and headed back to the main part of the cargo shuttle. "Kelsey and the rest will be here in a couple of minutes. I'm not going to feel safe until we have everything in the rooms. Do we need to worry about security searching our quarters? Some of the stuff we're bringing would get a lot of negative attention."

Weapons, high-tech gear to break and enter, specialized computers for hacking, and the small transport ring. Any of that would set security's hair on fire.

"They shouldn't," Veronica said. "We'll just keep our heads down and move forward with the plan."

Fifteen minutes later, Zia spotted Princess Kelsey leading a small crowd of almost two dozen people. A couple of them were moving a trolley with a couple of small crates, and everyone had packs just like the ones Veronica and she had retrieved from the shuttle.

Kelsey looked stunningly different. The shorter, darker hair and more pronounced makeup, combined with a sterner expression on her face, really did make the princess look like a stranger.

That didn't stop the small woman from giving her a hug as soon as they came together. "I was worried you wouldn't get everything set up by the time we arrived. I kind of jumped the gun."

Zia eyed the crates that Carl was hovering near. "We need to get these back to the rooms as soon as possible. Veronica made an arrangement with security to leave us unmolested, but I'm not sure that taking crates into the station won't get someone's attention.

"Veronica and some of our people are going to spread out and keep an eye out for security. If they spot someone, they'll signal us and we'll find a place to loiter until the course is clear. We probably should have someone trail along behind us just to make sure some enthusiastic security team doesn't come running up on us."

"Excellent idea," the princess agreed. "Let's get moving."

Veronica quickly conferred with the people assigned to scout. They spread out and headed into the station. A minute later, the main group moved to follow.

Zia was starting to relax when she spotted movement out of the corner of her eye. A couple of women exiting one of the restaurants near the cargo bay. Both wore lanyards that indicated they worked in the cargo bay.

It seemed as if they would walk into the bay without comment until one of them stopped and glared at Carl. "Hey! Where are you going with that? Has it been checked? Let me see your papers."

Oh crap.

* * *

TALBOT DIDN'T GIVE Carl a chance to respond. Before the young scientist could say a single word, the marine inserted himself between the two women and the crates.

"These were already cleared," he said smoothly. "There's no need for any trouble."

The woman who'd demanded the papers glared up at him. "I decide if there's going to be trouble. No taking cargo out of the bay without the appropriate clearance. Moving anything onto the station itself requires an examination."

He glared at her. "And who exactly are you? So far as I know, you're just some idiot trying to cause me trouble. And good luck talking yourself out of that category."

The woman bristled even more at his words. She grabbed the badge hanging from her lanyard and shoved it into his face.

"Associate Supervisor Marya Franzen, cargo control. You either trot out your paperwork, or I call security. I can tell you right now, your attitude is going to cost you."

He saw that Kelsey was about to step forward and insert herself into the conversation, but Zia beat her to it. The commodore extended some folded paper toward the supervisor.

"Sorry about that," she said, her tone bored. "He's new. Here's the paperwork. I think you'll find everything in order."

To Talbot's amazement, the folded paper turned out to be money. His friend was trying to bribe their way out of trouble. And not subtly, either. Right out there for everyone around them to see!

He waited for the supervisor to start shouting for security, but all she did was count the money and make a gesture for more. "This is light, and your mouthy friend just cost you even more. Take it out of his pay."

Zia counted out more money and handed it over.

The woman pocketed it and gestured for her companion to follow her as they departed toward the cargo bay.

Talbot watch them go in stunned amazement. Then he turned his attention to his friend.

"What the hell was that? Better yet, how could that *possibly* have worked?"

Kelsey waived a hand between Zia and him. "It doesn't matter right now. We need to get these crates out of sight. Pick up the pace a little, but don't be obvious about it."

Even though he was certain security would pounce on them before they arrived at their lodgings, Zia led them to a place called Statler's without trouble.

Only once they had the crates locked up in Carl's room did Talbot start to relax even a little bit. This was crazy. What had just happened? Time for some answers.

He found Zia in one of the rooms at the end of the hall with Veronica, Kelsey, and Doctor Parker. He walked right up to her and fixed her with a scowl.

"Have you gone insane? Offering bribes to an official? She could've turned us in. Second, how the hell do you know how to bribe anyone?"

The flag officer smiled a little and inclined her head toward Veronica. "I have to admit that I was just as skeptical as you were, until I saw Veronica bribe security to leave us alone. Apparently, that's a thing here. If you want to get anything done, you have to be a little free with the cash.

"Thankfully, the behavior is so prevalent that no one bats an eye when you offer them money to bend the rules. In fact, it seems to be expected."

She turned to fully face Veronica. "Is my understanding correct? Even for things that are supposed to be perfectly legal, adding cash to the equation is expected?"

The Rebel Empire Fleet commander nodded. "It's part of the cost of doing business. People along the chain of whatever you're doing expect to get a gratuity for doing their work. If you want them to step outside the bounds of what's normal, the required gratuity gets larger.

"From what I understand, Zia did exactly the right thing. That person wanted money in order to allow a violation to occur. You gave her what she wanted, and she went on her way with no one being the wiser. Excellent work."

Kelsey shook her head. "I don't think I'm ever going to understand the Rebel Empire. Some of this behavior makes my head spin. Still, I have to say I'm glad you were able to think on your feet, Zia. Allow me to second Veronica. Excellent work."

Talbot wasn't sure about that, but what was done was done. He checked the chronometer set into the desk. "It looks like it's fairly late here on the station. We should probably take the opportunity to get something to eat before we get down to really planning out what we need to do tomorrow.

"I'm sure this place is busy during the evenings and night, but we have a better chance going unnoticed if we do what we need to do during normal business hours. Frankly, it's been a stressful couple of days. We need to make sure we stay rested."

Kelsey nodded. "And as usual, I'm starving. Let's see if we can find a place to eat and bring something back for those of us that are staying here to guard the equipment."

Talbot was in favor of food and sleep. The stress of sneaking to Archibald Station and getting aboard had exhausted him. He needed to have his head about him tomorrow. That's when the real fun started.

22

B y the time Kelsey led the majority of the team out to find a local eatery, it was what she'd have called deep evening back on Avalon. In fact, most working people they'd seen earlier were probably at home now.

That didn't mean there were no restaurants open. The station had people working in shifts at all hours, and they needed to eat. Finding something interesting was as simple as walking a few hundred meters down the main corridor.

Carmona's purported to be something called Italian food. Kelsey checked her implants and found a reference to a region of old Terra. Apparently, it used to be quite favored in dining. Somehow, it had died off on Avalon, and thus the New Terran Empire had no record of it.

That wasn't to say that things like spaghetti and meatballs were unknown. They just weren't attached to the name 'Italian food.' Or to the other dishes on the menu, most of which meant nothing to her. Thankfully, there were pictures and short descriptions that allowed the diner to determine what they wanted to try.

She settled on something called lasagna. The server suggested fried mozzarella sticks as an appetizer, so Kelsey ordered enough for the entire group.

While they couldn't exactly discuss business out in public, they nibbled around the edges of what their plans would be during the next day.

Zia and Veronica would probe how difficult it was going to be to get over to the shipyard. Talbot, Doctor Parker, and she would scope out the research facility. Carl would be working remotely to see if he could get into the less secure sections of the computer network here on the station.

The fried mozzarella was good, but the lasagna was divine. The meat sauce gave it a spicy flavor that she immediately adored, and who didn't love cheese? Each table had breadsticks with some type of garlic flavoring that perfectly complemented the meal, particularly when dipped into something called alfredo sauce.

Once she'd finished devouring her main dish, she picked up a dessert menu and scanned it. So many options. There was one consisting of some squares of dough fried like donuts that could be dipped into chocolate sauce. It looked as if one order were meant to feed three or four people, but she selfishly ordered one just for herself.

Completely stuffed when she polished off the last square, Kelsey leaned back in her chair. "Somebody make sure Carl gets recipes for all of this stuff. The people back home have no idea what they're missing. We owe it to them to correct that great injustice."

Her husband laughed. "Be truthful. You just want all of this for yourself."

"Hell yes, but don't be petty. Everyone can revel in my victory."

"So in the most general sense, what are we expecting to accomplish tomorrow?" Talbot asked, his smile fading somewhat. "Do we think we'll get access to the medical facility? Will we get aboard the shipyard? How quickly are we expecting to execute?"

Kelsey double-checked to make sure no one was close enough to hear their murmured conversation. She also had her implants tag the locations of all the servers and started keeping a close eye on any coming toward them.

Veronica shook her head. "I don't imagine it's going to be easy to get onto the shipyard, but it's not solely a Fleet installation. It shouldn't be impossible."

"Getting into the computer system on the station shouldn't prove difficult," Carl said, dabbing his napkin at his lips. "The firewalls at the research facility will be another story. Until we get established in the general network, I'm not going to be able to guess at how long it will take to get in, if I can get in at all."

"And we don't dare try to physically enter the medical facility until we know we have to," Talbot said firmly. "A place like that is going to take a very dim view of people just wandering in."

Kelsey didn't disagree, but they were on a relatively tight schedule. With the arrival of the Rebel Empire warships, she really wanted to be gone by the time they finished whatever they were doing.

No matter how well they executed their raid on the shipyard, word was going to get out before their freighter could leave the system. That was an almost certainty. The same was true of an incursion at the medical research facility.

The best they could hope for was to sow enough confusion once they'd completed their initial moves that the locals didn't know what exactly had happened or who was responsible. They'd eventually figure it out, but the more time that took, the better.

Once the locals started going through the records on the battle station, they'd realize the freighter that Kelsey had brought had never actually entered the system. It had simply appeared there, and it was going to vanish in the same way. There was no way they'd miss that, but there was nothing she could do to fix that.

"Tomorrow is scouting day," Kelsey said. "Everyone is going to have to be careful how they approach anyone. Until we're ready to act, I'd rather not raise any suspicions.

"Until then, let's just focus on the pleasant evening ahead of us. We can rest a little easier tonight. Well done, people. And we can even order desserts to take back with us."

That made everyone laugh.

She was still smiling at her own joke—which really wasn't a joke—when a large group of men and women came through the front door to the restaurant and were seated nearby. They looked like a gaggle of low-to-mid-ranking Fleet officers, ranging from a single lieutenant commander down to a trio of ensigns.

Kelsey was about to call for the check when she realized the lieutenant commander was staring at them with a puzzled expression on his face. That's when she saw Veronica Giguere stiffen slightly out of the corner of her eye.

Oh crap. Something was going sideways. That man knew Veronica. Kelsey was certain of it. He hadn't placed her yet, but they'd met.

Things were about to get ugly.

* * *

VERONICA only barely stopped herself from flinching when she recognized Lieutenant Commander Don Summerville. It was far too late for her to conceal her presence. He was staring *right* at her.

She considered trying to bluff her way out of the situation but instantly rejected the idea. He'd known her for years. There was absolutely no way she was going to fool him. If she tried pretending to be someone else, he'd see through her act and his suspicions would be raised even higher.

Since she couldn't avoid the impending meeting, she decided to embrace it. With a brief prayer to the gods, she deactivated the stealth mode on her implants. If he checked her, she didn't dare turn up blank. That would raise questions they couldn't afford.

With that thought in mind, she sent a message to Princess Kelsey and Zia Anderson.

Activate your implants with your cover identities. Our first test is upon us.

Summerville was already heading their way, so she rose and came out to meet him.

"Don," she said warmly. "I never expected to see you here. How have you been?"

He took her hand and shook it with a friendly grin. "I could say the same. I've been good. Just transferred in. What brings you to Archibald?"

Veronica smiled but shook her head slightly. "I'm not allowed to get into the details because of operational security. This is a stopping point on the way to where the Lords have tasked us with accomplishing something, so even though I'm not actively on that mission right now, I'm not allowed to talk about it."

A convenient lie. Very convenient.

She turned to face her new friends, pleased to see that no one had stricken looks on their faces. Of course, a few of them looked a little strained, but the main players seemed unruffled.

"Everyone, allow me to introduce Don Summerville. He was the tactical officer on the heavy cruiser where I was first posted as an executive officer."

Once everyone had murmured their greetings, Veronica gestured toward Princess Kelsey. "Don, this is Captain Diane Delatorre. She's actually in charge of the excursion I was referring to."

They'd decided to give Princess Kelsey's cover identity a promotion. One step in rank would raise no eyebrows if someone checked. People often got promoted, and it took a while for the news to work its way through the system.

Kelsey extended her hand and rose to her feet. "It's a pleasure to meet you, Commander."

"The pleasure's all mine, ma'am," Don responded politely.

"And this is Commander Cordia Kellett, her exec," Veronica finished. "I'm number three this time around."

"Commander," Don said, shaking Zia's hand. "I didn't intend to disrupt your meal, but I was so shocked to see someone I knew. It's always hard when you're posted to a new sector. You never know anyone, so running into a familiar face was unexpected."

"I understand completely," Kelsey said. "It's happened to me too. I wish we had time to stay and talk longer, but even though we aren't in the mission's operation area, we still have a lot of planning to do.

"That said, we'll be here on the station for at least a few days more. You and Veronica could catch up. If, of course, your ship is going to be here for a bit."

Don laughed a little. "My ship isn't going anywhere. I've been assigned to the shipyard to work in the Fleet section. While the yard does mostly civilian work, it has a few of our ships under construction there and others undergoing refit."

He gave Veronica a wide grin. "If you're going to be around for a bit, I'd love to have dinner. Also, if any of you would like a tour of the yard, I'd be happy to act as your guide."

Kelsey smiled even more widely. "We have a little bit of discretion in scheduling, and I'm sure a couple of us would absolutely love to see the yard. In fact, we were talking earlier today about how we could arrange to get over there, so meeting you is a godsend.

"One thing, though. While what we're doing isn't precisely a secret mission, we *are* keeping a low profile. You've noticed that none of us are in uniform and that our associates are civilians. We're working on board a freighter and it would be a favor to both me and the Lords if you would be discreet about who you mentioned us to."

"Absolutely," Don said. "My lips are sealed. Veronica, if you'll give me a call sometime tomorrow, we can work out the details for both dinner and the tour. Everyone, it's been a pleasure meeting you."

With that, her old friend excused himself and returned to his table. His associates immediately started peppering him with questions, and Veronica could tell from their body language that he wasn't explaining things to their liking.

Kelsey gestured and everyone rose to their feet. "I'm stuffed," she said perhaps a tad louder than she needed to. "Let's get back to our rooms and call it a night."

Veronica made a point of waving at Don as she exited the restaurant with the rest of her team. Only when she was outside did she feel her hands starting to shake.

"Oh God. That was so close. Are we screwed?"

Zia put her arm around Veronica's shoulders as they walked toward the hotel. "You did great. No one could possibly anticipate randomly running into someone they knew like that. Your reaction was perfect. No way he saw anything wrong. We're still good."

The other woman's arm steadied her. Veronica took a deep breath and tried not to sag.

"I've been in combat. That was worse in some ways. I don't know if I'm cut out to be a spy."

"You did better than I did the first time," Kelsey said with a laugh. "Not that I've been a spy, but I have done things I'd never expected to do. You were fabulous. I didn't see a hint of tension in you, and neither did your friend.

"You also just solved our problem of getting into the shipyard. We don't have to sneak aboard or steal a cutter now. Obviously, we can't carry out the operation during the middle of the tour, but I'll bet we can make arrangements that will make getting back aboard a second time a lot easier while we're there.

"That's a huge stroke of luck. An opportunity that we can't afford to squander. Come tomorrow morning, I want you to contact him and arrange for Carl and me to accompany you on that tour. Zia can help Talbot."

Kelsey held up a finger toward the scientist. "I understand that you still have a lot of work to do regarding the research facility, but if there's a way to gain access to the shipyard's computer system, we need to take it. And to do that, we need you there in person.

"We're going to have to be fast on our feet to give you the time alone to get into their systems and do what you need to do, but we're not going to get another opportunity like this again. We have to seize it with both hands."

Veronica sighed. "I'm going to have to go out to dinner with him, aren't I? That's going to be a minefield. Probably a couple of hours of conversation where anything I say might trip me up. I feel a headache coming on."

"You'll do fine," Kelsey said. "In fact, you don't have to conceal a single thing. Other than the mission we're currently on, you can tell him the truth, though I'd leave out the mission to Erorsi. He can't check any of the facts in time to do him any good. Don't overcomplicate this. Like I said, you'll do great."

"You can say that all you want, but it's not going to make me feel any better."

She felt awful at playing on Don's friendship. Once they finished, they could leave. He'd face the wrath of the Lords with nowhere to hide. She truly was a traitor now.

Zia gave her shoulder another squeeze. "Don't let this eat at you. Come on. Let's get back to the hotel. Tomorrow is going to come early."

23

Z ia awoke to find herself alone in the room. A check of her internal chronometer told her that it was still a bit early. She'd set an internal alarm to wake her in about twenty minutes, so she cancelled it.

There was no sound from the darkened bathroom, and its door was slightly ajar, so she didn't think Veronica was taking a shower. Perhaps she was taking care of other business.

She slipped a robe on before knocking lightly on the bathroom door. When no one answered, she peered inside. Finding it empty, she turned on the main lights and made certain that Veronica was indeed gone. She was.

Dressing quickly, Zia let herself out of the room and went downstairs to see if she could figure out where the other woman had gone. In spite of Fiona having vetted Veronica's loyalty, Zia started to worry.

Her concerns dissipated when the lift doors opened and Veronica stepped inside with two cups of coffee.

The other woman blinked in surprise. "Did I wake you? I'm sorry. I just wanted to slip out and get us some coffee."

Zia took one of the cups and nodded her thanks as Veronica sent the lift back up to their floor. "Did running into your friend keep you up last night?"

The other woman nodded slowly. "I kept tossing and turning, running scenarios through my head. Seeing Don really threw me."

They traveled the rest of the way back to their floor in silence. Only once they were back in their room with the door closed did Zia speak.

"Let's sit over here and talk about it." She gestured toward the two straight-backed chairs. They wouldn't be comfortable, but it was what they had.

As Veronica sat, Zia sipped her coffee, finding the other woman had sweetened it and added creamer. Surprisingly, she'd gotten the mixture right. The woman was observant.

"How would you feel if you hadn't gone through the revelations you had?" Zia asked. "If you just ran across him in the course of your normal life?"

"I'd be happy," Veronica said, her voice sounding tired. "A lot of Fleet officers in the Rebel Empire are power-obsessed scumbags. He was one of the good ones. He *is* one of the good ones. It breaks my heart to stick a knife into his back."

"You're in a hard place," Zia agreed, putting her hand on the other woman's leg sympathetically. "It's one thing to fight back against a system that you completely dislike. It's another thing entirely when the face of that system is a friend.

"I can't pretend to understand what you're going through, but you're not alone. You don't know any of us. It's hard to pick strangers over friends even if you believe in the cause they're fighting for."

Veronica sagged slightly in her chair, setting her untouched coffee on the edge of the desk. "I can't see any way this ends well for Don. I'm using our friendship to start a chain of events that will probably end with his death.

"I have no idea whether he believes in the system or hates it like I do. That's not the kind of thing officers discuss with one another. It's not safe. People disappear when they do things like that, and one learns to keep one's opinions to one's self."

Zia's heart went out to the other woman. Having to choose between friendship and duty was one of the most difficult things a person can do. Veronica was obviously caught on the horns of a dilemma. No matter how things turned out, she'd be scarred.

"I've only been a senior officer for six months," Zia confessed. "After our people found and repaired the ships that we have now, we needed trained, experienced people to man them. And command personnel experienced in the new tech to run them.

"Before that, I was tactical officer on a destroyer. One very similar to the one you commanded, if far less capable. I don't have the depth of experience to even begin advising someone how to navigate the minefield you're walking through.

"What I can say is that if he's a decent man like you say, he would feel just as badly as you do but he'd end up doing what was right. Even if it hurt you. Even if it killed you."

The other woman sat silent for a few minutes, obviously lost in thought.

When she finally stirred, she picked up her coffee and took a sip, grimacing at the no doubt cool temperature.

"I'll do what I have to," Veronica said as she set the cup back down. "Maybe I can come up with some way to mitigate what happens to him. You know, stick him in a closet somewhere when push comes to shove. Maybe that will save his life.

"After all, the Lords can't expect him to be omniscient. There is no way he could expect me to betray him like I'm going to do. He's not psychic. It may ruin his career, but if I can save his life, I'm going to try my very best to do so."

She looked up at Zia. "I hope that's not going to be a problem because I'm not willing to negotiate the point. I believe the Rebel Empire has to be brought down, but I'm not going to murder a friend to make it happen."

Zia shrugged. "No one expects you to be a monster, Veronica. I think you can find a way to see your friend spared the worst consequences of our mission, but you're not going to be able to save him completely.

"Don't get so hung up trying to spare him that you put the mission in danger. There are billions of people counting on us. Trillions, if you count all the people in the Rebel Empire. One life is important, but you have to be able to keep your perspective."

Veronica rubbed her face with both hands. "I said I'll do what I have to, and I meant it. The Lords have demanded that I do distasteful things in the past, and I've complied. How can I do any less for the right reasons? That doesn't mean I can't mourn for a betrayed friend."

The two of them sat in silence, sipping at their cooling coffee until it was finally all gone.

She'd put off taking her shower for as long as she could—longer than she should have—so Zia finally rose to her feet. "Everyone else is probably already getting breakfast, but I need to get a shower. It's going to be okay."

Veronica looked up at her. "I'm not looking forward to today, but I think you've made it a little easier for me to do what I need to do. Thanks."

Zia smiled briefly and put her hand on the other woman's shoulder. "The only way any of us get through this is together. It may not feel like it right now, but this isn't necessarily a no-win scenario. If circumstances permit, you'll find a way to save your friend. I know that because it's what friends do."

* * *

KELSEY USED her foot to tap on the door where they were holding their morning meeting. Her arms were filled with bags of food and drink from a small place just up the corridor. She'd chosen it because it was so busy that it was unlikely anyone there would remember her presence after the fact.

She also hoped the crowd meant that the food was awesome.

Talbot opened the door, and everyone cleared the way for her to take the food over to the bed. The desk wasn't large enough for everything, so they'd have to spread the containers out on the covers and eat as they stood around talking.

Under any other circumstances, she'd try to find a conference room, but that would draw attention they couldn't afford. They had to stay off of everyone's scanners.

As soon as everyone had piled their plates high with whatever they wanted for breakfast and gotten cups of coffee from the large container she'd brought, she served herself. She ate quickly because she knew she'd be still putting it away once the rest were done.

That used to cause her so much embarrassment. She'd felt like a pig, continually stuffing her face. Now after years of stoking the furnace in her belly, it no longer bothered her. People would think what they thought, and that was no business of hers.

Besides, now that there were new Marine Raiders coming into existence, her appetite would hardly be unusual. If people thought she could eat, they'd be *stunned* over how much food Angela Ellis could put away in one sitting.

About halfway through the meal, the door opened to admit Zia and Veronica. The two women waved and began piling plates high. Their late arrival gave her a little bit more time to finish eating. By the time they finished, everyone else was sipping coffee and Kelsey was wrapping up her own meal.

Everyone put their trash back into the bags. Someone would dispose of it after the meeting.

Kelsey walked over to the desk and rapped her knuckles on the fake wood. "Everyone, if you'll let me have your attention, we'll get this rolling."

Once the various conversations ceased, Kelsey continued. "Veronica, today's work is going to be mainly on your shoulders. I want you to contact your friend and see if he can arrange for us to go out to the shipyard either this morning or afternoon.

"Then have dinner with him tonight, if you can. Any information you can get from him about normal operations at the yard and the situation in this system will be helpful. It's even possible that he might be able to tell us why there are Rebel Empire warships in Archibald's outer system, though we already have our suspicions."

Talbot cleared his throat. "I can shed some light on that. While you were out getting food this morning, I went downstairs and sat in the breakfast room while the other guests were eating. I went so that the management could see that some of us were taking advantage of the free buffet and to listen in on what was being said.

"No one seemed to be aware that there are ships in the outer system, but I did overhear a pair of travelers talking about how they'd been rushed out of a nearby system after some kind of ruckus at one of the system's flip points.

"Apparently there was some kind of fighting in the system next door. Nobody could say exactly who was doing the shooting, but it was serious enough that Fleet was locking everything down. They thought that was peculiar as the system in question only had the one flip point. They were wondering how Fleet had missed the intruders coming in."

Kelsey felt her heart sink a little. "It could be the Clans. Probably has to be."

Zia grimaced. "If that's the case, that one attack is only the beginning. They wouldn't have revealed themselves if they didn't intend to carry out a full-scale invasion of the Rebel Empire. They've had hundreds of years to prepare, with the Singularity building their forces, so they think they can win this fight.

"If the Clans are attacking other nearby systems—and we have to believe that there is more than one incursion—then the possibility of fighting here at Archibald in the very near future can't be ruled out."

Kelsey rubbed the bridge of her nose. "Perfect. That means we have to speed up our timetable as much as humanly possible. It also means that the Rebel Empire Fleet is going to be even more suspicious of anything unusual taking place. We'll have to act faster and be more careful at the same time."

She turned to Carl. "I don't suppose you brought enough equipment to clone yourself?"

"Sadly, no," he said with a shake of his head.

"Then we need you to get into the computer systems on this station as quickly as possible, as well as penetrate the medical research facility, and still be ready to go with us to the shipyard as soon as the opportunity presents itself. Is there anything we can do to help make all that happen?"

"I'm already one step ahead of you," Carl said. "I accessed the station network last night before I went to bed. It wasn't too difficult to get in. The secure areas are still locked away, but I believe that I've worked out which one is the research facility.

"I'm going to have to do a little more work to find a vulnerability that I can exploit to get complete access. Doctor Parker's computer specialist has been a big help. Together, the two of us might manage to do everything we need to do here before I have to go to the shipyard."

"Excellent. Keep it up."

She turned her attention to Talbot. "I want you to conduct an in-person reconnaissance of the area around the research facility. We need to know how we're going to get in. Take anyone you need to help and get the lay of the land."

"I can do that," he agreed. "If you don't need her right now, I'll take Zia."

The flag officer raised an eyebrow. "My schedule is open, but I'm not sure what I can add. I'm not exactly a superspy."

Talbot grinned. "No, but you'll keep me from standing out by being just one dude walking around looking at everything. A couple draws far less attention than a single male. Cain Hopwood and Bill Smith, his security guy, can look at what we record later and help devise an entry plan."

Zia considered his statement with pursed lips and nodded. "I'm in."

"Then let's be about it," Kelsey said. "If we can't get what we need before the Clans come calling, we're all screwed."

24

Talbot and Zia headed for the research facility at a slow stroll. They stopped at a couple of shops and browsed, making certain their progress toward their target didn't show any sign of urgency. Or, frankly, that they had a target at all.

"How's Veronica?" Talbot asked as they were looking at what appeared to be designer women's clothing. What precisely it was designed for, he had no idea. There were a lot of straps and snaps, but he couldn't discern any purpose for them.

"That thing last night really shook her up," Zia said. "But she's solid, and she'll pull through. What's the general plan? I've seen our destination on a map, but we've got no indication of how it's really laid out inside: how many levels, what type of security, that kind of thing. How are we going to get that information without going inside?"

"We *are* going inside. Not to cause any kind of scene but to make an inquiry. We have an injured family member, and we want to know if they have any hope. A child would be best, I think. Everyone has a soft spot for kids."

Zia nodded. "You're hoping we can pull somebody's heartstrings and get them to admit that kind of technology exists or to be very sad in saying that it doesn't. The only problem I see is that we're going to be talking to a receptionist. The odds this person is going to know what research projects are happening is fairly low, isn't it?"

Talbot laughed. "It isn't as if this is a secret military research facility. The different scientists and technicians working here are going to talk about their projects even outside the labs. While they probably won't chat over any classified details, the general thrust of their research is probably going to be mentioned outside the secure areas. Who do they walk past every day when they're leaving work and arriving? The receptionists.

"So, imagine this. A couple of scientists are arriving at work, getting ready to scan their badges and go in. They're already going to be talking about some of the experiments they plan on conducting that day. The receptionist is going to hear all about them.

"Or they've just finished a long day and had some successful or disastrous tests. They're leaving the building but they're not quite done talking work yet. While they're in the lobby, they're getting in that last little bit of discussion about what they're going to need to do the next day. And once again, there's the receptionist to drink it all in."

She gave him a look through narrowed eyes. "Exactly how do you know this?"

He grinned at her. "While I might not be on the market anymore, I've dated a number of receptionists in my time. They've told me quite a bit about things they're not supposed to know about. The people talking just consider them part of the furnishings.

"I have no doubt whatsoever that the receptionists in this building know virtually every single research project being conducted now and over the last few years. They probably have a decent idea of how far along each project is and whether or not they're feasible, just based on what the researchers are saying."

"That seems kind of risky," Zia said cautiously. "They're not involved in the work itself, and if we take their word at face value, we might be completely wrong."

Talbot gestured for them to change direction, and they headed down another corridor. "It's a risk, but we're not going to get the kind of information we need by standing outside the building and staring at it. Carl might get something when he finishes hacking his way in. We're just testing the water.

"If we can get verbal confirmation that something like this exists, we'll know that this mission is a go. If the receptionist doesn't know anything, then the odds of getting something once we get in are low and we might abort. That's going to be up to Kelsey."

They walked in relative silence for another twenty minutes, crossing through a number of larger segments inside the station. People around them hardly glanced at them. Or if they did, they just saw a couple out for a stroll and would barely remember them even one minute after they'd passed.

When they arrived near the research facility, their job became a little bit more difficult. The number of shops had gone down and the area seemed a tad more industrial in nature.

On the plus side, the facility had a large double door made of clear material with "The Michael Anderle Memorial Research Center" printed clearly for everyone to see. They weren't exactly hiding who they were or what they were doing.

Talbot had no idea who the man was or what he'd done to warrant having a research facility named after him, but that hardly mattered.

He raised an eyebrow toward Zia. "Shall we go in?"

"Let's."

Part of him expected the double doors to be locked so that only the receptionist could open it or an individual with a card could unlock it from the outside. Here in the Rebel Empire, the number of people with implants was restricted. Members of the higher orders had them and so did Fleet officers, but most members of society had to get by without them.

To his relief, the doors were unlocked, and they walked in without any issue. The receptionist, a young man with an earnest expression and a shock of dark, curly hair, smiled at them. His name tag indicated that he was Ralph.

"Good morning and welcome to the Michael Anderle Memorial Research Center," he said pleasantly. "How may I assist you today?"

Talbot held back just a little and nudged Zia forward. Since they were dealing with a man, she was more likely to get useful information. Hell, even if they were dealing with a woman, another woman was more likely to get the information they were looking for, now that he thought about it.

Before Zia had a chance to speak, however, the door behind the receptionist's desk opened and an older woman with a hatchet face set in a scowl stalked out. She wasn't wearing a name tag, but if she had, he wouldn't have been surprised to see her name was Helga.

"Take your break, Ralph. I'll handle the desk until you get back." Her voice was gravelly and held a sour note.

The young man rose to his feet with a smile for Zia and walked back the way the woman had come from. His expression held a note of regret or sorrow. Talbot couldn't tell which, but neither bode well for their mission.

Taking a seat, the older woman scowled at Talbot and Zia. "What do you need, and how may we assist you?"

From her tone of voice, Talbot guessed what she'd actually meant to imply was "I don't care what you need, but tell me now so that I can send you packing as quickly as possible."

Talbot hoped Zia was a much better conversationalist than he was, because he suspected that they were about to be unceremoniously tossed out the door.

* * *

Veronica didn't expect Don Sommerville to be available during what would normally be a work day. She was wrong, it seemed, because he said that he was available to meet with her right away.

That made her stomach do a slow roll. She hadn't been expecting to need to start the deception immediately.

"I'm not sure everybody will be ready to take the tour right now," she said. Since Zia was off assisting Talbot, she wouldn't be available to take the tour for a while yet.

"I can probably arrange another tour later, but going now would be perfect," he said with a slight shrug over the com link. "I got delayed on the station, so I'm heading for the Fleet bay in about half an hour. Maybe you could gather a couple of people and I'll give you the grand tour. I can try to arrange a second trip in a day or so. How does that sound?"

"Let me ask," she said and then put him on hold.

She sent an implant message to Princess Kelsey about the situation and received an immediate response.

Tell him we'll go. I'll grab Carl, and it'll just be the three of us.

That sounded exceptionally dangerous to Veronica, but it seemed they didn't have much choice. So, she told Don they'd meet him at the Fleet bay in half an hour.

After she disconnected the call, she went in search of Princess Kelsey. She found the woman already discussing the situation with the scientist.

"I'm not sure what equipment I can sneak through the Fleet bay," Carl was saying. "How thoroughly are they going to scan us?"

Veronica shrugged when Princess Kelsey looked at her. "We're under escort, so it could be no scan at all, or they might decide to examine us more closely. Two of us have Fleet IDs, so it might be better if one of us carries any unusual equipment. We're less likely to be searched."

"What kind of equipment do you think we should take?" Kelsey asked the scientist.

"There are a few pieces of specialized equipment that I can use to directly access the hardwired network inside the shipyard. None of them are very large. I could probably fit everything inside a small pouch. Something that would be concealable underneath normal clothes."

Veronica considered that and nodded slowly. "It might be best if I carry the pouch. Don has known me for years. If it comes down to being searched, I'm going to be the last person they look at. He'll vouch for me."

Knowing that was true made her feel guilty. Don was a decent guy, and she felt bad about the likely outcome of her using him like this.

Princess Kelsey put her hand on Veronica's shoulder. "You like him, and you feel bad?"

She gave the short woman a lopsided smile. "Zia said that your insight goes beyond what one would normally expect, but you continue to surprise me. Yes, I feel bad, but that won't stop me from doing my duty."

Kelsey squeezed her shoulder for a moment and then released it. "Duty can be a hard mistress. I've learned that lesson again and again over the last few years. Our plans are still fluid. There's going to be a lot of chaos when we leave. If we can, I'll try to work things so we take him with us."

"I'm not sure he'll thank either of us for that," Veronica said with a dark chuckle. "Still, with a choice between leaving him to the justice of the System Lords or kidnapping him, I appreciate the effort. Thank you."

"It's not a problem. With everything we've got in the air, what's one more ball?"

While they'd been talking, Carl had been going through his equipment. He came back over and handed Veronica a small pouch. One that would easily be concealable inside her clothing. So long as she wasn't searched, no one would ever know she was carrying it.

"Most of the hardware is shielded, so they're going to have to be looking exceptionally closely to spot this," he said.

Veronica tucked the pouch away. "Then let's hope they don't look. Shall we go? It wouldn't hurt to be just a little bit early."

She had no idea where the Fleet bay was, so she used her implants to consult with the basic station network and get an overview map. She'd been on a number of similar stations over the years and was quickly able to orient herself and lead them to the lifts that would take them to their destination.

Unlike the cargo bay they'd arrived in, the Fleet bay was segregated from the general areas of the station. The large hatches were closed, and a number of marines stood guard in front of them.

She knew that marines in the Rebel Empire were different than the ones used by the New Terran Empire. None of these men had implants, and their weapons had to be activated by an officer before each shift. The Empire didn't trust them very far.

Also unlike the marines in the New Terran Empire, these men would be more thuggish. Marines were brutes used to assault positions without regard to their own survival, so they tended to view life through the lens of what they could get away with before they died an inevitable and probably gory death.

A large man with a shaved head and what looked like a semipermanent sneer on his face stepped forward and raised his hand. His sleeve had corporal's stripes, and his name tag read Deacon.

"Fleet admittance only."

"We're expected. My name is Veronica Giguere, and this is Diane Delatorre and Carl Owlet. Commander Don Sommerville should have us on the list."

The man didn't bother looking at the clipboard one of his associates held. "You're not on the list. Come back once you are."

Veronica frowned slightly and restrained herself from snapping at him like she would have if she were in uniform. She was pretending not to be a Fleet officer, so she couldn't tear a strip off of him.

"Perhaps you should check the list again," she said firmly. "When the commander gets here, you're not going to like what happens if you continue detaining us."

The corporal grinned. "You want to see detention? We can do that too. Privates, take these three into custody for attempting to gain unauthorized access to a Fleet facility. I'll handle the pat downs myself."

That last was said with a leer toward Veronica.

The other marines smiled and stepped forward, obviously relishing the thought of manhandling two women and a skinny guy.

Oh, hell.

25

Somewhat disconcerted, Zia put on her best smile for the new woman. Her estimation of their chances at getting information plummeted from about fifty percent to around zero, but she was going to try anyway.

"Hi, we have something of an odd question. My sister's little girl had a terrible accident last year that damaged her spine. The doctors told us that they couldn't regenerate it. It's really hard, but we're trying to keep our hopes up. Is the center working on anything that might help her?"

The woman's scowl deepened. "It's against our policy to discuss research projects. The technology being evaluated and developed here is at the very edge of what's possible with Imperial technology.

"Even so, not all projects are successful. We don't want to get anyone's hopes up that a certain technology will be released for general use in the near future or even in the distant future. I hope that it becomes possible for your niece to recover, but I'm not going to be able to answer your question."

Talbot leaned forward, his eyes pleading. "We don't want to know any secret details. We just want to give my sister-in-law something to hold onto. Please. Even a hint that it might be possible would give her the strength to carry on for Rachel."

"I'm sorry," the woman said, her expression becoming fierce. "I'm doubly sorry that a little girl was injured, but that doesn't change the situation. I'm going to have to ask you to leave."

Zia considered pushing one final time, but since the woman had balked at Talbot's plea, she wasn't going to give in to anything Zia said.

"It breaks my heart to see a corporation that won't even say one word to give hope to those they claim they want to help," Zia said with anger that wasn't all that feigned. "We'll go, but you've made our pain worse. Remember that."

She took Talbot's arm and led him back toward the door, her back stiff with actual outrage. Part of her hoped the woman would call out and give them a clue, but she didn't. They exited the building no wiser than when they'd gone inside.

As they were walking away, Talbot grimaced at her. "Well, that was a bust. Not only was access to the building restricted enough that we got no information about what the layout is, the old battle-ax wouldn't even clue us in about any regeneration technology.

"You did good, by the way. If it'd been me, I'd have told you what you wanted to know and damn company policy. We'll just have to let Carl and the other nerds see what they can find out remotely."

She gave the marine officer a smile. "Don't sell yourself short. That last-minute plea of yours was genius. I figured she'd crack for sure."

Zia was about to add more when she saw someone walk around the corner ahead of them. It was the young man who'd been behind the receptionist's desk when they'd arrived.

He came directly to them and smiled a bit sadly. "I'd like to take a moment to apologize for my associate. Regina is somewhat of a stickler for rules. In any case, the company doesn't inform us about the various projects that are underway or their status. I'm sorry about that."

Seeing a second chance being dangled in front of her, Zia tried to pluck it. "I really do understand that confidential information needs to stay inside the company. You wouldn't want your competitors to get details on experiments and hardware and that kind of stuff.

"I'm not looking for any of that. All I want to do is tell my sister that her little girl might one day walk again. Might one day be able to feed herself again. I'm just looking for hope."

The young man glanced up the corridor and back down again before leaning close to her. "While no one has said anything to me directly about the matter, I've heard a couple of our senior researchers discussing a project that *might* lead to something like that.

"It sounds as if it's already in the testing stages, so if it passes the rigorous standards set for general release by the Empire, it might be available for your niece in a year or two. You didn't hear that from me."

Zia smiled widely. "Thank you. *Thank you.* You don't know what a difference you've just made in our lives."

She threw her arms around him and hugged him tightly for a moment before releasing him.

He coughed for a second and smiled at her as he stepped back. "I really hope your niece gets better. Good luck."

With that, the young man turned and walked briskly back the way he'd come. He turned the corner into a side corridor that probably led to another entrance to the facility.

Talbot hurried after the young man and peered around the corner. Zia joined him just in time to see the young man step into a side entrance. A discreet one with no identifying signs.

"Well, that's helpful," Talbot said as he led to Zia away from the area. "Unless he was just selling us sunshine, that means there's something in there that could potentially regenerate a damaged spine."

She raised an eyebrow at him as they mingled with the crowd. "You think he was lying?"

The marine shrugged. "It's possible. In his shoes, if someone came looking for something to hope for, it might be tempting to give them a comforting lie. It won't change the situation for that person, but it might make the near future more bearable. I'd consider doing it. Wouldn't you?"

Probably, now that she thought about it. That was the risk in putting forward a tearjerking story.

"On the plus side," Talbot continued, "we now know of a less obvious entrance to the premises. Better yet, we know someone whose ID card opens it."

Now she gave him a skeptical look. "We know that he can get in, but we don't know who he is or how to get a hold of his card. How do you propose we rectify that?"

He grinned at her. "Now that we know what he looks like, it shouldn't be that hard to put someone in the area to keep an eye out for him and follow him home. Once we know where he lives, I'd wager breaking into his domicile is going to be a lot easier that an assault on a research facility."

"That's not going to be the only security measures they have," Zia warned him. "That's just the first layer. A receptionist won't have access to the classified labs. Even the researchers that can get into the experimental area might not be able to access the specific project area we're looking for.

"In addition, we won't know where to look either. Even if we put that guy to the question, he won't be able to tell us what we need to know, I'd wager. And we don't dare make him disappear. That would raise all kinds of red flags.

"What we need to do is get access to his card and clone it. Then we leave the original with him, and no one will be the wiser. We've got to be subtle."

Talbot looked mildly offended. "I can be subtle."

Zia laughed a little and took his arm. "Only when compared to your wife. Trust me when I say that this operation is going to require a deft hand to pull it off without sounding alarms everywhere across the station."

In spite of their success, she was still worried about how they'd be able to carry out the penetration of the research facility. Getting in was just the first step in a long series of things that had to go right for them to succeed and survive.

That wasn't even counting the mission to the shipyard, which was their primary goal. If the attempt to steal regeneration technology failed, that would be unfortunate for Commodore Murdoch, but they'd have tried.

She was far more concerned about what could go wrong stealing a flip drive or manufacturing replacement parts. And the looming war between the Clans in the Rebel Empire. If, of course, that was really what was happening.

Well, if this kind of thing were easy, anyone could do it. They'd make it work. Somehow.

* * *

KELSEY STEPPED FORWARD, an angry look on her face. The look was mostly manufactured, though part of her was pissed that this idiot was putting them in such danger.

"My name is Diane Delatorre. Captain Delatorre to you. Stand down, or I will *break* you."

Following up on her words, Kelsey pulled her fake ID card out and shoved it into the man's face.

The marines that had been about to seize them stepped back a few paces. Based on the looks they were giving her, this was an extremely unwelcome revelation.

The corporal stared at the badge as if it were a snake that were about to bite him. Then he took a step back too.

"My apologies, Captain," he mumbled.

Kelsey took two steps forward, not allowing the man to increase the space between them.

"That's not good enough, Corporal. What makes you think that Commander Sommerville is going to tolerate your insolence to his guests? Is it your habit to offend officers in general or merely him in specific?"

The man raised his hands as if surrendering. "I meant nothing by this, Captain. I was only doing my duty."

Kelsey laughed, adding a harsh edge to her tone. "If you're going to be an ass, you're going to have to either learn how to lie better or accept the punishment for being a prick."

She jabbed a finger into the man's chest, putting enough force into it to be sure it hurt. "You can rest assured that if Commander Sommerville doesn't put you on report, I will. I'm not the kind of woman you want to cross. I leave my enemies wishing they'd never been born."

"You're hardly worth my attention, so I'll let it go at that. If you trouble me again, I'm going to make you my personal project. I'll be here on this station for another week. That would certainly make my time here more enjoyable."

The man recoiled from her, obviously cowed. "I'm sorry, Captain," he whimpered. "What can I do to make up for my wrongdoing?"

The smile that Kelsey felt creeping onto her face repulsed her, but it was in character for the person she was pretending to be. "Nothing. Now open the hatch and let us pass before I decide it would be more entertaining to start on you now."

The corporal raced to the controls and opened the main hatch. He saluted her rigidly as she strode past him and into the Fleet bay.

Kelsey didn't look behind her, but she knew her companions were following her. Right now she was trying to stop her hands from trembling.

"Remind me never to play poker with you," Veronica said softly. "You scared the hell out of me, and I *know* that wasn't you."

"I can second the thing about not playing poker against her," Carl said, with the wry smile. "I've heard stories. The marines were complaining at the start of the original mission about how she'd cleaned them out. That was years ago, back before everything happened. I'd imagine she's only gotten better."

Kelsey let her breath out and slowed her pace. "I've certainly gotten better at bluffing. What scares me is how easily I stepped into that role. It was almost like being on autopilot. Flip the bitch switch and off I go. Terrifying when you get right down to it."

"One of the things I've discovered in life is that it's easier for a civilized person to be a barbarian than for a barbarian to be civilized," Veronica said. "It's far, far easier to step down to someone else's level than for them rise to yours.

"In this case, that was the absolute right thing to do. When he thought we were civilians and that you were a pushover, he was going to take every advantage he could. Right up to and including sexual assault if he could've gotten away with it. That's how marines are here."

Kelsey sighed. "That would break Talbot's heart. Hell, it breaks my heart. Where are we supposed to go?"

Before Veronica could answer, Kelsey saw Commander Sommerville stepping out of a cutter and waving toward their group.

"Here we go," Kelsey said. "We need to see the manufacturing equipment and give Carl time to do his work, Veronica. Try to angle for something like that, and we'll keep Sommerville distracted while Carl works his magic."

The young scientist took a deep breath and nodded. "If we can find a network junction, it should only take me thirty seconds to install the splice. I brought four, just in case. One will do, but more is better.

"Best of all would be the opportunity to install a splice directly inside the manufacturing equipment. I could read its software and determine if what we're looking for is even here. That would make our lives a lot easier."

Kelsey clapped a hand to her friend's shoulder. "You'll do it. I have complete confidence in you. Now, let's get our game faces on. It's showtime."

26

Talbot finally relaxed when they arrived back at the hotel. He knew the odds of them having raised suspicions in someone this morning were low, but it only took one paranoid bugger to get them all into deep, deep trouble.

He found an empty room and pulled Cain Hopwood and his security guy, Bill Smith, in with them. It only took a few minutes to run down the information they'd gathered and pass along the imagery he'd captured through his implants.

Smith pursed his lips and slowly nodded. "The entry isn't going to be too bad, if we can get our hands on that guy and his badge. That'll get us into the first level of the restricted zone. From there, we'll probably run into segregated rooms, both large and small.

"The computers will be locked down, of course. We'll need to bring along the research hacker just to be sure we can force our way in. The goal is going to be getting all the hardware, reports, and research notes for whatever regeneration equipment we're looking at.

"We'll need to avoid suspicion moving in. Custodial coveralls would be perfect. Unless, of course, we happened to run into some *real* custodians."

"Okay," he said after a moment. "Are you going to be able to get us into the security system, Mr. Smith? Maybe we can make sure we have exactly the right kind of uniforms and possibly even avoid the real custodians."

"Once we're on site, I can physically get into whatever they have for a security system," Smith said. "I'm not a hacker, though. Not of the class we'll need to get in remotely.

"But that's actually fine. You don't realize it, but you're talking about two separate systems. What we need to get access to before we go in isn't the alarms. It's the monitoring side of the equation. That's where our hacker friend will help us."

Talbot nodded. "Have you worked with this guy before?"

Smith shook his head. "No, but Carl vouched for him. Considering how far out of my league Carl is, his word is good enough for me. Unless I miss my guess, the guy has been working on the various computer networks we have access to throughout the station already."

They'd go talk to the man shortly, but Talbot wasn't ready to move on from the planning session just yet.

"We're going to need to find a location in the research facility to set up the large transport ring. We can take everything we steal back to the freighter with no one being the wiser. Then all we have to do is move the small ring back to the cargo shuttle and off to the freighter."

Hopwood shot Talbot a grin. "That thing is *really* handy. Since nobody knows the technology even exists, they'll be scratching their heads wondering how the hell a big pile of boxes just vanished."

"Are you sure it's going to be a large pile?" Zia asked, raising an eyebrow. "It may only be a couple of machines and some files."

"Have you seen Carl's lab?" Hopwood asked with a laugh. "Scientists are like pack rats. There are going to be piles of equipment. Once we get to the lab in question, we won't even be sure what's important, so we're going to have to take *everything*."

The mental image made Talbot chuckle. Carl *was* kind of a pack rat. There was always some kind of experiment going on, and discerning what belonged to which project was never easy.

They'd have Doctor Zoboroski on hand to help them figure that out, but he was a practicing physician rather than a research scientist. They couldn't trust that they'd get everything without taking the whole pile.

"With Princess Kelsey and the rest making a scouting run at the shipyard, we should know by this evening how difficult the task is going to be," Zia said. "I wish that I'd had the chance to go with them and see things for myself, but I'll have an opportunity to go over everything they capture with their implants.

"And Carl knows what he's doing. He's more than capable of taking bold action if the need arises. He'll get the taps put into all of the appropriate computer systems before they come back, I'm sure. That'll give our hacker an opportunity to get us with the research center remotely."

Talbot sighed, rubbing the side of his head. "I wish we didn't have to risk everything on a couple of throws of the dice. It's going to be really easy to roll snake eyes.

"We can start off by seeing what the hacker has been up to. With any luck, he'll have already gotten into the research center's network. If we can tap into the security feed, we'll start mapping the place and devising our plan of attack. We'll know more when Kelsey and the rest get back. Let's hope for the best."

That was going to be the key, Talbot knew. They were going to need a couple of lucky breaks for things to go their way. Otherwise Rebel Empire security would come down on them like a Marine Raider drop capsule.

* * *

VERONICA WAVED as she walked up to Don Sommerville.

"There you are," he said with a smile. "Did you have any trouble?"

Deciding it would be less trouble if she glossed over the events at the main hatch, Veronica shook her head. "Nothing we couldn't handle. Just the usual marine nonsense."

His expression twisted. "I don't get why they put those people in positions over regular people like that. Marines are nothing but trouble."

She considered it ironic how she'd shared her friend's opinion until she'd met the marines of the New Terran Empire. It wasn't the marines that were the problem. It was the Rebel Empire and how they trained them. How they conditioned them to be brutal and then used them up like expendable munitions.

Maybe, with just a little luck, she'd be able to show Don what she'd learned. If they could figure a way to capture him as they were leaving.

"So, what's the plan?" she asked.

He gestured toward the cutter. "This is our ride. It's going directly to the Fleet section of the shipyard and from there I've got about two hours to give you as much of a tour as I can manage. We should be able to see just about everything interesting."

Without further ado, they trooped into the cutter. It was about half filled with Fleet officers of low-to-middle rank. The highest-ranking officer present was a lieutenant sitting in front, reading something on his tablet. He paid them no mind as they sat across from him.

As they sat down and secured themselves, Don turned to Princess Kelsey. "I realize you need to be circumspect in what you say, but I'm wondering if you could tell me anything about what you're doing traveling through here? Does it have anything to do with the Ghost incursion?"

Princess Kelsey, in the guise of the woman she was pretending to be, Veronica thought, scowled. "Tangentially. As I said before, I really can't discuss details. Now in a hypocritical twist, I'm going to ask you what you can tell me about the incursion. All I've heard is public gossip. Can you shed some light on the subject, Commander?"

Don shrugged. "Everything is still pretty confused. Word arrived by fast courier that Balladur was under attack yesterday. It's three flips from here, so we're on alert, but we should get word if there's a force moving toward us.

"Fleet had to withdraw from the system because there were too many ships coming against them. The funny thing is, no one knows where those ships came from. Balladur is a cul-de-sac. One flip point leads in and out. Units in the next system over didn't see anything until the few Fleet ships stationed in Balladur came running through the flip point, screaming for help."

"I don't understand that," Veronica said. "Ships just don't appear from nowhere. Where could they have come from? And if it is the Ghosts, how could they have so many ships?"

"Frankly, I kind of thought they were a myth. Every once in a while you'd hear a story about some strange ship being cornered and blown up. Or about supply ships that vanished without a trace. Or even small warships like destroyers disappearing. I really never gave the rumors much credence."

Don nodded. "That's about how I felt too. I guess we can definitely put their existence into the confirmed category at this point. Weirdly, the reports on the kind of ships being used doesn't match up with the few cases Fleet was rumored to have engaged in the past.

"Some of these new vessels are larger than a heavy cruiser and with commensurate weapons. That's scary, and it really has the higher-ups freaked out."

"Is it just Balladur under attack?" Carl asked. "Are other systems being hit too?"

Don shrugged. "We haven't heard of any, but word might come in at any time. The contingency invasion plans that Fleet maintains for each system are being dusted off, and we'll figure out something if they come here.

"We don't have a lot of offensive force, other than the battle stations. If the Ghosts get into the system, we'll evacuate what we can and probably destroy the shipyard. Based on the positioning of the flip points, and the fact that we have scout ships in the adjacent systems, we'll have at least a day's warning."

A tone sounded announcing they were close to docking. Everyone on the cutter began making certain they'd gathered their possessions. None of Veronica's group had taken anything out for the trip so they'd be able to depart quickly once docking was complete.

A few minutes later, the cutter docked, and people began streaming out into the shipyard. Veronica walked with Don out onto the Fleet section of the shipyard.

A trio of people in fleet security uniforms stood near the only hatch leading out of the room. Two large enlisted men with sidearms stood behind a slender woman with strawberry blonde hair and lieutenant's tabs.

Since Veronica wasn't in uniform and expected to have her ID checked, she made certain to look relaxed. In fact, she might as well be proactive.

Smiling, she stepped over to the woman and pulled out her identification. "Commander Veronica Giguere."

The woman took her ID and examined it closely. She then looked up and directly into Veronica's eyes. Moments later, Veronica's implants informed her that they'd just been queried for her identification.

That surprised her. Thankfully it wasn't going to be a problem, but it hinted at a somewhat higher state of readiness than she'd expected.

The woman handed Veronica's ID card back to her. "Thank you, Commander. I'll need to see everyone's identification, please."

Princess Kelsey handed over her ID next.

The woman spent an equal amount of time examining it before looking up at the princess. This time, the woman's gaze seemed a little sharper.

"You might want to see someone about updating your identification photo, Captain. It seems a little out of date."

Princess Kelsey scowled a little. "Did you just say that I'm getting old?"

The security officer smiled without a hint of humor. "Age catches up with us all, Captain. In your case, it's the opposite. Whatever treatments you're getting for your skin and the work you had done on your nose have made you look younger and somewhat different than your photo. My congratulations on finding an excellent cosmetic surgeon."

The woman turned her attention to Carl, her expression showing a little more interest than before. "Identification."

The young scientist handed over his card and waited, his nervousness apparent to Veronica. She hoped it didn't trigger more attention from the security officer.

This time the woman's examination of the ID took almost twice as long and she looked up at Carl twice.

"There may be an irregularity with your identification, Mr. Owlet," she said at last. "I'm going to have to ask you to step aside for enhanced screening." She gestured toward a hatch set off to the side of the compartment.

Dammit.

27

Z ia walked down the hall and knocked on the door where the research hacker was working. The man's response was muffled, but she assumed it was an invitation to come in. Hopefully she wasn't about to catch him just coming out of the shower.

To her relief, she found him sitting at the desk, working on a portable computer. It was more substantial than a tablet by a significant margin, and there were extra drives and equipment scattered around the room, probably providing additional resources for his work.

The man bore a striking resemblance to Carl in the fact that he was somewhat scrawny and extremely nerdy. He was also about thirty years older than her friend and wore anachronistic glasses perched on the end of his nose.

He was turned in his seat, facing her as she came in. "Commodore Anderson," he said as he slicked back what was left of the hair on his balding head. "What can I do for you?"

"Doctor Rehnquist, right?"

The man nodded with a slight smile. "That's right. Andy Rehnquist."

"Excellent. You mind if I take a seat?"

Without waiting for his answer, she sat on the edge of his bed. "We've made some progress on identifying potential ingress points at the research facility as well as identifying potential sources for access to the building. I just dropped by to see how you were progressing on getting into their network."

The man smiled widely. "I think I'm ahead of schedule. I've penetrated the outermost layers of the onion, so to speak. In fact, I believe I now have complete access to the nonclassified systems used by them for interfacing with the public."

"That's good news, Doctor. Can you break down exactly what that means for us?"

He nodded briskly. "In effect, I've accessed the systems used by their administrative personnel. That system does interface with more secure areas, but I'm going very slowly. I don't want to trigger any kind of unexpected security response by poking around in a haphazard manner."

"I'm all for caution, Doctor," Zia said with a smile. "In fact, the work you've done thus far might be able to help us get into the building. Do you have access to the service files for the receptionists?"

"As a matter of fact, I've managed to access their version of human resources. Never really liked that term. It makes it sound as if people are property. Of course, in my *particular* case, that wasn't very far from the truth."

"Well here's a chance for you to strike a blow against people like that. I'm looking to identify one of the receptionists I met today. A young man with dark, curly hair. His name tag indicated that he was Ralph.

"I'd like to know where he lives, what his schedule is, and any other juicy details his file might be able to provide for us. The more we know, the better chance we can take him without causing problems."

The scientist spun on his chair and typed on the physical keyboard at what to her was a blinding pace. Data began scrolling up the screen, and what was obviously a file image of the man she'd spoken to appeared.

"Ralph Halstead," the scientist intoned. "He's been with their company for two years. According to HR, he's a diligent worker with no marks against him. His supervisor indicates that he's 'a personable, dedicated young man with a true desire to help people.' I'd say the young man is going to go far in his profession."

"Does it list an address for him?"

"Indeed it does." He rattled off an address that she'd be able to parse later and locate where the man lived.

"There's one more piece of useful information that I think you'll want," the scientist said. "Mr. Halstead is related to one of the research scientists, a Doctor Adriana Lipp. She's listed as his maternal aunt."

That might be useful. If they could use the receptionist to get to his aunt and subvert her access, that might get them very close to their goal when the time came.

"Do you have any idea how long it might take you to find a list of their research projects?" Zia asked.

"In a perfect world, I'd prefer to do that over the next twenty-four hours.

I believe with that amount of time I can gain access with no one being the wiser. Better yet, I should be able to access the video from the security feeds at that point. I might not be able to override anything, but I should be able to at least see it in read-only mode."

"What about twelve hours?" Zia countered. "That would put us in the overnight hours. Otherwise, we'll be working during daylight tomorrow, and that's not really the way we want to do this. A late-night heist is exactly the kind of thing we're wanting."

He scratched his chin thoughtfully. "If nighttime is your goal, I suggest that you aim for thirty-six hours as opposed to twelve. That would give us the largest margin for success, in my considered opinion."

She rose to her feet, satisfied. "That sounds good, Doctor. If we can put it off until tomorrow night, we will. The problem is that we don't know what our time frame is going to be. Honestly, if things go poorly enough for Princess Kelsey, we might have to abort this part of the operation entirely. Or we might have to rush it through tonight.

"I suggest you do what you can to gain access without being too overt. Perhaps you'll catch a lucky break and get what we need without having to take too many risks."

He didn't look pleased but nodded. "I'll do what I can and keep you informed of my progress."

That was the best one could ask for.

"In the meantime, Colonel Talbot and I will see if we can get into the young man's apartment. If we can compromise his security system, we'll be able slip in and get his ID card tonight with him none the wiser.

"I'll need an address for his aunt as well. It sounds like she's someone that we need to take captive and question."

The balding man nodded. "You're going to need to be careful. According to her file, she has a husband. If you're expecting to take her, you're going to have to deal with him too."

Zia grunted. "Perfect. I suppose we should also assume the worst about our young man. He's a handsome and polite boy. He might just have a live-in of his own. And pets.

"Unless things go to hell, I have no intention of moving forward tonight. We need to scout these individuals and get an idea of as much of their behavior as we can. When we strike, we're going to have to take them all prisoner."

The doctor nodded. "Then I'd ask that you consider what you're going to do with them when you're finished. When the full scope of what we're doing becomes evident, I have no doubt that security will come down on them hard.

"I doubt very seriously that civilians will be killed for cooperating with armed intruders, but we can't rule that out. The Rebel Empire is an ugly place filled with ugly people. It might be prudent to take them with us so that they can't tell anyone what they've seen. Or so that security doesn't torture them for information they don't possess."

Zia considered that and slowly nodded. "One more complication but a relatively minor one in the scale of things. I'll consider that, Doctor. Get us the access we need while I go talk to a marine about breaking and entering."

* * *

KELSEY WAS SERIOUSLY CONSIDERING GOING in after Carl. Veronica had subtly shook her head any time she'd looked toward the door. Even though she knew the other woman was undoubtedly correct, that didn't stop her from worrying.

Finally, after what seemed an eternity, Carl came back through the door. He looked shaken, his face pale. Whatever had happened, it hadn't been pleasant.

The female security officer swaggered out behind him and gestured toward her men. "Let them through. Have a pleasant visit."

Commander Sommerville had an expression of mild distaste as he nodded toward the woman and led the three of them into the shipyard.

The corridors beyond the entry point looked like the kind one would see in any station or shipyard. People either dressed in Fleet uniforms or civilian clothes moved about on tasks that Kelsey couldn't begin to guess at.

"I'm sorry about that," the Rebel Fleet officer said. "For what it's worth, Mr. Owlet, I'm sorry you had to go through that."

Carl just nodded, his expression pale. "I understand. Thank you."

Veronica moved up to engage Commander Sommerville in conversation while Kelsey pulled Carl a little behind them.

"What happened?" she asked softly. "Did she hurt you?"

He licked his lips a bit nervously. "I'd rather not discuss the specifics. Imagine whatever humiliating search procedures you like, and let's just say I'm glad Veronica has the gear because I couldn't have hidden it anywhere on me."

A bolt of pure rage shot through Kelsey, and she almost turned on her heel to start back the way they'd come before he grabbed her shoulder.

"Don't," he said softly. "We have too much riding on this mission. People are counting on us. What happened was incredibly demeaning, but I did what I had to do. Let. It. Go."

"I'm so very sorry, Carl," she said at last. "Let's do what we need to do and get the hell out of here. Veronica and I will distract Sommerville when you need us to. Just give me the high sign when you're ready."

He nodded, not saying anything more.

She let the subject drop and moved forward so that she was once again involved in the conversation between Veronica and Commander Sommerville.

He was gesturing toward a cross corridor. "That way goes toward the main viewing area. A lot of construction takes place inside the confines of the shipyard, and they've built a transparent wall so that visitors could see the hulls.

"And up ahead we're going to get into the place where they manufacture the various parts that have to go over to the ships. Everything from the drives to life support. Nothing is imported. Everything is built right here on this shipyard."

Veronica nodded. "Without getting into any classified information, what kind of ships are being built here? Freighters? Destroyers? Maybe even a light cruiser or two?"

"All of that and more," he said. "The civilian side builds just about any kind of ship you can imagine. The Fleet side builds every class of ship we need up to and including heavy cruisers. This is a full-service shipyard. If you need it, we can build it."

Out of the corner of her eye, Kelsey saw Carl raise his hand and meaningfully glance at a junction box on the corridor wall. It was time.

That's when she remembered that Veronica had the equipment that Carl needed. She'd need to distract Commander Sommerville while the other woman slipped the pouch to Carl.

"So, you build flip drives here?" Kelsey asked, stepping between Veronica and Sommerville. "I had a long discussion with one of my engineers about flip drives. There's a lot of rare materials that go into making the damned things. Are they mined locally or imported?"

As she spoke, she walked around him so that Veronica was able to pass the pouch to Carl without Sommerville seeing the act. It only took a moment, and then Carl started working on planting the patch.

"No," Sommerville said. "Those have to be brought in, but luckily the closest source isn't very far away."

Carl's estimate of the time required was conservative. Inside twenty seconds, he had everything closed back up and was listening politely to Sommerville's answer.

One down, three to go.

"You mentioned manufacturing equipment that built all of this stuff, including flip drives," Veronica said, stepping up beside them. "If you don't mind, I'd like to see those next. That sounds fascinating."

Somerville smiled and gestured for them to continue down the corridor. "It's not very far from here, and it really is an amazing thing to watch. Come on. We'll go take a look at that, and then I'll treat you all to lunch. It's the least I can do."

28

Talbot sat in a small café just down the corridor from where their young target lived. He wasn't alone, but none of his companions were in sight at the moment.

Bill Smith, dressed in nondescript coveralls and wearing a hat that came down over his eyes, was in the building where Ralph Halstead lived. Talbot wasn't certain exactly how the man was going to manage it, but it was his job to figure out if the receptionist lived alone or if they were potentially going to have to deal with a second person.

Rather than communicating by implant, since that might end up being traced back to them, they were using standard com units. Talbot's was linked to an earbud so he could listen without worrying about being overheard. A throat mic meant he could murmur his responses safely.

"It looks like the apartment is empty at the moment," Smith said. "The hall was empty, so I stuck a flexible camera under the door and took a peek. The lights are off, and the unit didn't pick up the sound of any pets."

"So, what's next?" Talbot asked.

"Come on up. I can pick the lock and bypass his security system but not while I'm watching over my shoulder for random passersby."

"I'll be right there."

Talbot left a tip on the table and dropped his disposable coffee cup into a recycle unit. Unhurried, he walked up the corridor and into the residential building. Since he would stand out more than Smith, he made certain to do nothing that would draw anyone's eye.

The building didn't seem to have any cameras in the lobby, but one never knew. The technology could be so small that no one would be able to see it.

Knowing that the elevator would almost certainly have a camera, Talbot used the stairs. Minutes later, he exited onto the target's floor. Smith was standing just down the corridor working on a panel recessed in the wall.

He walked up to the man and looked over his shoulder. "What are you doing?"

"Just passing the time until you showed up. As long as I was working on something, nobody that saw me would give me the slightest bit of attention."

Smith closed up the panel and walked a few doors down to the target's apartment. "I'm going to be focused on the lock in the security system. If anyone pops up, I want you to go ahead and start reading me the riot act for not getting something fixed. Make sure you have something in mind before you start talking."

"Copy that."

Even though he mentally rehearsed a little segment chewing Smith's ass about his toilet not working, no one intruded before the specialist had the lock undone and the door open.

"Inside," Smith said with a hurried gesture.

Already, there was a low beep sounding from an illuminated keypad on the wall. Smith focused on that as soon both were inside and the door was closed.

Rather than ask an idiotic question about whether Smith was going to be able to disarm the alarm before it went off, Talbot reserved his gaze for the apartment itself.

The furniture matched, so young Ralph made enough money to buy his own stuff. It wasn't of the highest quality—in fact, it was somewhat worn—so it might have been hand-me-downs.

Rather than art on the walls, the young man had photographs. A lot of photographs. Not of people but of places. All of nature scenes. He wondered whether the receptionist took them himself or just fancied them.

The beeping stopped. Since there was no alarm blaring, Talbot assumed that Smith had disarmed the security system.

"You're pretty handy," the marine admitted.

"That's what the ladies tell me," Smith said as he tucked his equipment away and relocked the door. "What are we looking for? The guy isn't here, and he's going to have his security badge with him."

"Mainly evidence that he lives alone. We'll be going over everything just in case there's something useful, but I'll be happy if this is just a dry run for breaking in tonight to retrieve his badge."

Talbot had his stunner out. It had been among the equipment they'd smuggled aboard the station. After all, if security found the transport ring it hardly mattered if they found a couple of illegal weapons too.

He didn't need it. There was no one else in evidence. In fact, it seemed their target lived alone and had no pets.

The only thing that stood out as unusual was what would normally have been a spare bedroom. In this case, it seemed to have been converted into a home office. One with a lot of computer equipment and large screens. There was also a VR suite.

Smith looked around with a smile and whistled softly. "My, my. What have we got here?"

The intrusion specialist walked over to the computer—or perhaps Talbot should've said the largest computer—and examined it without turning it on. "I'd have to look inside to be sure, but this is probably a very powerful unit."

"Don't they all look the same from the outside?" Talbot asked. "It's just a computer. The Rebel Empire can make some really small ones, so why would a big one be a shocker? Maybe it's old."

Smith shook his head. "I don't think so. That VR unit and some of the equipment on the shelf beside it make me think this is a gaming computer. Those have to be powerful. In fact, the more powerful they are, the better a player can perform. Gamers tend to have the most advanced equipment in the general population."

Okay, Talbot admitted that was interesting, but it hardly seemed relevant to what they were doing. "If you can stop panting over the equipment, we should finish searching the rest of the place."

The man waved them on. "You go on. I want to call in some computer support. If the hacker can help me get into this system, we might have just hit the jackpot."

Talbot frowned. "I don't follow. How so?"

Running his hand across the top of the computer, Smith grinned. "I'm just following a hunch. I might be wrong, but the thing that gives a gamer the most edge is lots of processing power.

"Our young friend has a relative in a research department with some very serious computing power, I suspect. If he managed to get any kind of access through her—or he's a hacker too—then this computer might be linked into the research facility to use its raw power.

"If we can get into this machine and that is true, our guy can bypass all the stuff that's been keeping him from going through the firewall. Our little hacker might have already done all the work for him."

Talbot considered that. There was a potential for gain, but there was also a risk that someone would catch them in the apartment the longer they stayed. Still, it was a regular workday, so they should be okay.

"Call him. Is this going to be something that requires his physical presence, or can he do it remotely?"

Smith shrugged. "I'm not sure. Let me contact him while you search the rest of the apartment."

Talbot spent fifteen minutes going through the rest of the apartment without finding anything useful. Ralph seemed to be a relatively normal guy living on a fairly regular income, massive computer aside.

He was about to head back to the gaming room to find out what Smith and the hacker had decided when he heard the front door unlock.

* * *

VERONICA HAD to admit that the automated manufacturing setup impressed her. The compartment holding all of the industrial equipment seemed to be as large as her old destroyer, and that was not an exaggeration.

The multilevel room held row after row of massive machines that were being fed raw materials by small automatons, and the finished products were then picked up by those same machines and taken away.

The entire room was visible from the bottom level because the central part of the room had no ceiling. The open space went up seven levels and showed her the entire operation at a glance. It was massive.

The machines seemed to have very little human interaction. Everything was done by computer-controlled machines and seemed to operate at very high speed. Which she supposed was necessary as they were building a number of vessels at the yard and would be continually in need of fresh parts.

Frankly, she couldn't see how they kept everything straight.

"Okay," she said to Don after a few minutes. "This is damned impressive. What I don't understand is how you keep track of everything. That part over there, for example—whatever it is. How does it get to the appropriate ship to be installed? What if there's a delay? Does it get put on a shelf somewhere?"

Her old friend grinned at her. "Everything is tagged so that it can be tracked down. Once a part is on the schedule, it gets built. If the schedule slips, so does the manufacture of the part. If there's some type of short-term holdup, the part gets put into one of the storage rooms for retrieval.

"With computer assistance, it's not hard to keep track of everything that needs to be built for a given project. Or even for a project that is already complete. I could look back at any of the ships previously constructed here and tell you when each and every part for it was made, shipped to the construction site, and installed."

She cocked her head. "If it's so automated, what do they need you for? To stand around and look important?"

He laughed. "It seems like that some days. I spent a lot of time wandering between systems and making sure everything is operating as it should and that all parts are accounted for. I suppose you could say I'm a glorified bean counter and maintenance man."

"That seems like a lot of work for one person," Kelsey said. "Shouldn't there be a team of you?"

"All joking aside, Captain, there *is* a team working on this. We work on different shifts to make sure someone is always here. There are always three of us on shift. It's such a large facility that we occasionally work an entire shift without seeing one another, but we're here."

At that moment, one of the machines one level up began emitting an insistent beep, and a small red light started flashing on top of it.

"And speaking of the devil, there calls my master," Don said with a sigh. "I'll go see what's wrong with that unit and be right back. It should only take me a couple of minutes to get whatever is out of alignment back on track. Just wait here, I'll take care of it, and we'll go have lunch."

With that, Don set off for a lift serving that side of the compartment.

As soon as he was out of sight, Carl stepped over to one of the machines near them. "Keep an eye out for anybody coming by. I'm going to install a shunt on this machine so I can access the computer system inside the facility."

Veronica watched one way, while Princess Kelsey watched the other. There was no one in sight, but that didn't mean someone couldn't just appear without warning.

The young scientist quickly took off an access panel and dug into the guts of the machine. Sixty seconds later, he had it back together and was standing beside them as if nothing had happened.

"I'm accessing the shunt now just to see what I can get to," he said. "This machine doesn't look like it's set up to manufacture flip drive parts. I need to figure out where exactly the machine we need is located and how to get into its programming."

He closed his eyes for about thirty seconds and then smiled. "Found it. It's on level three just above us. As it's a specialized piece of equipment, I'm going to have to access it directly. I'm not getting much more than the location from here."

"What if Don comes back?" Veronica asked, concerned. "If you're not here, that's going to make him suspicious."

Carl shrugged. "It's not as if we have a choice. If we skip this opportunity, we may never get another one. Tell him I went looking for the bathroom or something."

With that, the young man headed for the lift on this side of the compartment, moving quickly and pressing the button. The doors slid open, he stepped inside, and he was gone.

The next three minutes dragged by with incredible slowness. Veronica willed the scientist to reappear every few seconds, but of course, he didn't.

Instead, the first lift opened, and Don walked out. He grinned at them as he walked over. "Problem solved. Let's go get something to eat."

Then he frowned. "Where's Mr. Owlet? This is a secure facility, he can't just wander around. Technically, I shouldn't have left any of you unescorted."

"He had to go find the bathroom," Princess Kelsey said. "I promise he'll be right back. While we're waiting, can you tell me how this room is broken down? Do specific sections of machines work on specific parts, or is it all random?"

Don hadn't stopped frowning, but he did turn to face the short woman. That put his back toward the lift that Carl had used. With any luck at all, he wouldn't see the young man return.

"It's complicated, but each of these sections holds machines that work on related parts. That simplifies the process of getting the raw materials segregated. I can break down which floors do what kind of work, but I really shouldn't be talking about that level of detail. Which way did he go? We should go find him."

Out of the corner of her eye, Veronica saw the lift doors open. Her relief was short-lived, though. An unknown man in a Fleet uniform stepped out from the lift, pushing Carl in front of him.

They'd been caught.

29

Zia made her way to the receptionist's apartment carefully, being absolutely certain to look casual as she walked down the corridor but keeping an eagle eye out for anything that looked out of place. Ralph Halstead knew what she looked like, so an inopportune meeting would be a very, *very* bad thing.

Doctor Rehnquist followed along behind her, looking completely out of place and somewhat shifty as he attempted to sneak along.

"Just walk, Doctor," she said softly, shooting him a glance. "You look like you're up to something."

"I *am* up to something," he said in something close to a stage whisper. "I've never done anything like this before."

"Talk to me in a soft, but normal, tone of voice," she said firmly. "Don't whisper. That looks suspicious.

"Once we get to the apartment, what are you hoping to find in the computer system? How is it going to help us determine if what we're looking for exists?"

The older man cleared his throat. "If, as Colonel Talbot suspects, the computer system is linked to the research facility to use its computational resources, that means some kind of connection has already been established that bypasses the firewalls. Perhaps not all of them, but it will get us into a better position to assess what needs to happen next.

"From that vantage point, I should be able to get into the files detailing what research projects are currently underway. Perhaps even those that are shelved or completed. Probably not the classified data, but at least summaries of what the research entails."

She nodded as they turned into the apartment building. "What about the security feeds from the classified section of the building? Will you be able to access those from here as well?"

The man shrugged as they entered the stairs. "Perhaps. At a minimum, I should be able to get the security feeds in the nonclassified areas of the building. I hope to also gain control over the side entrance so that I can allow our people access."

No one was in the hallway when they exited the stairwell, so she walked up to the man's apartment briskly and opened the door.

Inside, she found a surprise. Talbot had Ralph Halstead at stunner point. The young man was seated on his own couch with his hands folded in his lap. He looked a little frightened. Understandably so.

"He showed up out of the blue," Talbot said grumpily. "This is probably going to upset our schedule."

"I don't suppose I can ask what's going on," the young man said. "I'm not exactly certain how breaking into my apartment and kidnapping me is going to get your niece medical treatment sooner."

Yes, this was going to severely upset their schedule. They could probably stash the young man for a day and get away with it. If he went incommunicado for longer than that, someone would come looking for him.

"This is a complication we could've done without," Zia agreed with a shake of her head. "Doctor, why don't you head back and see what you can find. Make the most of this opportunity. We may not get one like it again."

She considered what to tell the young man. The truth was definitely off-limits. They needed a lie that made sense but didn't give the Rebel Empire a clue to what they'd *really* been up to.

"Industrial espionage," she said as if she were admitting something she'd rather not. "You discovering us does complicate our schedule, but we'll get what we need and be gone before anyone else on this station is aware of what we're up to.

"If you cooperate, we'll leave you unharmed. If you attempt to cause us trouble, we're going to have to disable you until we get away. I'd much rather not harm you, so I suggest you do the smart thing and cooperate."

His expression was somewhat unreadable, but he nodded. "I'll do whatever you want. Just don't hurt me."

Talbot stepped close to her while still keeping the stunner aimed at the young man. "What the hell do we do now?" he asked softly.

"We play this by ear. Follow my lead."

She raised her voice slightly so that the boy could hear her. "Is your computer system tapped into the research facility computers? Don't bother lying. My compatriot is examining it right now, and he'll be able to tell us the truth in just a couple of minutes."

With a sigh, Ralph nodded. "They have a lot of computer power that they're not using, so I borrowed my aunt's login credentials to get into the external systems without them being aware. It won't get you into the classified research computers, though. Those are isolated."

"I suppose that's the best we can hope for," she said with a sigh. "Why did you come home early?"

The young man looked embarrassed. "Since I live so close to the research center, I often eat lunch at home. It saves me a little bit of money and lets me get away from Regina for little bit. She's something of a pain."

His admission made Zia laugh a little. "I can completely understand that. I really am sorry that you've gotten caught up in this. Honestly, all we were doing was casing your apartment so that we could sneak in tonight and clone your identification. Under other circumstances, you'd never have known we were here."

"I realize you probably can't answer this question," Ralph said slowly, "but I'm not certain why you're so interested in what could only be a specialized kind of regeneration. Normal medical regeneration is good enough for just about any kind of injury. I don't understand why any company would be looking for something so focused."

She raised an eyebrow. "And yet the research center is working on just that."

Ralph shrugged. "The research is funded by the Lords. If we were doing this for profit, that might be a different thing, but our research center is kind of specialized. I can't tell you for certain what use this technology would be put to, if it actually exists, but the Lords won't be pleased at having someone meddle in their affairs."

If only he knew how pissed they'd *really* be if they knew the truth.

Zia was still pondering how to answer his very logical questions when Doctor Rehnquist stepped out into the living room and cleared his throat softly.

"Excuse me," she said as she stepped over to the doctor and drew him back into the hallway. "Have you found something?"

The man nodded, a grin on his face. "Your intrusion specialist and I have been going over the young man's computer closely. He has all the access we desire, though I must confess that he's hidden it rather well. I'm quite impressed with his skills."

She frowned. "I'm not certain I understand. What exactly did you find?"

The research scientist turned so that his back was facing toward the living room. "That's not a gaming computer, though it's certainly meant to look like one. In fact, I suspect our young friend uses it as such, but that's not its true purpose.

"What he has in there is a very powerful machine dedicated to hacking into secure systems. Buried underneath its disguise as a gaming computer, it has a sophisticated array of penetration tools.

"The young man has completely hacked into the research center. Not just the public areas of the system, either. He's penetrated the secure firewalls. We have *complete* access to everything but the labs themselves."

Zia found herself blinking in shock. "Wait a minute. You're telling me that that earnest young man is some kind of criminal and that he's been busy doing exactly what we want to do all this time?"

The scientist nodded energetically. "Indeed."

Well, holy crap.

"Good work, Doctor. Get back in there and make certain we can duplicate that access, just in case we have to run. Also, go through their files and see if they really do have a research project that matches what we're looking for. This is our big chance. Let's not waste it."

Zia walked back into the living room and smiled at Talbot. "You're going to like this."

Before he could respond, the door burst open, and two men came rushing in, weapons in their hands. Their attention zeroed in on Talbot, likely because he was armed.

At the same moment, Ralph Halstead drew a hidden weapon from between the cushions on his couch, raising it to point directly at Zia.

That instant seemed to last an eternity, and then everyone started firing.

* * *

KELSEY FORCED a relieved smile onto her face. "There you are, Carl! Did you find the restroom?"

He shook his head and gave her a wry smile. "No such luck. I ran into this gentleman and was hoping he'd point me in the right direction, but he's pretty annoyed to find me unescorted."

The man pushed Carl forward as the pair got closer to the group. "I found this guy wandering on level three, Commander. Should I call security?"

Sommerville stared at Veronica for a few seconds. "I don't think that'll be necessary, Jack. I'm sure it was just an honest mistake. Head back to your post."

The man looked unsure about that, but he headed back for the lift.

Once he was gone, Sommerville put his hands on his hips and focused his attention on Carl. "What were you really doing, Mr. Owlet?"

"He was just looking for the—" Kelsey started.

Sommerville held up a finger toward her. "If you don't mind, I'd like to have Mr. Owlet answer for himself, Captain Delatorre. Depending on how satisfied I am with what he says, I might end up calling security after all. Be forewarned, I'm not buying the restroom story."

As Kelsey watched apprehensively, Carl sighed. "You're right. I'm their tech guy. I just wanted to get a closer look at some of the other pieces of equipment to see if they were like the ones down here. I meant no harm, Commander. I have Fleet clearance, and I wouldn't jeopardize our mission. I'm sorry."

Kelsey held her breath wondering if Sommerville was going to believe them or call security. If he seemed doubtful, she was going to have to take him down and then they'd have to go hunt the fellow that had seen Carl. That would screw their primary mission, so she really hoped it wasn't necessary.

The man kept his attention focused on Carl for a long few seconds and then nodded. "It's not very respectful to my position here or me personally, but I can believe that. Unfortunately, it means that our little tour is over. Trust only goes so far. I'm afraid you've abused mine, and I'm going to have to ask you to leave."

Veronica sighed but nodded. "I understand. I'm sorry, Don."

"So am I. I'm afraid that I'm going to have to cancel lunch. I need to perform a walk-through on level three to make certain that nothing has been tampered with."

He turned his attention to Kelsey. "I wish you the best of luck in your mission, Captain Delatorre. If we meet again, I hope it's under more auspicious circumstances."

Fifteen minutes later, Commander Sommerville had escorted them completely out of the Fleet area before turning around and returning to his duty station without a word.

His unspoken message was perfectly clear. They were not welcome in the Fleet section of the shipyard. Kelsey wouldn't be surprised if he'd put a flag on them and would be notified if they attempted to go back inside the Fleet area.

Kelsey led the others to a nearby café, and they ordered some coffee and sweets. The large window nearby had a stunning view of Archibald's red moon as the shipyard orbited around it. She wondered briefly what caused the intense shade of scarlet but set that aside. They had more important things to worry about.

Once the waiter had departed, she leaned in toward Carl. "What happened?"

"It isn't as bad as it looks," he assured her. "I put one shunt into the machine that makes the flip drives and the last into a general computer hookup in the main bulkhead. That one should give us a lot of information about all of the systems and what they've been doing.

"The guy that caught me did so after I'd closed everything up and was headed back for the lift. I didn't have a chance to hide because he was inside it. I gave him my cover story, but he wasn't having any of it. He dragged me downstairs, and you know the rest."

Kelsey turned her attention to Veronica. "Is your friend going to let this go, or is he going to keep digging till he finds something? Is he going to report us?"

Veronica looked uncertain. "I don't think he's going to report us, but that doesn't mean he won't look very closely at everything on level three. It's possible he could find the shunts."

"That's not very likely," Carl said with a shake of his head. "The shunts are designed to look like other components. Nothing he sees will look out of place unless he's *intimately* familiar with what should've been there to begin with."

"We'll just have to hope for the best, then," Kelsey said. "What do we know? Can we do this?"

"It looks like they've already been building a ship that needs a flip drive that might work for our purposes," Carl said. "One of those freighters that Veronica was talking about earlier is about to enter its final trials, or so the construction logs say. I've looked over the design parameters for its flip drive. It's weak for what we need, but if we're cautious, it might work."

"That doesn't sound very promising," Kelsey said with a sigh. "I was hoping we'd be able to get something perfect for what we need, but I suppose that was a long shot. Can't we just have the manufacturing equipment make us a perfectly designed flip drive?"

The young scientist shrugged. "Sure. I can have it build one and put it into storage, but we'd still have to get it out. With Commander Sommerville's suspicions raised, that's probably a lot more dangerous than slipping on board a freighter with a small crew and stealing it during the test flight."

"I have an idea," Veronica said. "Don said something about the system being able to automatically deliver parts where they're needed. Could you have the manufacturing equipment build the perfect flip drive for *Audacious*, deliver it to the target ship, and then erase all traces that you had done so?"

Her young friend pondered that for a moment and then nodded. "I have the plans. I even have updated plans that have the modulator installed that would allow the ship to use multiflip points without risking another burnout.

"The problem is that I'd have to be here to direct things. It's a new drive, and we don't want a problem with it to attract Commander Sommerville's attention. Then comes the order to ship it to the freighter. I can't give it that instruction until the manufacturing is complete."

"How long will it take to build the flip drive?" Kelsey asked.

"Based on what I can see, the machine takes premanufactured parts where it can and puts them together. It only produces unique elements when the design calls for something that's not in storage.

"I think I can have the new flip drive finished in about eight hours. If I then schedule it to be immediately delivered to the ship and placed into one of the storage holds, that means it'll be ready sometime tonight. I'll have to stay here and oversee that though."

Kelsey shook her head slowly. "This is where we take a big risk because I'm not leaving you here where they might pick you up. We'll call for a shuttle to come pick us up and have them bring one of the FTL coms.

"Fiona can direct the construction of the flip drive and see that it's shipped to the right place. She can then erase all evidence it was ever built. If anyone saw those plans, they'd deduce what kind of flip point it's useful for.

"That will also give her some access to the Fleet computer systems. How much access would Fiona have?"

Carl shrugged. "A lot."

Kelsey nodded. "There's undoubtedly a lot of interesting information in there, but that's a bonus. We have to have the right flip drive, and we'll take this risk to make it happen.

"Get things in motion, Carl. We'll need to recover the FTL com when the drive is complete, but we'll figure out that part when the time comes. This means that whether the other team is finished or not, we're getting out of the Archibald system tonight."

30

T albot had just a moment to bless all the fighting practice he'd had with Kelsey over the last year as he responded to the unexpected attack. Her speed had honed his reflexes to a razor's edge, though she still trashed him every time.

As he had his weapon out, he only had to pivot slightly to fire at the intruders coming through the door. He knew where they were, whereas they hadn't had a firm grasp of where he'd be standing when they rushed in.

Talbot's stunner bolt took the lead attacker in the chest and dropped him to the floor. Even as the second man was firing at him, Talbot was dropping below the shot. A grunt behind him told Talbot that it had still found a target in Zia.

He fired as soon as he hit the floor, taking the second man in the lower torso and dropping him as well.

A stunner bolt struck the carpet right in front of Talbot's face, coming from the couch. Somehow, their prisoner had gotten his hands on a weapon. Perfect.

Even as he was rolling onto his side to return fire, Bill Smith appeared in the doorway leading into the rest of the apartment and shot the young hacker on the couch with his stunner.

Talbot leapt to his feet without waiting to see the results of the shot and threw himself into the hallway. He suspected there would be more intruders waiting to rush into the apartment, and he wasn't disappointed.

Two more people waited in the hall, a man and a woman. The man was armed, so Talbot shot him first. The man's return fire missed the marine by scant centimeters as he gripped his weapon spasmodically.

The woman opened her mouth to say something or maybe to shout, so Talbot shot her as well. Miraculously, no one else in the building seem to notice all the commotion. At least not yet.

Smith stuck his head out, ready to assist in the fight, so Talbot drafted him into getting the two new prisoners into the apartment.

Moments later, they'd dragged the man inside and dropped him on top of the other two. Talbot was a little gentler with the woman and set her on the couch next to the unconscious hacker.

Smith locked the door again. Talbot had been certain he'd secured it after Zia had arrived, so one of these people undoubtedly had an entry code. This wasn't a random attack.

"Doctor Rehnquist, you need to hurry up," Talbot called out as he made his way to Zia's unconscious form. "Now that we've had visitors, we can assume there'll be more. We need to get out of here. How much longer?"

"I'm wrapping up what I need to do now. Give me three minutes, and I'll have us our own access to the facility computers, independent of this hardware."

"Make it two if you can."

Smith was watching the door, so Talbot holstered his weapon and went to examine the prisoners. He swiftly searched through their pockets and found their identification. Not that they'd mean anything to him.

The woman had an identification badge that indicated she worked at the research center. It showed her name as "Adriana Lipp, PhD." The man from the hall was Kevin Lipp.

"Well, well, well," he muttered. "It looks as if this is a family affair. I certainly wish we could take everyone back to our place for a more detailed questioning, but that seems unlikely considering we'd have to wander through the corridors with them over our shoulders."

"It's not out of the question, if you know what you're doing," Smith said. "Keep an eye on the door, and I'll be right back."

He ducked out into the hallway and was back a minute later pushing a large laundry hamper.

"Where the hell did you find that?" Talbot demanded.

"I saw a sign at the end of the hall. Apparently, this apartment building has a central laundry that the tenants are eligible to use. I tossed out the bags of personal clothing and left the sheets and pillowcases in the cart. We should be able to cover everyone up with those and not suffocate anybody."

Talbot eyed the size of the hamper and slowly nodded. "Maybe. It'll be a tight fit, but I'd rather not leave any witnesses that could describe us later."

Doctor Rehnquist came out and stopped abruptly as he saw all of the bodies lying around the living room. "Good heavens! What happened?"

"You really need to work on your situational awareness skills, Doctor," Talbot said. "These are our young hacker's allies. Did you get everything you needed?"

The scientist nodded. "I physically removed all the storage media. I'll have plenty of time to go over everything the young man has stolen, and I took the time to add another access pathway through the firewalls to allow us to use my equipment for the operation."

"Excellent," Talbot said with a sharp nod. "Smith, you're on lead. We want to make sure nobody raises an eyebrow when we come by. If they do, we're going to have to stun them and make a run for it. I'd rather not do that, but if push comes to shove, that's the plan."

The intrusion specialist signaled his understanding. "Just push that thing like you have every right to do so, and no one will pay you any mind. If anybody asks what you're doing, I'll handle it.

"Doctor Rehnquist, I want you to follow along behind us. Stay back at least thirty meters and pretend you don't know us. Don't even look at us. Just walk back to our hotel."

The scientist raised an eyebrow. "Speaking of our hotel, exactly how are you planning on getting that thing through the front door? I suspect the management is going to object if you try to bring it through the lobby."

Smith smiled. "Our hotel has a freight entrance. I've already taken the liberty of bypassing the security. We'll go in that way and head up the service lift to our floor. If we run into anyone, I'll bribe them to look the other way."

Talbot certainly hoped that worked, but it wasn't as if they had a whole lot of choice in the matter. They needed to get back to their rooms as soon as possible. The research center might not miss their wayward receptionist, but a misplaced research scientist could potentially raise the alarm.

They'd certainly be aware if she failed to show up at work as expected the next day. That pretty much guaranteed they'd have to carry off their intrusion and theft tonight.

"Doctor, did you find anything in the files to indicate they were working on the kind of regeneration equipment we need?" Talbot asked the scientist.

The older man nodded with a smile. "Indeed. As a matter of pure luck, I suppose, Doctor Lipp here is the chief researcher on that project. Sadly for us, her nephew was primarily interested in other projects."

"I'm glad to hear that they have something suitable," Talbot said. "Is there any indication of exactly what projects young Ralph is most interested in?"

The scientist shrugged. "He has a number of files that I haven't had a chance to peruse. I can take care of that once we get back to the hotel. Perhaps by dark I can have a status report for you."

Talbot knew that was the best he was going to get, so he didn't push the matter. He and Smith carefully placed everyone into the cart and covered them with sheets and pillowcases. They then headed down the hallway toward the freight elevator. It took both of them to move the heavy cart.

He crossed his fingers as they walked, praying they didn't run into any trouble. If something went wrong now, it could go very badly for all of them.

"Once we get back to the hotel, I want you to go hit Doctor Lipp's apartment," Talbot told Smith. "We might get lucky, and she'll have copies of her files at home."

"We can't count on that," Smith said with a grunt, "but I suppose it doesn't hurt to try."

Talbot felt better the further away from the apartment building. He hoped Kelsey's side of the operation was going more smoothly than his. It felt as if he were just staying just one step ahead of disaster.

* * *

VERONICA WALKED into chaos as she arrived back at the hotel rooms on the station. It seemed that Colonel Talbot had run into a little more excitement than he'd planned on while scouting out the research center.

They'd apparently gotten into some kind of firefight in the receptionist's apartment and now had five prisoners. That raised a lot of interesting questions about who the receptionist and his aunt were really working for.

Zia wasn't going to be pleased when she woke up either. Stunner headaches were a bitch.

Doctor Zoboroski was monitoring everyone and assured Princess Kelsey that there would be no lasting damage. At his best guess, the everyone would regain consciousness in about two hours.

They'd put Zia in the room she shared with Veronica while the prisoners were cuffed and secured in separate rooms under guard. They'd also put a blocker in the aunt's room. It only had a short range so it didn't affect any of their people.

Unlike her nephew or the others, she'd had implants. They couldn't allow her to wake up and communicate with the station, or she'd call for help. They also couldn't allow others to track her based on those same implants.

Bill Smith had disabled everyone's com units the moment they'd captured them. He'd be overseeing any data extraction when he got back from Doctor Lipp's place.

On the positive side, it seemed they'd gotten information and access into the computers at the research facility. Doctor Rehnquist started cheerfully explaining everything he'd found to Carl Owlet as soon as the young man had walked in the door. Together, the two scientists were firming up their access and knowledge of the facility in preparation for a raid tonight.

Princess Kelsey was closeted with Colonel Talbot and Cain Hopwood discussing the particulars of both missions. They'd invited her to join them, but Veronica decided to do a little bit of scouting on her own.

Something felt off to her about the way people had been behaving on the station since they got back. They seemed a little bit jumpy. More worried. She suspected something had happened, and she needed to find out what that was.

Before heading out, she stopped in her room to change into something more appropriate. Once she'd dressed, she let herself out quietly and made her way down the corridor to a local bar. One that seemed to have a solid Fleet presence.

If anyone knew what was happening in the system, they'd be in this room. The presence of alcohol made it much more likely they'd share something they probably shouldn't too.

The bar was a fairly upscale establishment, not some dark hole where serious drinkers went to drown their sorrows. The lighting was good, the clientele well dressed, and based on the prices, the liquor was of good quality.

A glance around told her that there was a significant amount of serious conversation taking place. Every table seemed to hold people with their heads bent close together, discussing something. There was definitely something afoot.

None of the Fleet officers were seated alone, so Veronica made her way to the bar instead. Bartenders seemed to hear everything. Perhaps she could get the information she needed that way.

She ordered a fairly upscale drink and left enough cash beside it to make for a hefty tip. As the woman was taking it, Veronica leaned forward so that she didn't need to raise her voice too much.

"What's everyone worried about? They all seem so nervous."

The bartender leaned toward her. "You hear those rumors about the Ghosts attacking some system nearby? It seems like they're coming our way. From what I hear, all Fleet elements are being put on alert. They're worried the shipyard might be a target. That Archibald itself might even be a target.

"I don't know about anyone else, but when I get off shift in an hour, I'm headed straight down to the surface. I've already got a ticket on one of the evening shuttles. As soon as I heard about the trouble, I picked it up while I was on break.

"It won't be long before everyone is trying to get off the station, so if you haven't gotten tickets down to the surface, you might want to go ahead and get them now before the rush starts. I wouldn't want to be stuck here if the Ghosts come calling."

Veronica shook her head as the woman moved off to serve someone else. Perfect. Their already tight schedule had just gotten significantly more complicated.

As she finished her drink, Veronica chuckled bitterly. With their luck, it was an almost certainty that the Clans would arrive tonight. She had to get back to the hotel and let Princess Kelsey know.

They'd have to begin preparing to hijack that ship as soon as the new flip drive was delivered. Time was no longer on their side.

31

Zia sat up, clutched her pounding head, and wondering what had happened. Then she remembered the attack in the apartment.

A glance around the room told her she was back at the hotel, so they'd won the fight. Well, that was a pleasant surprise. Considering how abrupt the ambush had been, she'd been afraid they'd lose.

She staggered to the bathroom and washed her face. A small package of painkillers sat beside the sink with a note to take them. That was thoughtful.

It only took a few minutes to find Princess Kelsey and Talbot. They were closeted with Cain Hopwood. Only Veronica was missing.

Kelsey smiled as she came in. "Oh good, you're awake. Feeling okay?"

"That's debatable," Zia grumbled. "My head is beating like a drum. I hate stunners."

Talbot grinned at her. "They beat the heck out of flechettes. As you've already figured out, we won the fight. Our little friend wasn't just a receptionist. It turns out he was an industrial spy or something. He, his aunt, and her husband were stealing technology from the research center. I guess they won't be thrilled with the competition."

"Probably not." Zia sat down and poured herself a glass of water from the handy pitcher. "Did we get what we needed?"

The marine nodded. "We have several bits of good news. First, the project his aunt was working on is indeed an advanced regeneration machine that can probably take care of what we need done for Commodore Murdoch. I realize that we'd be in better shape if we could focus on just one mission, but at least we're past guessing.

"Second, the receptionist had thoroughly penetrated the center's firewalls. He had complete access to the restricted areas and even files from some of the projects. Unless it was on a stand-alone computer, he could get to it. And third, we have both his aunt and uncle stashed in a room nearby under guard.

"I expect they're waking up about now. I'll question them before we make our move. They might be able to give us some clarity about the project. Anything that speeds us along is a good thing."

She nodded in spite of her pounding headache. "That's good news. Tell me the bad news."

"You're a pessimist," Kelsey said gloomily.

"I'm an optimist with a sense of history. The bad news."

"He didn't have any files from his aunt's project," Kelsey said with a chuckle. "Either she has them elsewhere or it's on a stand-alone computer. We have Bill Smith checking her place, but we probably still need to get the files from the center as well as any hardware to be certain we have everything we need.

"Thankfully, Ralph has their security thoroughly penetrated. We don't even need his identification card to get in. Carl said he can create false identities for everyone involved and print up cards that will work if you're confronted. Basically, you should be able to waltz right in, steal everything you need, and waltz back out."

Zia laughed as the door opened and admitted Veronica. "Nothing ever works that easily for us. There will be some major complication along the way."

"I'm not sure what we're talking about," Veronica said as she took a seat, "but I'm here to deliver the mandatory complication. Word is out that the Ghosts are moving toward this system. Fleet is on alert, expecting an intrusion at some point in the next few days.

"We're going to have to move tonight if we expect to get clear before they get here. If I was a betting woman, I'd wager they'll show up at the worst possible moment. For example, while we're busy carrying out our plans tonight."

Kelsey swore. "I wonder what that's going to do to security around the shipyard. Are we still going to be able to slip onto the freighter once our new flip drive is delivered? If we can, are we going to be able to get away without Fleet coming down on us like a ton of bricks? Will Carl be able to retrieve the FTL com?"

Zia cocked her head? "Freighter? FTL com? What did I miss?"

Her short friend shrugged. "We got caught planting Carl's shunts, but they didn't get the shunts themselves. I ordered Carl to hide an FTL com on the shipyard so Fiona could direct the manufacture of the flip drive we need, have it delivered to a freighter we can steal, and plunder their computers for any interesting information.

"The original plan was for Carl to retrieve the com before we leave, but we might have to send a destruct signal to it if we don't have time. Or if we can't get back aboard the yard to get it. We can handle that. I'm worried about getting away when we steal the ship."

"If the ship is in operable condition, then it's going to be ordered to flee as soon as things start looking bad," Veronica said. "If we can get our people on board and ready to secure the vessel ahead of that, we can wait for the real crew to get orders to make a run for it and then take them out."

"What if those orders never come?" Talbot asked. "What if the attack doesn't make it to Archibald?"

"Then the ship will be ordered to do its trials. There's also a good chance it will be used to move critical equipment out of this system. That freighter is a big ship. So long as we hide ourselves well, there's not going to be enough crew on board to find us. We can wait until it gets away from the shipyard to take it over at our leisure."

Cain Hopwood nodded. "If we can get my crew on board, I'd say we have a pretty good chance of taking it over without anyone being the wiser. We can install lockouts on the communication and control systems to make sure.

"Even though the Rebel Empire Fleet might be at a higher state of alert, they'll have their eyes on the flip point. They're not going to expect someone to try stealing a ship right out from under their noses. We can use that to our advantage."

"It sounds as if both plans are advanced enough to execute," Zia said slowly. "What are we going to do at the research center? Sneak inside with the small ring and bring the larger ring through inside the center? Then move everything out to our freighter and walk back out?"

Kelsey nodded. "Something very much like that. Since Carl has access to the security system, he should be able to cancel any calls for help. That's going to be the initial response of anyone that feels like you shouldn't be there. With him watching over your shoulder, you should be able to get the equipment you need and get the hell out of there pretty fast."

Zia certainly hoped it worked out like that, but she'd wager there would be complications. There always were.

"Do we have any idea what *Persephone* is doing?" she asked. "We might have need of the marines on board that ship and even their weapons if things get really hairy. And what about the Rebel Empire Fleet ships at the outer gas giant?"

"We risked contacting Angela. The Rebel Empire ships arrived at the gas giant and haven't left. Our probes say they're sending cutters and pinnaces from all ships down into the atmosphere. I'd wager they're sending crew to the battlecruisers hiding there so they can use them to fight the Clans."

Veronica rubbed her eyes. "I think it's a fair bet that those ships are going to move back toward the flip point or come to Archibald orbit before too much longer. We're going to have to take that into account. If they show up while we're in the process of stealing the freighter, that could get ugly really fast."

Princess Kelsey crossed her arms and nodded. "Both missions have to be carried out tonight."

"I think your best bet is to make the attack at the research center about one in the morning," Cain said. "It's far enough past closing that they won't be expecting trouble, but it gives you enough time to finish everything before the early risers come in the door tomorrow morning. All you'll need to deal with are the researchers and staff there overnight."

"What about our new prisoners?" Talbot asked. "I'm going to hit them up for more information, but they know what Zia and I look like. That might get the Rebel Empire on our trail sooner than we'd like."

Kelsey grimaced. "We'll have to take them with us. Stun them again before you go, and take them with you. Send them through the transport ring to the ship with the equipment. It'll be good to have the aunt with us in any case, since this is her project. If we have questions about the process, we can ask her.

"We'll want to make our move on the freighter around the same time. There are a lot of small craft flitting around the shipyard, so we shouldn't draw undue attention if we don't come too close."

"The ship is ready for trials, so it won't be inside the yard itself," Cain said. "It's going to be orbiting a short distance away. My people can get off the shuttle at range and use suit thrusters to land on its hull and gain access. We should be able to settle ourselves into a hiding place and wait to make our move with no one the wiser."

"There we go," Kelsey said. "That gives us about ten hours before we need to execute both missions. Zia and Talbot, brief your people and get some sleep if you can. Have someone take your noncritical gear back to your shuttles before go time. Leave nothing here at the hotel for the Rebel Empire to find.

"Veronica and I will go with Cain to our freighter. We'll eat and sleep too. Remember, if the Clans attack, we'll be leaving in a hurry. If the Rebel Fleet warships come in, we might have to sneak away a bit more stealthily. If push comes to shove, *Persephone* will have to create a diversion."

Talbot rapped his knuckles on the table. "This is it. We're either going to succeed tonight or go down in flames. Let's make sure we give it our best effort."

"I'm feeling good," Kelsey said. "Only one thing is bothering me. After disguising myself as Delatorre and everything, I never got to blackmail anyone."

Zia laughed. "Maybe next time."

* * *

KELSEY, Talbot, and her team moved back to their cargo shuttle as nonchalantly as they could. They traveled in small groups and did nothing to draw undue attention to themselves.

Even though she expected someone to stop them and try to extort money, everyone arrived at the shuttle without having been harassed. They returned to the freighter without problem.

There was enough time before they were to execute their plan for her to grow nervous and twitchy. With her implants, she didn't require nearly enough sleep to get through until departure time.

Instead, she spent the time going over their scanner readings and refining her thoughts on how they'd get on board the freighter and what they'd do when they did. Cain Hopwood was smarter than she was and was sleeping until just about an hour before they were ready to launch, but she ran what she'd thought about past him as they were making final preparations.

"I think that looks good, as far as it goes, but we're going to have to play this by ear. Once we get on board that freighter, anything can happen. I think it's going to be relatively safe for us until then. Our suits are made to avoid detection so no one is going to see us coming.

"The problem is going to come in once we get inside the ship. There's no telling where the crew is located. I'm hopeful most of them will be in their quarters asleep. Or if we're lucky, not even on board. A skeleton crew would be ideal."

She nodded at him and headed to suit up. "We'll deal with the situation as we find it. Thanks again for your help. You guys have made our successes possible in so many ways. Rest assured that the Empire will remember this when we get home."

A little bit more than an hour later, their shuttle detached from the freighter and headed away from the station. Word from Fiona had come in that the flip drive was complete and had just been delivered to the freighter. One major milestone complete.

Their cargo shuttle wasn't passing close enough to the shipyard to be challenged, though it was at the very edge of what they thought they could get away with. The target freighter was still too far away to be seen visually. Even the shipyard was only a bright speck in the distance.

Thankfully, their stealth suits had overpowered thrusters, and they had no lack of fuel to get to where they needed to go.

Even with all the pressure on them, Kelsey took a moment to admire Archibald after they stepped out into space. The planet was all greens and blues, just rising above the curve of the red moon. Wispy clouds covered a substantial portion of the planet's surface. It was a beautiful world. Perhaps not as pretty as Avalon, but she had to admit she was biased.

"We'd best be on our way," Cain said. "By my best estimate, it'll take us almost an hour to get to the freighter. If everything goes to hell, I'd rather not be floating in space when it happens."

The slow trip to the freighter was rough on her nerves, but Kelsey had gotten much better at dealing with that sort of thing over the last few years. She distracted herself by going over the deck plans that Carl had gotten for them. They needed to find a good hiding place, and she wanted to be sure they were picking the right one.

The final approach was nerve-racking. If anyone observed them visually, they were screwed. She barely breathed until they finally touched down on the ship's hull.

They'd decided not to use even low-powered radio because of the risk of being detected. This was Cain's operation now. He'd get them inside without detection and deal with any unfortunate incidents involving the crew.

She couldn't help feeling a sense of impending doom. This was the part of the mission where things usually went wrong. Often catastrophically wrong.

Five minutes later, Cain's people had the outer airlock door open, and he made a hand gesture for everyone to move into the airlock in groups. This was it.

32

A fter Kelsey and her people left, Talbot felt like a sword was hanging over his head. He kept expecting a call saying that they'd run into terrible trouble or to hear alarms outside the hotel and see security people rushing around.

That hadn't happened. In fact, the shuttle had made it back to the freighter without any problem, reporting that the drop-off had been smooth and without issue. That didn't stop him from fretting.

He'd distracted himself by interrogating their prisoners. Not that they were being very cooperative. He'd thought the boy would be easier to get information from, but he'd proven exceptionally recalcitrant. He'd smiled and told them nothing.

That impressed Talbot. That level of resistance spoke to either a lot of training or some serious willpower. In either case, he'd had written off getting timely assistance from the young man.

Doctor Lipp was more talkative but still told him nothing. She'd denied everything and claimed she'd received a call for assistance from her nephew.

Neither of them believed that, of course. Any reasonable person would've called security in that set of circumstances, not grabbed her husband and some "friends" to go fight it out in her nephew's apartment.

Bill Smith had gotten back from the woman's dwelling a few minutes ago. He'd gathered a lot of data, but nothing about the project she was working on or the criminal activity she was apparently perpetrating on her employer.

To add to the complexity, the man had also brought back Lipp's cats: a pair of kittens about four months old, both male. One was black and had a stubby tail, and the other was a gray tabby. Both were playful and friendly.

What Talbot was supposed to do with them, he didn't know. Still, the man was right in that he couldn't leave them there. If no one came to check on them, they would die of neglect. Bringing them was the right thing to do.

As far as problems went, they were the least of his worries. Someone would take them back to the cargo shuttles and see them safely on the freighter.

The fact that Lipp had argued with him at least raised the potential that Talbot could get her to tell them something, so he made his way back to her room half an hour before he and Zia would leave for the center.

He entered the room without knocking. It wasn't as if he was going to find her running around loose. She was restrained and under guard. One of the female marines he brought along on this mission even escorted her to the restroom.

When he came in, she was sitting up in bed. Two marines stood against the far wall and the female assigned to watch over her was seated at the small desk.

"My, doesn't this look homey." he said. "How are you feeling, Doctor Lipp?"

She gave him a hard look. "Let me be blunt. I don't know who you are, but you're not going to get any useful information from me, and security is undoubtedly already searching for me and my family. Do yourself a favor and let us go so that you can get the charges against you reduced."

He leaned against the desk and gave her a flat smile. "We both know that's not going to happen. You, your husband, and your nephew were engaged in industrial espionage. If we get caught, you get caught. It's unfortunate for you that we came along and upset your applecart, but your only path out of this as a free woman is in cooperating with us."

She laughed, a bright sound under the circumstances. "You think highly of yourself. If what you said were true—which it isn't—all we have to do is keep our mouths shut until you're gone. It's not as if you're going to take us with you. You're after information, not hostages."

"Maybe. We're after the research project you head at research center, and we need that project to work. Taking you along might suit me fine."

The woman shook her head. "Getting the data I can buy, but you'll never get off the station with the equipment. It's not just a couple of small handheld items. It's easily double the size of a standard regenerator. Not something you're going to put into your pocket and stroll away with, even if you could get access to the lab."

Talbot grinned. "We're not without our tricks, but let's set that aside for the moment. Say you're right and we get caught. We can tell them about you and maybe get a reduced sentence. You're still screwed. Don't forget that we have your nephew's computer access and system as proof."

The woman eyed him for a few seconds. "Just for the sake of this ridiculous discussion, let's say that your fantastic story is true. How does it benefit us to help you? If you succeed, you'll bring all kinds of attention down on the research center. It's going to ruin our operation no matter what."

"Indulge me. It certainly seems as if your nephew has already penetrated the research center's computers quite thoroughly. Why are you still here?"

The woman smiled slightly. "Hypothetically, let's just say that some researchers are more paranoid than others about isolating their research from the network. But, given enough time, they'd have to turn something over to the managers. That gets critical details out into the general research network where a resourceful—if theoretical—thief can access them."

"So, you have some specific project that you need information on that you've been unable to access. We've gotten a basic list of projects from your nephew's computer. Which one are we talking about?"

"Let's pick one at random," she suggested. "Just pulling one out of the air, research project 471DC-3."

"How startlingly specific," Talbot said, amused.

He accessed the list of projects in his implant storage. The receptionist/hacker had picked up a vast amount of data on current and past projects during his intrusion. All of them had the same kind of identifiers. If a project name got out, it wouldn't tell anyone what the researchers were exploring.

Interestingly, there was no data available on the project she named. No indication it even existed.

To avoid hinting at the woman that he had implants, Talbot stepped out of the room for a few minutes and got a cup of coffee before coming back in. He sipped at the hot drink and stared at her.

"Your nephew doesn't have any information on a project like that," he said coolly. "Your hypothetical example might just be too hypothetical."

Doctor Lipp chuckled. "Or perhaps it's so classified that all information revolving around it is kept isolated from even the research network."

"I suspect we're going to need your assistance in using the equipment, and contrary to what you think, we can get you off this station. You're going to be coming with us simply because your knowledge will be helpful. That's happening one way or the other.

"As an incentive, what if we broke into that other research area and stole the data for you? We're already going to be in the facility, so it shouldn't be too much additional trouble to take an extra set of computers."

She raised an eyebrow at him. "That would hardly do me any good if you killed my nephew and me. How do I know that you're not planning something dastardly for us?"

He laughed. "Dastardly. I like that. Look at it this way. We used stunners when you attacked us. Why would we suddenly change to something more lethal?"

"No one had seen your faces at that point," she pointed out somewhat reasonably. "You didn't expect my nephew to come home early, and you certainly didn't expect me and my husband to come after him. Now that you have us, you might decide we've seen too much."

"Want proof we're taking you with us and will let you live? Life doesn't allow for that level of certainty, but we broke into your house and rescued your kittens. A black one and a gray one. They're already off on our ship where you will join them. If we intended to murder you, we probably wouldn't save your cats."

She stared at him with hard eyes but slowly nodded. "I'm inclined to believe you. Since I'm in a bind, I'll take a chance and help you. Getting caught at this point might cost my life, and I no longer have any control over events."

* * *

VERONICA WAITED for her turn through the freighter's airlock a little nervously. Cain Hopwood and his recovery agents had led the way inside and had already reported no contact with any of the crew, but that didn't stop her from feeling on edge.

Princess Kelsey was leading a team to find a hiding place near the bridge. With deck plans provided by Carl Owlet, she had a couple of places in mind that would allow half their force to be ready to seize control of the ship at a moment's notice.

She was in charge of a second team that would seize engineering, but she had one task to perform first. She needed to make certain the flip drive Carl had ordered was safely stored away in the cargo holds.

Team one had already headed out for the bridge, leaving her people waiting for her to give them direction. Veronica consulted the map and pointed down the corridor. Their initial target was a computer interface rather than a hold.

It was positioned on the bulkhead exactly where she'd expected it. Doctor Rehnquist stepped forward and quickly unlocked the interface for her.

Since she had a delivery number, it was a simple matter of consulting the cargo database and having it spit a hold number back at her. Five seconds after she had access, they were on their way to the correct hold.

It was roughly on the way to engineering. In fact, it was close enough that they could wait inside the hold for Princess Kelsey's signal to attack.

The scouts in front kept a close eye out for any randomly encountered crewmen. If someone popped up, they'd have to stun them and that would be bad. Anyone that went suddenly quiet could have their friends looking for them in just a few minutes.

They arrived at the hold without encountering anyone. A different specialist applied her talents to opening the hatch. After a few moments, it slid aside and gave them access.

Half the team entered the hold with their stunners up, searching for trouble. The compartment was unoccupied, and Veronica made her way to join them. The tech closed the hatch behind them.

Veronica quickly realized that the scale of the hold was significantly larger than she'd envisioned. A carrier might be roughly the same size as this ship, but she hadn't seen any open areas this large aboard *Audacious*.

The large hold reminded Veronica of the manufacturing area at the shipyard. The ceiling rose far above their heads and various crates of cargo were strapped to the deck and piled high. It looked somewhat risky to her if the ship had to maneuver, but all the crates were stoutly strapped down.

They spread out looking for the flip drive. Less than a minute later, one of her teammates called her over. She'd found the flip drive.

Only, she hadn't. The order number indicated this was a *different* flip drive.

"Keep looking for our cargo," she ordered, somewhat confused. "It has to be here somewhere."

They found it after another five minutes of searching. It looked *identical* to the first one they'd found. That made Veronica wonder what was going on. Why would someone be shipping a flip drive on this freighter? It was only scheduled to be doing in-system trials.

"Commander Giguere," Jon Paul Olivier said quietly at her shoulder. "I found something I think you need to see."

His expression was unreadable. This probably wasn't good.

The man led her a couple of aisles over, and she stopped dead in her tracks. Stacked on the deck were at least a dozen flip drives. They came in various sizes and configurations, but this was more than just a fluke. What was going on?

Then she saw what was in the row on the other side of the flip drives, and her blood ran cold. Crates and crates of missiles. Based on their size, they looked like Fleet standard munitions.

She walked over and took a closer look. There were several rows of missiles. This cargo hold was filled with weapons.

This didn't make any sense. It had taken days to load all of this cargo.

Probably weeks, if other cargo holds held similar load outs. It couldn't be related to evacuating before the Clans attacked.

And, with this amount of equipment stored on the ship, there might be more than just a skeleton crew aboard. In fact, it wouldn't surprise Veronica if there were marines around somewhere and perhaps even a Fleet crew.

The plan called for com silence, but she had to let Princess Kelsey know. The odds were good that there was a lot of trouble waiting just around some corner for them to find.

33

Z ia stood in the alley beside the Michael Anderle Memorial Research
Center and kept an eye toward the main thoroughfare. Traffic was
exceptionally light at this hour, but that didn't mean they were alone
in the corridors.

Carl was working on the card reader, if one could call waving a forged
card that he'd printed earlier in front of it and having it click open could be
called "working."

"Are you sure this isn't going to show up on the security monitors?" she
asked in a low voice.

He shook his head. "They're watching a repeated loop of the last two
hours. There's been no traffic in or out through this door or inside the
corridor housing the research labs. I've blocked the door from logging our
entry, so no one is going to be the wiser."

It was about an hour after midnight so she wasn't surprised at the lack of
activity. After all, that's why they'd picked this ungodly hour to carry out
their raid.

One of the benefits of having penetrated the center's security so
thoroughly was that Carl had been able to watch the guards. "Watching the
watchers," he'd jokingly said.

It hadn't taken long to figure out the pattern of patrols. At roughly half-
hour intervals, a single guard left the security center and tested the exterior
doors. Once that was accomplished, the guard returned directly to the
security center.

While they could see the long corridor of doors leading to the individual labs in the restricted area, there were no cameras inside the labs themselves, so it was always possible they'd run into unexpected people, but the lack of overt traffic did present them with an opportunity to get in and out without being seen.

Being able to monitor the comings and goings inside the building also allowed their recovery specialists to see the custodial crew in action. They now knew exactly where the cleaners stored their carts and wore coveralls that were identical to the ones in use by the regular workers.

They'd cobbled together a cart of their own to move the small transport ring. It had gotten them a few glances as they'd made their way through the station corridors, but no one really paid them much mind.

Talbot led the way into the research center, his stunner at the ready. Several marines followed him in. Carl was using his implants to monitor all the security feeds, so he'd be able to warn them if security became concerned.

This was Zia's first time on one of these adventures, and she had to admit her adrenaline was really pumping. Her heart thumped in her chest as she led the follow-up group with the cart.

The side entrance to the research facility led into an employee only area that was deserted at this hour. Security had their own break room to make certain no one could easily breach their area at any time. As the rest of the employees were off shift, this section of the building was deserted.

They made it to the single door leading into the research area without incident. Carl's falsified identification got him through. That one door led into a long corridor with four doors on each side that gave no indication of what lay in the labs behind them. Each of the doors had a number on it. Odd numbers on the left, even numbers on the right.

The walls were an unbroken dark gray, as were the doors. No windows. Beside each lab door was a card reader and keypad. Gaining access to an individual lab required both a card and a code, according to Doctor Lipp. Zia was certain that a failure to enter the correct information more than a few times would signal security to come running.

The one they were looking for was lab three. Only once they were certain they had access to the lab they absolutely needed and had set up the large transport ring would they go looking for the second target.

They had Doctor Lipp's identification card, and she'd given them a code, but Zia didn't trust the woman. Carl would probe the system to see if he could get in without it.

Her young friend had brought along a specialized tablet with a series of cables that could plug into various sockets inside this kind of equipment. He carefully pried the keypad apart and examined what he'd found.

To Zia, the electronics would've been indecipherable. If it had been up to her to break in, they'd have been doomed.

Thankfully, Carl was made of sterner stuff. Less than sixty seconds after opening the panel open, the secure door slid aside to admit them. He hadn't entered the code Lipp had given them.

She raised an eyebrow at him as Talbot and his people moved in to sweep the lab. "You're handy to have around. I'm wondering exactly how secure this thing is if you're able to break in so easily."

He grinned at her. "I cheated. Since Doctor Lipp gave us her access code, I was able to double-check it without actually entering it. Systems like this aren't supposed to retain codes, but I've discovered over the years that it rarely works that way in practice.

"People will use parts from other types of equipment when designing something, and they may not always be as secure as they should be. Basically, I used her code to scan all of the electronics to see if I could find a match. Once I'd located it, it was simple enough to verify that the code would open the door and make it do so."

Zia nodded, impressed. "Give you another fifty years, and you're going to be a master criminal. Is this flaw going to be useful at the other lab?"

He shrugged. "Potentially. I started out with a lot of information here, including having cloned Doctor Lipp's identification card. I'm hoping that I can backtrack from a code in the other door to get identification for the user out of the security system. Needless to say, that might be complex, and it's going to take me longer than sixty seconds."

Talbot came back over to the door. "There's nobody in here, and the description of the equipment matches what she told us to expect. We're going to have to go through everything with a fine-toothed comb to be sure, but I think this is the place.

"I'm going to have my folks set up the small transport ring and use it to start bringing in the large ring. Once I get it in place, we'll be able to get everything out of here pretty fast."

"What about the other labs?" she asked. "Just because this lab is empty doesn't mean there aren't people inside them."

"I looked over the feed starting at about five in the afternoon," Carl said. "While I can't see into each lab, I could tally who went into each lab and who came out. If anyone is still working right now, they've been in there since before quitting time."

"I'll keep a couple of marines here in the corridor," Talbot said. "If anyone unexpected pops out, we'll stun them and rush the lab they came from."

Not the most comprehensive plan, but it would have to do.

Zia stepped into the lab as Carl began putting the keypad back together.

A quick look around revealed no cameras watching them, so she was fairly confident there would be no record of their presence after they left. Well, except for all the missing equipment and files. People were going to tear out their hair trying to figure out how they'd done it.

"I can oversee this," she told Talbot. "Take Carl and go get what we need from the other laboratory. Be careful. If that project is really hush-hush, there may be extra security measures."

"Relax," he said with a reassuring smile. "We'll make this happen. If you're going to worry about someone, worry about Kelsey. If she can't steal the other freighter, we're screwed."

"You sure know how to make a girl feel better. Get moving."

Zia hoped Kelsey didn't run into trouble. If things went sideways over there, it didn't matter how well she and Talbot did. They'd probably still end up being caught, and that wasn't a fate she wanted to contemplate.

* * *

KELSEY HAD BEEN SEVERELY ANNOYED with Veronica Giguere risking that transmission. At least until she saw the images that went with the warning.

"Holy crap," Kelsey muttered.

Image after image scrolled past her view as she went down the message. There were enough missiles in that hold to completely rearm *Audacious*. There were also a *dozen* flip drives, not including the special one they'd ordered built.

And that was just one hold. There were plenty of others scattered around this ship. What the hell had they stumbled into?

With the time to reflect on it, she realized Veronica had done the right thing in warning her. With this amount of equipment on board, the chances that there were more crew members than she'd planned on were high. They'd be better trained too. If they weren't already on the ship, they might show up at any time.

She turned to Bob Noble, Recovery Incorporated's computer specialist. He'd been working with Jason Young, the company's security specialist, to gain access to the freighter's computer system.

"How is it going?" she asked, hoping her growing worry didn't bleed through into her tone.

"So far, so good," he assured her. "We've got access to the noncritical systems, and Jason is helping me hack our way into the critical systems. Once we have a way to control those, we'll be able to force the bridge hatch open on command and lock down the communication and propulsion systems remotely."

"How long are you anticipating that to take? Can we access the video feeds from the rest of the ship? I'm concerned there may be a larger crew on board the ship than we've anticipated and that they might be more heavily armed too."

Considering that they hadn't anticipated running into armed crewmen at all, even men with stunners would prove problematic. If there were marines aboard, this could turn into a bloodbath very quickly.

"I don't suppose this ship is equipped with anti-boarding weapons," she added. "Just about now I'm thinking it would be a good thing to be able to stun everyone other than ourselves and just sort it out later."

"We won't know until we get into the critical systems, but they aren't standard on a freighter of this class," Young said. "I didn't see any on the way here, but I'll admit I had other things on my mind. Bottom line, don't count on it.

"As far as the time frame for gaining access, we're going slow and careful. I figure another ten or fifteen minutes should give me something. That's for the firewall. After that, each critical system will take more time."

That wasn't the news that Kelsey that had hoped for, but it was what they had to work with. At least Veronica and her people were safe in their cargo hold. Even if someone came into it, they had a lot of space to hide in.

Kelsey and her people were a little bit more constrained. They had to be near the bridge and that ruled out the cargo holds. Instead, they'd secreted themselves into one of the maintenance tubes. She made a mental note to have sensors installed in the maintenance tubes back on their ships because these things were far too convenient for hiding in.

The next fifteen minutes went by so slowly that she thought an hour had passed. Every time she felt like asking if they had made a breakthrough, she'd check her internal chronometer and find out that only a few minutes had passed. It was maddening.

Finally, Bob Noble gave her a thumbs-up. "We've got access to the firewall. I'll start working on getting into the communications and propulsion systems. Jason is working on tapping into the video feeds to see what he can find."

Jason's expression was one of intense concentration as he used his implants to invade the system. "I found the video feeds, and I'm starting to cycle through them now. They aren't even locked down. Sloppy."

Kelsey took a deep breath and forced herself to wait patiently.

"Interesting," he said after a minute. "We have four people on the bridge and one of them is in a Fleet uniform."

"Shunt the feed over to me," Kelsey ordered.

When the image popped up in her implants, she cursed under her breath. It was Lieutenant Commander Don Sommerville.

"What the hell is he doing here?" she asked rhetorically. "This can't be good."

"I've got more bad news," Young said. "I can see a number of people down at the cargo dock. It looks as if we've got an incoming crew. And that's not all. I see some marines in unpowered armor."

Kelsey searched for and found the feed he was watching. There were dozens of crewmen exiting a pair of cargo shuttles. A third shuttle was disgorging what certainly looked like a marine platoon.

What the hell was she going to do now? She couldn't just call everything off. They *needed* that flip drive.

She gritted her teeth. They'd find a way to make it happen. She'd come too far to give up now.

Noble cursed softly. "We've got another problem. A Fleet all-hands notice just came in. There's been an incursion at the flip point. It looks like the Clans have arrived, and they're attacking the battle station. They've come in force."

Perfect.

They needed to take out an armed crew they hadn't expected, steal a ship while the area was under a heightened state of security, and evade an invading hostile force. What could possibly go wrong?

34

Once the small transport ring was set up and the pieces of the larger ring were coming through, Talbot gathered Carl and half a dozen marines to make the side trip to the second laboratory.

Part of him wanted to wait until they'd cleaned out the first lab, but he knew they didn't dare waste the time. If something went wrong on this side mission, they might not complete their primary work before they had to withdraw.

The go-to-hell plan was to barricade themselves in, evacuate through the large ring, and set off explosive charges to destroy the ring past the point of any analysis. They'd rigged plasma grenades all along its circumference.

The blast would wreck not only the lab holding the large transport ring but all of the other labs too. It would probable cause critical damage to the entire building, but the lethal zone should be restricted to the research area.

Destroying the ring would be a terrible loss, but it would get them clear of the station with everything they needed. Security would flip out but wouldn't be able to link this back to his people quickly enough to do anything, he hoped. Best case, he wouldn't need to do that.

He was curious what the medical center could be working on that warranted the level of industrial espionage that Doctor Lipp and her nephew had been engaged in. The woman was either operating under her own name, or her organization had constructed a false identity capable of fooling someone who was undoubtedly very careful about who they hired.

That strongly implied that Doctor Lipp was a real person using her own identity to steal something from a company she'd invested two years of her life insinuating herself into. He had no idea what was worth that amount of commitment, so he wanted to see it for himself. It was like something out of one of the movies that Kelsey favored.

He shook his head and led his people down to lab six. Much like the first target, it had a card reader and keypad. That was something of a relief as Carl wouldn't have to deal with unexpected hardware.

With quick, sure motions, Carl took the reader apart and connected his tablet. He scanned the screen and nodded.

"It looks like the key code is in the same location in this hardware. That's the good news. Now comes the risky part. I can't be certain the last person to access this door was the senior researcher. If I guess the wrong identity, I'll be applying someone else's code and the system will reject it. At best that will earn us one strike for a failed entry attempt. At worst it could set off an alarm."

Talbot nodded. "You have access to the security system. If it signals to the guards, you'll know. Do it."

The scientist tapped a button on his screen and grimaced. "Access rejected. On the plus side, it doesn't look like any kind of alarm went out to the security center. The guards aren't aware of our presence."

"Do you have the names of any other researchers authorized to enter this lab?" Talbot asked as he looked back up the corridor toward the main entrance to the research zone.

"Doctor Lipp gave me a couple of names. Since we can scratch the lead researcher off the list, I'm going to try his chief assistant."

Moments later, Carl cursed under his breath. "Second failure. Still no indication that the system has sent any kind of alarm to the guards. I've got one more name to try. If it's not this one, I'm going to have to figure out a new way to break into this lab and that's almost certain to get us into serious trouble."

Talbot felt his muscles tensing as the young scientist tapped on his tablet a few more times. This could be it.

Instead of an alarm, the hatch unlocked and slid aside. As he already had his stunner out, Talbot stepped into the lab and took a quick look around for potential threats.

To his shock, a pair of men in lab coats were staring at him from one of the many tables set up in the room, their mouths agape.

"Who the hell are you?" one of them demanded. "You're not cleared to be in here! I'm calling security!"

So much for being all alone in the labs.

Talbot shot the man and then took the other one down before the first one had hit the table and collapsed to the floor.

"Spread out," he ordered his marines. "Make sure no one else is hiding in here."

The lab was set up in a pattern similar to the first one and seemed to be of about the same size. Rather than a large piece of equipment resembling a regenerator on steroids, though, this room held rack after rack of computers.

Talbot stepped over to the table where the two men had been working and saw that it was covered with what looked like parts of another computer. The two men had taken this machine apart far beyond what anything Talbot had ever seen.

Or even thought possible. They'd not only disconnected everything that could be disconnected, they'd taken chips off of the board and set them aside. Nonremovable chips, or so it seemed.

"Carl?" he asked. "What the heck are they doing here?"

The scientist took in the contents of the table in at a glance. "Completely disassembling a computer of some kind. They've used specialized equipment to remove the chips from the boards they normally reside on. That's pretty unusual."

"Why are they doing it, and how does it relate to whatever medical research they're doing here?"

His young friend shrugged. "I haven't got the slightest idea. Yet I don't see anything else in the room. This has to be the project they're working on."

Talbot looked at all the computers in the room and shook his head. "It'll take forever to get the files off these things."

One of the marines waived at Talbot. "Colonel, I have something."

He headed over to where the woman was standing and found himself looking at a hatch built into the wall. Based on its location, it led into the lab next door, lab eight. That would be the one at the very end of the corridor on this side of the hall.

This was a very different layout than what they'd seen in the previous laboratory. It had been completely self-contained. Were there even more computers next door that they'd have to worry about?

Or worse, more people. People that could come in at any moment looking for one of the two men he'd stunned.

Unlike the exterior hatch, this one didn't seem to require an access code. Talbot summoned half his marines and triggered the mechanism. With their weapons out, they stepped into the other room.

Unlike the lab they'd just exited, this one looked as if something had exploded inside it. Hunks of debris littered the floor and the smell of burned circuitry and hot metal hung in the air.

Having been around devastation for much of his adult life, Talbot recognized this wasn't fresh damage. Something had blown this equipment apart weeks or months ago. Possibly years.

That made sense. If Doctor Lipp was here looking for information from this lab, all of this had to be here before she was hired. Call it a minimum of two and a half years.

"Carl, I need you to come in here and tell me what I'm looking at again."

Moments later, Carl stepped into the room and goggled. "Holy crap. Someone blew up a computer. A big one. That must be where the pieces parts on the table came from."

"Is this the hardware from a sentient AI?" Talbot asked.

The young scientist stepped over to some of the damaged equipment and began examining it. Moments later, he shook his head.

"While it's big enough for that, this is something different. It matches up with what I was seeing in the other room, though. There are markings on the chips and boards that aren't in Standard. Since the Rebel Empire is just like us linguistically, that implies this hardware comes from outside the Empire."

He looked up at Talbot and patted part of the damaged equipment. "This is made very similarly to Imperial hardware, though I can see some differences even at a glance. Our technology and this share a common ancestor."

Talbot grunted. "The only group we know of like that is the Singularity. If this is one of their computers, it might have critical data we absolutely have to have at some point. They're helping the Clans and this might have come from one of their ships."

He checked his internal chronometer. They probably had four or five hours before people started showing up for work in the labs. These two rooms were absolutely filled with equipment. It would take every second they could beg, borrow, or steal to get the majority of it.

Coming to a decision, he gestured at the damaged hardware. "I'll send as many people over as I can. Have them start taking this and the other computers back to the first lab. Keep an eye out for security. Don't let anyone come and catch us in the corridor with this stuff. We're taking everything we can."

* * *

Veronica covertly monitored the video feeds that Kelsey's associates with Recovery Incorporated had shunted to the cargo hold where she and her people were hiding. Part of her worried that someone on the other side would detect the access, but Jason Young seemed pretty sure they were on safe ground.

The crewmen that had arrived on the cargo shuttles had quickly hurried to various sections of the ship and began making it ready to move. That made sense if they intended to flee.

Yet it still didn't explain what Don Sommerville was up to. He was assigned to the shipyard, yes, but her old friend was obviously taking command of this ship with the expectation that he was going to be leaving in it.

Kelsey had indicated that the third shuttle had held Fleet marines, but Veronica disagreed. Those people were wearing unpowered marine armor, but they were not marines. She'd been around enough Rebel Empire marines to know that these people were too disciplined. Too controlled.

Her suspicions were confirmed when a fourth cargo shuttle docked and disgorged a mixture of crewmen and more individuals in armor. The last one off the shuttle was the female Fleet security officer that had "greeted" them when they'd docked with the yard earlier.

Veronica opened an audio-only communication channel to Princess Kelsey. Hopefully the lower bandwidth would help keep the signal from coming to anyone's attention. It should mix in with any number of other signals going out through the ship right now as the other crewmen spoke to one another.

"I have an update," she said without identifying herself, trusting the other woman to recognize her voice. "Another shuttle has docked, and I see that security officer your friend Carl got to know earlier."

A few seconds of silence greeted her, but she waited, knowing that the princess was probably reviewing the feed right now.

"It looks like you were right," Kelsey conceded. "The people in armor are Fleet security. Which, in its own way, is even more confusing. Why would Fleet security be helping Commander Sommerville take control of this freighter?"

"I haven't got the slightest idea, but I'm not sure we can overpower this many people. I hope you've got a good plan in mind."

"I'm still working on that," the other woman admitted. "Once I figure it out, I'll let you know. Out."

That was fairly brusque coming from Princess Kelsey, but the young woman had a lot to worry about with the Clan warships having just destroyed the battle station at the flip point and begun boosting toward Archibald at maximum acceleration.

Doctor Rehnquist cleared his throat. "I think I might have a few answers to the situation we find ourselves in."

Veronica raised an eyebrow at the scientist. "That sounds refreshing. Do tell."

The older man swiped a hand over his balding head. "I've been reviewing video feeds from other sections of the ship. I think I have a few items that you'll want to see. Why don't we start with feed twenty-seven?"

She accessed the feed in question and frowned. It looked like a small control room. Three people sat in the center of the compartment facing one another over a trio of consoles. Veronica had to admit that she'd never seen anything quite like this particular configuration.

"Do we have any idea what they're doing?" she asked after a few seconds.

"Use the zoom feature and go in close to the consoles. Two of them are visible from this angle."

Veronica did as instructed and then swore. What she was looking at had no business being on a freighter. That was a tactical console. One that indicated it was in control of a dozen missile launchers.

She switched to the other console and saw that it was more defensive in nature. The interface she was examining was designed to manage a heavy warship's battle screens and antimissile defenses. But only cruisers had defenses like that, not freighters.

The third console wasn't in direct view, but it probably had to do with weapons of some kind too. Beams, perhaps? Yet one more impossibility on a freighter.

"You said that you had more than one thing to show me," Veronica told the scientist after a moment. "What else have you found?"

"I've been going over the feed from main engineering. This revelation is less obvious, but the drives seem quite muscular for a freighter. The grav drives in particular seem designed to achieve a level of speed comparable to a much faster vessel. The gravitic compensators are similarly overpowered."

Veronica considered his words for a long stretch of time before finally nodding. "Honestly, I'm not certain if that really affects what we're doing in the slightest. We're already inside the ship so they can't stop us from boarding with those weapons or run away from us with their drives.

"This is all very interesting, but we need to find an edge that'll let us overpower them. I don't suppose you have anything for me in that arena, do you?"

The scientist grinned at her. "As a matter of fact, I have. I've been looking over the manifests from a number of crates in this hold, and I think you'll be pleased to discover some of the things we have to draw upon. Come take a look at this."

He led her across the cargo hold to a series of large crates lined up against one of the bulkheads. "I think these might go quite some way toward evening the odds."

She used her implants to access the manifests built into each crate, and her eyes widened in shock. "That can't be right. These don't have any more business being here than the weapons this ship is apparently armed with. Still, I'm not going to look a gift horse in the mouth."

The row of crates sitting in front of her indicated that they were filled with powered marine armor and all of the associated weapons that went along with those suits. None of the people with her was trained in using them, but they'd be virtually invulnerable to standard weapons inside the things.

If they could use them, of course. She knew the suits were wired with explosives to make certain they didn't get into the wrong hands. Or to put down a rabid marine, if needed.

"Start opening one up," she told the doctor. "I'll see if Princess Kelsey has any idea how we can make them safe to use. Good work, Doctor."

As she stepped back, she considered how this might change the equation. If they could make the suits operational, that just might give them a chance.

35

Z ia was relieved when they finished assembling the larger ring and opened the connection to their freighter. The crewmen aboard the ship poured into the lab and began helping to disassemble and move everything in sight.

Even though they had a direct connection, it was still going to take a while to transfer everything. And until they were finished, things could still go terribly wrong.

Just a few minutes after this process had started, Talbot hurried back into the room. From his expression, there was trouble.

"What's wrong?" she asked as her gut started tightening.

"It seems the good doctor was holding out on us," he said as he took in the activity around them. "The lab she wanted us to break into isn't involved with medical research. Unless Carl is gravely mistaken, they have some kind of large computer down there that was blown up a couple of years ago. He thinks it's a Singularity computer."

Zia blinked at him, shocked. "Seriously? How the hell did the Rebel Empire even get their hands on something like that?"

The marine officer shrugged. "I haven't got the slightest idea. The problem is, we're not going to be able to pass it up. Whatever it is, it might be critical to the war with the Clans. We're going to have to take it with us, and that's going to really complicate this raid. They have a lot of equipment down there. Two labs full, in point of fact."

She rubbed her face. "We only have a few hours to get everything that we need. I suggest that you tell Carl to get the most important things first."

"Already done," Talbot said. "He's is going to have everything moved here and queued up for transport through the ring as quickly as possible. He's got one eye on the security officers so we'll stop if they send someone in our direction. If anyone shows up early for work, we're going to have to stun them."

That would work for a little while, Zia knew, but there was going to come a point where too many people were coming into the research area for them to stop them all.

"Have him expedite as much as possible," she finally said. "As soon as they figure out what's going on, they're going to start screaming. We need to be gone by then."

As soon as Talbot headed back toward the other lab, Zia stepped through the ring and into the freighter. Thankfully, there was plenty of room in the massive hold to store everything they were stealing today. Crewmen were already securing pieces of equipment against one of the far bulkheads.

Zia stepped over to one of the communications consoles built into the bulkheads and called the bridge. "This is Anderson. What's the status on the last shuttle from the station?"

"They're on final approach now, Commodore," a young male voice said. "They're not reporting any issues and are less than five minutes out."

"Excellent. Get everyone off it and send it back so the last of the team can use it. Also, have the ship ready for departure on short notice in case we have to expedite. What's the status of the incoming Clan vessels?"

The voice on the other end paused for a moment. "It looks like the incoming hostiles are still about six hours out. The Rebel Empire Fleet ships that went to the gas giant are moving to intercept the incoming vessels, so that time frame might grow.

"It looks like they picked up the four battlecruisers that we suspected might be out there. Even so, they don't really stand a chance, considering that the Clans had more than enough firepower to destroy a battle station. That's pretty brave of them in my book."

"Never fall into the trap of thinking that your enemies are cowards," Zia said. "They may not believe in the same things that you do, but human beings can be gallant and brave even when they're doing the bidding of terrible people. Do the Clans have a force heading toward the other flip point?"

"Yes, ma'am. None of the ships at Archibald are going to be able to escape the system through the usual methods."

She nodded. "They'll come in and take over the station and shipyard, and then start hunting for ships that ran. They're not going to hurry after us as long as we get moving on schedule. Have someone come through the ring and inform me if the situation changes."

Once the man acknowledged her order, Zia headed back through the ring and into the lab.

The hatch to the corridor was open, and Carl was helping to move a cart full of scorched computer parts into the room. He waved a hand at her and stepped over.

"I'll need more of the crewmen from the freighter to come help. We can get a lot of the equipment as long as we have the hands to move it."

"This is risky," she told him. "Every time you move something out into the open, there's a chance that someone will open the hatch at the end of the corridor and see us."

Her young friend shook his head. "Not happening. I've tasked one of the marines with monitoring the video feeds in the corridors leading up to the research area. If anyone shows up, we'll have at least sixty seconds notice before they arrive."

"While that may be true, I'd rather not get into a fight that makes us blow up the rings. They're irreplaceable."

Her friend nodded. "I know. I'd rather not put them at risk, either, but it's not as if we have a choice. Those computers might have information about the Singularity that could make a difference for us in the future.

"It's obvious the Singularity is involved in this war, and it's only a matter of time before they realize the New Terran Empire exists. When they do, they're going to come for us. We have to have these computers and the wreckage that the lab rats were studying."

Zia's implants pinged. It was a message from Talbot. Someone was coming toward the research area. She took a moment to tap into the feed and recognized the lead researcher for the project that Doctor Lipp had been trying to steal. What the heck was he doing here in the middle of the night?

Well, that hardly mattered. They'd have to take him down and hope that no one else came looking for him.

She opened a channel to Talbot. "Let him come to you. Stun him as soon as he comes through the hatch. Put him on the next cart over."

"Copy that. I've got two prisoners that were here when we broke in to send with him."

"Really? You should've mentioned them."

"Sorry. Other things on my mind. I'll handle it. Out."

She sealed the hatch leading out into the corridor and began waiting. Hopefully this was the only interruption they were going to have to deal with.

Inside, she laughed. No, this was probably only the first of a cascading set of complications. Life had a way of throwing curveballs at them, and they were going to have to deal with them.

"Uh-oh," Carl said. "We've got a problem. Two of the security guards

are exiting security central and are headed this way. It looks like they're
going to arrive about the same time as our guest."

* * *

KELSEY LISTENED with a frown on her face as Veronica explained what she'd
found. She wanted this to be a game changer, but she wasn't certain they
could make it work.

"You know those suits are booby-trapped and require a specific code to
activate, right?" she asked. "Not only do we not have the right tools for the
job, the only person we brought that has ever done this successfully is back
on the station."

"I'll admit that adds a certain level of complexity to the task," Veronica
agreed. "Yet, I don't see that we have a lot of choice. I'm hoping we find
some additional weapons that we can use if this doesn't pan out."

Jason Young waved a hand in front of Kelsey's face. She blinked at the
distraction and then raised a hand to let him know she'd seen him.

"We can't do anything until we're further away from the shipyard and
Archibald," Kelsey said. "Get one uncrated, and we'll see what we can do."

"Copy that," Veronica said. "Out."

Kelsey focused her complete attention on the young security specialist.
"What have you got, Jason?"

"The bridge crew is preparing to move the ship. They've received
clearance from control to depart the shipyard and try to hide in the outer
system. I suppose it's possible. Every hour without pursuit makes it
exponentially more likely they can elude detection for as long as their
supplies hold out."

"How long do we have and in what direction are they planning
on going?"

"Just a couple of minutes, I think. I've tapped into the controls, and it
looks like they're headed away from the multiflip point. I'm not sure that's a
negative at this point because that will draw any pursuit away it."

Kelsey pulled up a map of the system in her implants. This was going to
add time to their escape, but it might make it difficult for any of the forces
currently here to track them. Jason was right about that.

She checked the current location of the Clan warships and saw they had
about five hours remaining before the hostile vessels engaged anything in
orbit. The Rebel Empire warships were going to intercept them a couple of
hours out. Even with the four battlecruisers, the Clan vessels would be able
to take them apart without much trouble.

Tapping into the scanner feed, she watched as the freighter pulled away from the shipyard. She was able to link to the ship's passive scanners and saw that a number of ships were leaving both the station and the shipyard, running in any direction they could. Some smaller Clan vessels were pursuing some of them. Odds were good they'd get one too.

She sat down and gave herself over to thought, checking the scanners every ten minutes or so. Less than an hour later, her fears were confirmed. The freighter was making good time—though not using its full acceleration, she noted—and had drawn what looked like a frigate in pursuit.

While less powerful than a destroyer, a frigate was more than capable of chasing down a freighter and forcing them to stop or be destroyed. Since this vessel was actually a Q-ship—an armed freighter made to look harmless— the fight would be brutally short and certain to give victory to the freighter.

That would draw the Clans' attention. They'd send follow-up ships with more powerful weapons. If the Q-ship went to full acceleration, it might very well elude detection, but they wouldn't just let it go.

More worrisome to her, their original freighter was still in orbit around the station. Talbot and Zia had not yet completed their mission and pulled out.

At this range and lacking the ability to communicate, it would be impossible for her to get an update. She'd just have to hope that her husband and friends managed to get out of there before the enemy arrived in force.

They could call Fiona and *Persephone* if they needed to, but the FTL com she'd intended to use was on the shipyard. The AI was monitoring the situation and would blow it up if it was discovered or when the Clans attacked the shipyard. The damage would then be blamed on them.

The Clan warships had altered course to meet the Rebel Empire warships and were spreading out into a battle formation. That was going to delay their arrival at Archibald, which was a good thing.

Still, Talbot and Zia really needed to speed things up. If they delayed much longer, they were never going to escape the station at all.

If things went really badly, *Persephone* could intervene, but that would cause a whole new set of problems for them. Secrecy was still their best weapon. If they couldn't keep themselves and their mission quiet, the Pandorans would be the ones paying the price.

Well, worrying about her friends wasn't going to help Kelsey do her part. She needed to capture this ship.

She examined the internal video feeds and allowed her combat implants to sort the various enemy personnel inside the deck plans. Her people needed to strike simultaneously and with overwhelming force on the bridge and in engineering when the time came.

Then they'd have to hold those areas against a determined

counterattack. How they'd manage that might revolve around the armor Veronica had found. If it could be rendered safe.

That was outside her personal control, so she'd have to pray the other woman figured out a path to success. If not, they were probably screwed.

36

T albot waited inside the second lab for their unwanted visitors to arrive. He was crouched behind a computer on the right-hand side of the compartment. Everyone was under cover except for two marines who now wore the white lab coats and stood at the worktable with their backs toward the hatch. They were the distraction.

"I've put the corridor feeds back to real time," Carl said over the com. "There's someone in security central monitoring it now."

"Acknowledged," Talbot said. "Be ready to put it back on the loop when we have these people in custody. We'll have to take out security central as soon as we can. They'll be worried if these clowns are too quiet."

"You bet. Our guests are in the main corridor and will be at your location shortly. Good luck."

A minute later, the hatch slid open, and the intruders stepped inside. The security guards didn't have their weapons out, but their hands hovered near them. They were definitely expecting trouble.

"Did anyone come in here half an hour ago?" the project lead demanded. "I was notified about several unsuccessful access attempts."

All three of the men had taken several steps into the lab so Talbot stunned one of the security men. The target dropped without a word. Two other marines took out the remaining hostiles a moment later.

Talbot stepped over to the hatch and closed it. "Start that corridor loop, Carl," he said over the com.

Several of the marines searched the new prisoners and removed the weapons from the security men. They then bound all of them and put them into the corner with the original researchers.

"The loop is playing now," Carl said. "I'll meet you in the corridor."

Getting to the security center wasn't difficult since Carl was able to monitor all the corridors for wandering people and block out any images of them moving through the facility. That didn't make things less tense for Talbot, though. There were still plenty of things that could go wrong.

When they arrived outside the security center, he motioned for Carl to stay to the side. "How many people inside? Where are they located?"

"Two people, both almost directly ahead of you. Since they didn't have any indication of people in the corridor, I suspect the door opening is going to cause them some consternation and surprise. Both are seated but armed."

Talbot nodded and motioned for three marines to join him directly in front of the hatch. "Two of you down on your knees, one of you stand next to me. When the hatch opens, we open fire. If you're on the left, take out the person on the left. You're on the right, take out the person on the right."

As soon as they were ready, Talbot made a gesture to Carl and the young man got to work on the lock. His friend was turning into quite the expert at breaking and entering.

Twenty seconds later, the hatch slid to the side and all four of the ambushers fired at their targets. The security men had barely begun to turn their heads toward the hatch and hadn't even reached for their weapons.

As soon as they were down, Talbot led the marines into the security center, and they spread out to make certain there were no unexpected surprises waiting for them. Sixty seconds later, they were sure the facility was secure.

"Get these two down to the lab with the others," Talbot said as he holstered his stunner. "Let's make them a priority and get them over to the freighter now. If things get chaotic later on, I don't want to have to worry about leaving witnesses behind."

To be certain they weren't surprised again, he stationed two of the marines in the security center to keep an eye on all of the monitors and to handle any incoming calls. He picked two that could wear the security uniforms and had the prisoners stripped.

He didn't anticipate much action this late at night, but with the lead researcher having shown up unexpectedly, he wasn't going to rule it out. Having a few men that looked like security might come in very handy.

Talbot took Carl back to the research area. Zia had been working hard with her people and their primary target was almost cleaned out. He estimated they probably only had another fifteen minutes or so to strip the room bare.

She stepped over to him as he looked into the lab. "Everything taken care of?"

He nodded. "I'm worried that they're going to come and find us, though. We really need to get this done. Moving all of that equipment from one lab to the other is a pain in the ass."

She shook her head and smiled at him. "You're not thinking this through. As soon as we finish clearing this lab out, we can disassemble the large transport ring and move it over to your lab. We'll set it up there and finish cleaning everything out. It'll be faster that way."

Talbot blinked in surprise at the idea and then laughed. "That's thinking outside the box. It's still going to be close, though. I'd like to get every single thing we can out of the other lab, but I don't want to get caught or need to destroy the transport rings. Any word on Kelsey?"

Zia shook her head. "The other freighter left the shipyard over an hour ago. It's making for the outer system. Not exactly in the direction we'd like them to go, but beggars can't be choosers. It looks as if the Rebel Empire warships in the system are going to try to intervene with the Clan warships. I don't think we're going to see anyone here sooner than six hours now."

"With that in mind, I want to be done in four. Sooner, if we can. Let's say it takes another hour after that to get the small transport ring back to the cargo bay, onto the shuttle which is on its way there now, and back out to the freighter. That still gives us an hour to get clear of the station before the Clans arrive in force."

"That doesn't sound like a lot of time," Talbot said with a scowl. "They'll send someone after us."

Zia nodded. "Of course they will. Unfortunately for them, *Persephone* is going to be shadowing us once we get clear of Archibald. The Clans aren't going to send a large ship to chase us down. At most, they'll send a frigate. A Marine Raider strike ship should be able to take it out in one salvo.

"It's not my favorite plan, and it certainly is going to let them know something is wrong, but I don't see that we have a choice. Let's get moving. We've got a lot of work to do if we're going to make that timeline."

* * *

VERONICA EYED the uncrated combat suits uncertainly and then turned toward Doctor Rehnquist with a look of suspicion. "So, let me get this straight, you didn't remove the explosives but you *think* you have them all disabled. Exactly what order of probability would you give to that assertion?"

The older man shrugged. "Nothing in life is certain, Commander. All Princess Kelsey could do is give me a general idea of how the self-destruct system worked. She didn't have plans for exactly what needed to be done to make these absolutely safe. Even if she did, we don't have the tools to disassemble the armor. Or the time."

The scientist and his impromptu assistants had cleared six suits of armor in the last three hours. There was plenty more, but they didn't have time to prep another one. The Clan frigate was almost upon them.

When the confrontation came, her old friend would probably blow it out of space. Based on the weapons she suspected the ship had, he would pretend to surrender to draw the enemy in as closely as possible, then use the beams to eviscerate it. With lightspeed weapons, the frigate would never see what was coming for him.

If the enemy commander was a little more canny, Don would need to use missiles. However, unlike the frigate, this ship had battle screens to protect it while her missiles finished the frigate at knife range.

At that point, Don would go to full acceleration and get as far into the outer system as he could. On a ship this size, he probably had enough supplies to last for many months. Perhaps even years.

All he had to do was outwait the Clans. They'd move on in time, leaving a holding force. Eventually, the Rebel Empire would reclaim the system, or he could find a time to use one of the flip points to get clear.

Princess Kelsey's plan would disrupt everything for him. Of course, timing was everything. They couldn't spring into action until the frigate was no longer a threat. Attacking during the fight would only disrupt the crew defending the ship.

They'd found a few crates of regular flechette weapons, so if they had to fight, they wouldn't be completely reliant on their stunners.

She shook her head, dismissing the worry. "I certainly hope you're right because if they manage to set off any charge you missed, I'll wager the blast would be more than enough to set off all the ones you've disconnected. From what I understand, these make a pretty significant fireball when they go off."

The scientist shrugged slightly. "We've done the best we can, Commander. At this point, we have to trust that we'll come out ahead in the end. If not, I'm certain the princess's ship will come and rescue us. Those of us that survive, that is."

"I'd like to avoid the need for rescue, and we really can't count on anything. We play this straight. Total victory is our goal."

Her com chimed with an incoming call. It was Princess Kelsey.

"Are we ready?" Veronica asked. "I'll need a few minutes to suit up."

"The frigate just demanded the freighter surrender. Commander Sommerville cut acceleration and accepted their terms. Of course, he's powering up his beam weapons. He gave the order, so we can now confirm that the ship has them. We also have battle screens because they're on standby. The missiles are also ready to fly.

"Based on my experience, I think we have maybe twenty minutes before this fight is over. The frigate is only going to have a single pinnace, so they're going to be very careful how they use it. Get suited up and be ready to hit main engineering as soon as the fight is over."

"What about those Fleet security goons?" Veronica asked. "As soon as the attack starts, they're going to come after us. Do we know where on the ship they're congregating?"

"Right now, they're spread out preparing to repel boarders. They're also armed and armored. I think our best bet to deal with them is to wait until this fight is over and they've returned to the area they've set up as their armory and barracks. Once that happens, they'll mostly be gathered in one place and out of armor. Their guards will be down."

That sounded like a solid plan to Veronica. "Which of us is going to deal with them? I can cut aside a group of marines."

"No," Kelsey said. "You need to focus on engineering. It's going to be a much more difficult target than the bridge, so I'll deal with the security forces. You focus on overwhelming everyone in engineering quickly enough that they don't damage this ship. That's the critical part."

"Can do. We'll be ready to go in twenty minutes, just to be safe."

She really hoped she wasn't overpromising with that. None of them had ever used this kind of armor before and getting into it in fifteen minutes might be a challenge.

"I'm thinking more like thirty to forty minutes," Kelsey said firmly. "Getting that armor on isn't something you can rush into, especially if you've never done it before. Also, we need to give the security forces time to stand down. Don't rush this, Veronica. I'll let you know ten minutes before we execute and even if it takes you longer, we have time. Good luck."

Veronica rubbed at her face as the call ended. She wasn't afraid of a fight, but this wasn't what she was used to. Well, she'd rely on Kelsey's marines for guidance and make it work. Or die trying.

37

The next three and a half hours felt like weeks to Zia. They quickly finished emptying the first lab and relocated the transport rings to the second lab to get as much of the computer equipment as possible.

Carl oversaw the removal of the destroyed Singularity computer and all of the support equipment that had been analyzing it like a madman. He rushed from one end of the lab to the other, seeing that the various server towers were removed and hustled through the larger ring as quickly as possible.

As the clock ticked down, Zia made more frequent trips to the freighter to check on the status of the Clan warships. They'd delayed their arrival at Archibald to deal with the Rebel Empire ships, but that wouldn't delay them much longer.

She and her people only had until that fight was done to get everything they could. There were a lot of vessels fleeing the planet, and she didn't want to be the last one out the gate.

By her estimates, they were about half an hour away from emptying the second lab when the research center employees started arriving. They'd run out of time, and she had a hard choice to make. Leave the remaining stuff in the lab with the Singularity computer or destroy the large transport ring.

That was a tough call, but that's why they paid her.

"Carl, finish emptying the lab," she told him. "Then get everyone to the freighter. Send the small ring next because I don't want to leave it here when we go."

He blinked at her. "How will we get the large ring out?"

"We won't," she said harshly. "We're blowing it when we leave."

The scientist grabbed her arm. "No! We can leave what we didn't get. We still have time to get the large ring out and slip away with the small ring."

Zia shook her head. "We can't afford to lose any of this equipment since we don't know what's important. Stop arguing and get moving. You have ten minutes maximum. Maybe less. Don't waste it."

The young man nodded, his expression filled with anguish, and ran off.

"The marines we left in the security center ran into some trouble," Talbot said, walking over to her. "It seems their replacements have begun arriving for shift change. Thus far they've stunned two new security officers. What are we going to do with them?"

"They'll need to take them to the exit in ten minutes. We're scraping the plan and blowing the large transport ring."

The marine winced but didn't argue. "Copy that. We need to evacuate the building. The blast will wreck the labs and potentially bring the whole thing down. That means I need to get back to the shuttle with the last of the marines rather than going back with you."

That was an added complication that she hadn't really planned for. Still, she wasn't a terrorist and didn't blow up innocent people. "We do this together. I'm coming with you."

The marine officer scowled at her. "That's a needless risk. I've got this."

"I'm sure you do, but this is my operation, and I'm going to make absolutely certain that everyone gets home."

She could see the calculation in his eyes. He wanted to argue, but he really didn't have any options. Well, she supposed he could stun her and send her back to the freighter with the rest of the prisoners, but even being married to the heir wouldn't save him from that kind of decision.

He must've finally come to the same conclusion because he sighed. "Then I suppose we best get this finished."

Minutes later, everyone except for Talbot, herself, and two marines dressed in security uniforms were back on the freighter, and they'd sent the smaller ring back to the freighter.

"Time to get out of here," Talbot said. "I've armed the plasma grenades and set them for ten minutes. We need to go help move the disabled security people."

As a group, they left the research area and headed for the security center as the fire alarm went off. The marines on guard had triggered it so that they could clear all the workers out of the building.

A minute later, they arrived at the security center and the marines soon had all four unconscious security guards over their shoulders and the group was on the way to the exit.

For this brief window of time, her people weren't going to have any access to the internal video feeds. They were on their own.

They'd almost made it to the exit when an older man in a suit confronted them. He seemingly popped out of nowhere, coming around the corner when the exit door was just in sight.

He scowled at them from under bushy white eyebrows that looked like caterpillars crawling across his face and put his hands on his hips. "What the hell is going on?"

Zia grimaced. They *literally* didn't have time for this.

* * *

KELSEY HAD to admit that she admired how Commander Sommerville had handled the Clan frigate. He'd waited until he was certain the ship was as close as it was going to get before he'd opened fire. His unexpected beams had torn through the other ship in multiple places, crippling it instantly.

Unfortunately for him, his shots hadn't destroyed the ship. It had been able to return fire with its missiles. He'd brought the freighter's battle screens up in time to absorb the hits, though, allowing the Q-ship to strike again.

That time, the frigate had exploded. One of the beams must've hit its fusion plant. The destroyed vessel had already launched its pinnace, but the blast took it out as well. The enemy had been efficiently eliminated.

Sommerville had immediately ordered the freighter to maximum acceleration. He only had a brief window to vanish from the Clan scanners and had been determined not to waste it.

That had been twenty minutes ago, and the Fleet security elements were back in their barracks, presumably stripping off their armor and storing their weapons.

Timing was going to be tricky. She wanted to allow them enough time to disarm but not enough to scatter.

The Clan warships had just engaged the Rebel Fleet elements with crushing force. The fighting wasn't over, but the victor was never in doubt. Only the battlecruisers remained, and they were going down fast. She gave them no more than five minutes more.

It was time to get this party started.

"Tell me that we're into all the command systems," she told Bob Noble.

"Almost all of them. We have access to communications, propulsion, and navigation. We're focusing on the tactical systems next."

"What about scanners? Could we spoof them if we need to?"

He nodded. "With a little warning, yes. What do you have in mind?"

"I'm worried what will happen when *Persephone* turns up. I feel pretty sure Angela is closing in on us. This ship has better scanners than we'd planned for. If they spot her, I'd like to make the sighting look like a scanner ghost. We have to keep them from detecting my ship."

The young man chewed his lip. "That's doable. It would help if we knew where to find her. Can we send them coded instructions?"

Kelsey frowned. "The Clans will detect the transmission. That'll make them wonder who we're talking to."

"It's not as if this ship didn't just paint a huge target on itself by blowing up their friends."

"True enough. I'll code a message for them to come in from behind. This ship is fast for a freighter, but *Persephone* is faster. Once Angela gets the message, she can communicate with us via tight beam, and they'll never know, right?"

Noble nodded. "Sure. We have control of the com system so I can lock out their detection of incoming signals directed at them. It's not as if they're expecting anyone to want to chat."

It only took Kelsey a few minutes to code a brief message explaining everything to Angela. Bob Noble took it and had it sent moments later.

"We're not waiting for her to respond," Kelsey said. "It's time to take this ship. If she gets back to us before then, I'll let you handle the coordination."

"Yes, ma'am."

With that task handled, she turned her attention to the marines and recovery specialists awaiting her orders.

"Cain, you and your people take the bridge. There shouldn't be much resistance there. I didn't see any weapons, and they can't be expecting an attack from inside. Have your people lock out every system they can right before you go in or as soon as the alarm goes up from another group."

"Got it," he said with a nod. "Since Jason and Bob are into the systems, we shouldn't have any problems."

"I'd like to keep the command crew alive," she stressed, "but if they resist too strongly, don't hesitate to use deadly force to protect yourselves."

She gestured for the marines to form up behind her and opened a com channel to Veronica. "Are you ready?"

"My marines are in armor, and we're ready to rock," the former Rebel Empire officer said. "We'll be in engineering in less than five minutes, whether we run into resistance or not."

"Don't get cocky," she warned. "Those suits are powerful, but they don't make you invincible. Mostly."

"Yes, Mother."

Kelsey laughed in spite of the grave situation. "Be glad it's not a case of like mother like daughter. You're go to execute your attack. Everyone, move out."

She killed the com channel and led her forces into the corridor. They had access to the internal video feeds, but that didn't guarantee they'd spot any enemy crewmen before they saw her or her people. They had to plan on an unexpected encounter ruining the element of surprise somewhere along the way.

To her astonishment, her group made it all the way to the Fleet security compartment without running into anyone. So far, Veronica's team and Cain's group had avoided discovery too. This was going to be a devastating surprise for the Rebel Empire forces.

The hatch slid aside just as she approached. Time to make the magic happen. Or to make the donuts. She could never remember which was the correct saying.

It only took a moment to dump Panther into her system, and the world seemed to slow as her cognitive response time raced far faster than a normal human could manage. She was ready for this fight.

Her implants were already in combat mode, but unlike the first time, she now knew how to retain full control of her actions and work in concert with the tactical computer inside her head. No one was going to die if she could help it.

That didn't mean she wouldn't seriously hurt someone. Like that bitch in command of these sadists.

The man coming out of the compartment barely had time to note her presence before she punched him in the diaphragm. His breath exploded out of his lungs as she ghosted past him.

Kelsey drew her stunner with her off hand as she stepped inside. The compartment was filled with people, most of whom were staring at her with shocked expressions.

"Hey there!" she said brightly. "Time to party!"

Her combat computer immediately flagged those who were armed and assisted her in aiming her stunner as she danced between two of the enemy. She had her primary target sighted and wasn't about to let the enemy commander escape retribution for the indignities she'd heaped on her friend.

The marines flooding in behind her made the outcome of this fight a foregone conclusion since no one was armed with anything more than a stunner. Their timing had been excellent.

That didn't stop a few people from bolting toward the compartment where they probably kept the lethal hardware and armor. Odds were good at least a few people were still in there too.

To her credit, the security commander tried to delay Kelsey while her people dove toward the real weapons.

"You!" the woman hissed as she swung at Kelsey's face.

Kelsey leaned her head just far enough to the side for the blow to miss before slamming the heel of her free hand into the woman's face like a hammer.

The woman's nose shattered under the blow, and she somersaulted backward, already unconscious even before she slammed full length into the deck.

Payback was a bitch.

Two men were hauling weapons out of the makeshift armory when Kelsey reached the hatch, but they were far too slow to stop her from stunning them or their friends the security commander had been trying to protect.

By the time she'd made sure the compartment was secure, the fight was over. A few of her people were down but only stunned. They'd knocked out the biggest threat to their dominance and capturing the ship suddenly became a lot more likely.

"All teams, status," Kelsey said over the com.

"We're at engineering," Veronica said. "We had a surprise a few corridors back so expect trouble."

As if summoned by the words, an alarm began hooting over the speakers. Don Sommerville's voice came on a moment later.

"Intruder alert. All hands repel boarders. They're near engineering."

Well, he was a little late for that, but it would still make things more exciting than Kelsey preferred.

"Cain, tell me you're about at the bridge," she said.

"Just got here. The hatch is closed and locked. Jason, can you open it?"

Moments later, the security specialist came on the channel. "Negative. They've manually locked it down. We've cut most of their controls, though. They're deaf and blind in there."

"They'll wait," Kelsey decided. "Veronica, we'll mop up the rest of the ship, but you've got to take engineering intact. We're counting on you."

With that, she killed the com and started directing her people to secure the weapons and to start clearing the ship of hostile crew. That would take a while, but without heavier weapons, the enemy was screwed. The ball was in Veronica Giguere's court now.

38

Talbot spun the old man around. "The fire is spreading, sir! Come on!"

The man tried to resist. "Let go of me! We have to clear out lab seven and eight."

"Can't. That's where the fire is."

Or it would be in a shade over five minutes.

Based on the way the man was dressed, he was an executive here. One that was bound and determined to run in where a bunch of plasma grenades would end him.

When the man made to argue more, Talbot clamped a hand over his mouth, picked him up, and ran for the exit. Awkward to say the least but not impossible when death was racing up behind him.

He didn't stop at the alley either. He kept running toward the cargo bay. He didn't stop until a low thump behind him told him the plasma grenades had detonated. Only then did he release the man.

Thankfully, the man was content with swearing at him and running back toward the now burning research center.

"The clock is ticking," Talbot said he gestured for the marines to set the unconscious security guards down. "We need to be gone before station security gets spun up."

Fifteen minutes later they were at the cargo bay. They got in without issue but found a large cluster of men and women in cargo-handling coveralls trying to bypass the locks on their cargo shuttle.

"Can we help you?" he asked dryly when he and his marines arrived behind them.

The group turned to him almost as one. They each had an expression of fearful despair on their faces.

One woman stepped forward. "Is this your shuttle? Please, take us with you. We can pay!"

He recognized the woman who'd given him a hard time smuggling the small ring onto the station. What had her name been? Associate Supervisor Franzen.

He was about to shut her down when Zia put a hand on his shoulder.

"We're not going to the planet," she said. "We're going to make a run for the outer system in our freighter. We might never get back here if we escape the system."

"We don't care," the woman said hoarsely. "Those Ghosts destroyed all the Fleet ships in the system and are on the way here. We don't want to be here when they arrive. We can work our way. We know cargo better than anyone else you'll ever meet. And we can pay. Whatever you want."

"Step away from the hatch," Talbot ordered, shooting Zia a look that expressed his basic disagreement with what she was doing. Not that he was going to dispute her right to make the call. She was the flag officer, after all.

He let her get inside and head for the shuttle's control area before he allowed the cargo handlers in. Even that was more than he'd bargained for as others came over and joined the first group once it became obvious the shuttle was about to depart the station.

If there'd been more people in the bay, he'd have had to start turning people away. Cargo shuttles could hold a lot, but even so, the large crowd only barely fit.

Talbot noted with some irony that there were a few station security uniforms in the crowd. Even a number of enlisted Fleet crewmen. All told there were probably a hundred people packed into the shuttle.

He entered with the last two marines and sealed the hatch behind him. "Search them. Confiscate anything that could be used as a weapon. We'll off-load them as soon as we get back to the freighter and lock them up."

That done, he joined Zia on the flight deck as she was lifting off. To be safe, he locked the hatch behind them and strapped into the copilot's couch just as she turned the shuttle to face the main bay hatch.

"Did we get clearance?" he asked.

"No one answered," she said as her hands moved across the controls. "I assume control has abandoned their stations because of the impending attack. Let's hope they didn't lock the hatch, or this will be a very short trip."

He felt his gut tighten, but the main hatch began opening before he had a chance to really get worried. It led into a massive airlock so they weren't clear just yet. Still, if one hatch opened, odds were good the other one would too.

A few minutes later they were clear of the station and on their way to the freighter. It had left orbit as soon as Zia signaled they were in space, so it took a bit longer to catch up with it than would be normal. With the incoming ships, it was best to be sure the freighter was one of many others running away, so he understood the need not to delay.

They docked with the freighter half an hour later, and he finally started breathing a bit easier. They still had to get clear of the system, but that was Zia's problem. Nothing he could do from this point forward would make a difference in their escape.

She unstrapped and stood. "I'm heading for the bridge. We'll boost for the outer system, away from the other freighter. The Clans should be busy with conquering Archibald and not worried about the scattering civilians. Get everything secured, including our new passengers. Then get some rest. I'll call you as soon as I get word from Kelsey."

Once Zia had departed, he directed the crew to start unloading the new prisoners. He had no idea what they'd do with these people once they got to Pandora, but that was a problem he could solve later. For now, he wanted a beer and a place to rest while he waited for word on wife and the rest.

* * *

VERONICA RAN behind the marines as they rushed toward main engineering. The crew there knew they were coming, and the hatch was already sliding closed.

The lead marine did the opposite of what Veronica would have expected and sped up, the feet of her powered armor gouging the deck as she launched herself at the shrinking opening. She sailed through the air sideways and bounced through the narrow opening right before the hatch slid shut with a clank reeking of finality.

"Lewandowski?" Zia shouted over the com. "Are you okay?"

"I'm a little busy. Hang on."

The next fifteen seconds dragged by before the hatch began opening. The opening revealed the marine threatening a group of crewmen with her armored fist from beside the hatch controls. They were trying to stun her with zero effect. The thick armor was proof against that.

Since the massive suits were immune to that kind of weapon, they didn't come equipped with them either, so Brenda Lewandowski had no way to stop the people attacking her without maiming or killing them. A standoff of sorts.

The balance of forces changed as the unarmored marines and recovery crew opened fire with their stunners. That quickly cleared the Rebel Empire forces nearest the hatch and got them into engineering.

"Suited marines, dig the enemy out of any pockets of resistance," Veronica ordered. "Everyone else back them up. Clear engineering before someone does something we can't fix."

Veronica led the charge to the drives. She figured the attack had been far too sudden to give anyone the idea of sabotage, but she wasn't going to take any chances when their future depended on it.

A few crewmen tried to use the drives as cover, but an armored marine simply tossed them out into the open where they were stunned. Veronica verified the drives were intact with a sigh. Then she went to make sure the fusion plants were equally secured.

Ten minutes later, she was reporting to Princess Kelsey that engineering was theirs. She'd heard that the bridge was locked down, but without Fleet security and their weapons, clearing the ship would be simple enough, if time consuming.

Of course, any strays might get their hands on a crate filled with weapons, so clearing the freighter quickly was critical.

She left two armored marines inside engineering. Her people would lock the hatch behind her and keep any intruders out. If someone somehow managed to blow the door, the marines would come down on them like an avalanche.

Two other armored marines would secure the Fleet security armory. The final two would join the search for holdouts.

She hoped it didn't come to it, but depressurizing sections of the ship was an effective method of flushing them out. Drop the pressure slowly while calling for anyone hiding to come out. When they couldn't breathe, people tended to see reason.

Her primary task done, Veronica took a couple of unarmored marines to guard her and headed for the bridge.

Princess Kelsey hadn't summoned her, but she owed it to Don to get him out of there alive. His friendship had meant a lot to her back then and she wouldn't allow him to die for the Lords.

She found Jason Young working on the hatch while Princess Kelsey and a team of armed marines and recovery specialists waited impatiently in the corridor nearby.

Veronica didn't have much hope for the man's success. The bridge hatches were designed to keep people out. They'd have to talk Don out or use plasma cutters to burn the hatch off.

"What's your status?" the princess asked as she approached.

"Engineering is secure," Veronica assured her. "I sent some armored marines to guard the Fleet security armory and others to help with the search. I came here to get Don out."

The short woman nodded. "You know him better than I do. Can we end this peacefully? We don't need bridge access right now, but it makes my spine itch to have hostile forces in there, even if all the primary systems are locked out. One never knows how resourceful they are."

"Don is *very* resourceful. We have a bond. Let me use it to save him."

Kelsey's eyebrows rose. "As in a romantic bond? That could prove awkward if he feels betrayed, since you… ah, betrayed him."

Veronica shook her head. "No, not that. He's not my type. I'm more into… well, that's not important right now. What matters is that we were friends. I can get him to surrender."

Princess Kelsey gestured toward the door. "The com at the hatch works. By all means, give it a try."

Veronica walked over to the com and pressed the button. A moment later, her friend's voice came from the speaker.

"We're not opening up."

"I really wish you would, Don. We don't want to hurt you. Quite the opposite, really."

There were a few moments of silence. "What are you doing, Veronica? I never saw you in the role of a traitor."

She leaned her back against the hatch. "Me, either. Then I found out the Lords had been lying to us all along. Enslaving us. Now I'm working with people determined to throw off the yokes of our electronic overlords.

"We've locked you out of all the critical systems. I'm sure you have hopes of regaining control of something. I'll grant that you're resourceful and can probably pull something off. What then? The Ghosts have control of this system, and neither one of us wants them to catch us, trust me on that."

Her friend sighed gustily. "You ruined a perfectly good escape and literally years of hard work and planning. Now you probably have most of my people out of action, and we're both going to pay the price for that. Why?"

"You're not the only one with secrets," she assured him. "We can and will get out of this system, if you don't screw up *our* plan."

When he didn't respond for a minute, she figured she'd failed and the conversation was over, but the hatch slid open. She stood and turned to face the bridge. All four men inside stood there, their hands raised high.

Princess Kelsey wasted no time in sending her marines in to secure them.

Don's eyes never left Veronica. "If you're working against the Lords, I deserve to know who you're working for."

Veronica gestured at Princess Kelsey. "Her. She's a descendant of people that escaped the Lords. They aren't Ghosts. They call themselves the New

Terran Empire. There are elements of resistance in our society, and she's working hard with some of them to help us free ourselves.

"We needed this ship because we had to steal something critical. We had no idea you were doing… whatever it is that you're doing here. What *are* you doing with all those flip drives, armored marine suits, and this ship? How did you even get it built?"

He considered Veronica for a few seconds before shaking his head. "I suppose the ship and its contents are more than enough to condemn us if you're working for the Lords, so I might as well take a chance you aren't lying. You know that resistance you mentioned? I work for them. I always have."

Veronica blinked in shock. "I… see. Then I suppose we need to sit down and have a long talk while Princess Kelsey gets us out of this system. We might still be able to be friends after all."

Don frowned at Kelsey. "Princess?"

"That's a *very* long story," the short woman assured him. "Let me get this ship on its way to safety, and we'll have lunch while we tell it. I'm starving."

39

Zia hadn't relaxed until all their ships had eluded the Clan warships in the system. She and her freighter hadn't drawn any pursuit, but Princess Kelsey had drawn the attention of the invaders.

They'd had to go far out into the outer system to be sure they'd escaped pursuit. It had taken more than a day for them to join Zia at the multiflip point with *Persephone* guarding her.

In that time, the Clans had consolidated their control over the Archibald system. More and more ships had continued to pour through the flip point, emphasizing the point that this war had been long planned. Raul Castille might have kicked it off with his unprovoked attack, but it would have happened anyway.

The invading forces had seized control of the station, but the Rebel Empire had chosen to blow up the shipyard just before the Clans reached orbit. At least after the chaos of the attack, no one would put together what they'd done.

Fiona hadn't had to destroy the FTL com. The Rebel Empire had done it for them. Sadly, they'd lost the large transport rings. Carl was despondent, and she wasn't much better.

He'd thrown himself into going over everything they'd stolen. She hoped it was worth the loss they'd suffered.

If Commander Sommerville was to be believed, he was working for the resistance and had stuffed the Q-ship with all kinds of illicit goodies. He wasn't saying where he'd intended to take it all, but he'd seemed fairly certain he could get it out of the system.

She supposed it was possible they knew about the far flip points, but he wasn't saying. Maybe once he laid eyes on *Audacious* he'd be more forthcoming.

They dropped an FTL probe to keep an eye on the Archibald system and flipped back to Pandora. The Q-ship was large, though not as big as her carrier. Carl assured them that this segment of the multiflip point could handle something that size, but she still fretted until they were all safely across and in orbit around the planet.

She virtually snagged Carl by the ear and had him move her ship's new flip drive over to the carrier. Getting it into engineering wasn't a simple task, but a few hours later, her people were maneuvering it into place. They'd had no reason to leave the old one there, so it had been removed while they were gone.

"How long will the installation take?" she asked her chief engineer, Commander Tony Hastert. "Not that we're about to rush off or anything."

"Getting it into the compartment was the difficult part," he assured her. "The unit is basically plug-and-play on a massive scale. We'll have it locked down and fully connected in a shift. I'd prefer to spend another shift testing it before we head to a flip point to make absolutely sure it's working correctly.

"We'll want to flip into an empty system to test out the frequency modulator that Carl built into it. That's unproven. We'll flip once without it and then use the tuner on the way back. At that point, I'll declare us fully fit for action, barring any issues."

Being fully operational in a day sounded excellent to her. "Call me if you run into any problems."

She was about to head for the flag bridge to get an updated tactical briefing when her com chimed with an incoming call. It was Carl.

"What now?" she almost barked. "What else has gone wrong?"

The scientist shook his head sadly. "Someone needs a nap. In fact, we have some good news for a change. Can you come down to my lab?"

Zia considered begging off, but decided she needed to know what he'd found. It might have a bearing on the briefing she'd been planning.

"I'll be right there."

Ten minutes later, she was ensconced in his office. It wasn't much of an office as he didn't have a desk, just more workstations, so she snagged a rolling chair and sat. "Talk to me."

He grabbed an identical chair and settled in across from her. "The researchers have been continuing to work on the FTL anomaly while we were at Archibald. They made a breakthrough right after we got back. It's a big one and has implications on what we do going forward."

When he stopped talking, she gestured for him to continue. "Don't make me drag this out of you. What did they find, and why do I need to know about it right now?"

He smiled widely at her. "They discovered the communications throughput was going down because they'd found a way to enhance the range. That's the tradeoff. Longer range means less bandwidth.

"They tested it by selecting an FTL pair where the other end was far outside our normal transmission range. They couldn't send a message, but they pulsed it to see if they got a status response on the quantumly entangled pairs. They did."

Zia blinked at him. "Are you telling me that we can talk to someone back home? Seriously?"

"Not exactly," he cautioned. "We know the paired com detected its other half, but that end isn't configured correctly to link up with it. I doubt an actual call would be successful without some reconfiguring on the other end.

"The hardest part will be making them aware of us at all. There's likely no indication on that end that we've tagged them for a status. The coms weren't designed to make anyone aware of that sort of thing."

"So, let me see if I understand," Zia said slowly. "We know that we can potentially communicate with home, but we need to somehow make them aware we're out here. They would have no reason to look more deeply because they know we're far too distant and a real call from us would cause their com to signal them."

He nodded. "That's about it. I have a few ideas that might bear fruit, but it's going to be hard going. Also, it's not all the coms at home. It's a single com. We've tried others, but the range limitation is still too great.

"That said, I think you'll be pleased to hear which com we've connected to. The researchers had no luck with the ones on *Audacious*, so they started working the sets aboard *Persephone* as soon as we got back into orbit. They hit pay dirt with the one Admiral Mertz keeps with him that's linked to a special one for Kelsey."

Zia felt her eyes widen. "That's terrific! If anyone can help us get home, it's Admiral Mertz. It's kind of odd that his com is the only one in range, though. What about *Invincible*?"

Carl shook his head. "No dice there. Wherever the admiral is, he isn't aboard *Invincible* or any of the other ships we have FTL coms for. I'd wager, based on the timing, that he's in the captured destroyer giving the report about Harrison's World to the Rebel Empire."

That made sense. It also gave them an opportunity with a limited shelf life. The admiral would deliver his report and go home as quickly as he could.

"Keep working on this," she ordered. "Make it priority one."

"I have everyone working on it," he assured her. "We'll figure this out."

Zia checked her internal chronometer. The briefing could wait. Kelsey would want to hear about this right away.

* * *

KELSEY WATCHED Don Sommerville stare at Derek while Veronica explained where they were and what the New Terran Empire was all about. Since the Rebel Empire had no history with aliens, the man's poleaxed expression made sense.

The Pandoran prince and his human friend Jacob Howell had been waiting for them, and it tickled Kelsey's sense of fancy to have them there for the briefing. They were still curious about their new associates, and it wouldn't hurt to have them see the Rebel Empire was made up of normal people too.

She still hadn't told anyone what the doctor had told her about the Pandoran DNA. It might be a long while before she felt comfortable with the revelation. In any case, at some point they'd be leaving, and it would hardly be worth wrecking the Pandorans' view of themselves before setting off.

Veronica was just finishing her basic overview of the New Terran Empire but hadn't started on how she'd been captured when Zia arrived. Kelsey left her to it when the commodore gestured for her to join her in the corridor.

"What's up?" she asked when they were alone.

Zia proceeded to fill her in on what Carl had told her.

When the other woman finished, Kelsey was grinning. "Carl will figure out how to make contact. We need to start prepping for departure. Even if we don't leave today, it won't be very long."

"I want to go with you," Jacob said from the hatch. He'd slipped up on them quietly and must've overheard most of what they'd said.

She turned to face the man. "We'll be going a long way from here, and I can't say that I'll ever come back, though the Empire might eventually send someone. That could mean a one-way trip. I'm sorry, but no."

"Don't you think that's my decision to make?" he asked seriously. "And I know that Derek will insist that he and some of his people come along. We've heard stories of the Clans for decades. Now those crazy bastards are on the loose. Add in the Rebel Empire, and our people have to know what's going on and do our part to set things right."

Kelsey started to reject him again, but Zia put a hand on her shoulder. "Maybe he has a point. In any case, if his people want to send a group back to the New Terran Empire, we should consider it."

"All I ask is that you consider my words," Jacob said as he bowed his way back into the compartment. "I'll leave you to discuss things without prying ears."

She didn't have to make a decision right this moment. Instead, she turned her head back to Zia.

"How goes the flip drive replacement?"

"So far, so good. We'll know by tomorrow if all this was worth it."

Kelsey laughed. "It was worth it. I've been looking over the master manifest on the Q-ship. Add in the ship itself, and we've come out a lot better than when we started.

"Doctor Zoboroski tells me that he's relatively satisfied that the new regenerator will be effective on Commodore Murdock. Doctor Lipp is helping with that. Not that we can trust her very far, mind you. She's a spy.

"On the positive side, even with the loss of the large transport ring, we have the Singularity computer and its data. That's going to be fascinating. I can't help but wonder what it might tell us that bears on our Singularity prisoner. Or how his tune might change if he knew we had it."

"The next few days should be interesting," Zia agreed.

Kelsey excused herself and sent a message to Veronica that she'd be elsewhere. She needed to get a handle on what they did next. Wherever Jared was, she had to find a path to him via multiflip points and far flip points. The regular network was far too dangerous.

They'd have to start mapping with FTL probes and that meant sending *Persephone*. Now that Angela was a fully operational Marine Raider, Kelsey could pass command of the ship to her.

Not that she really wanted to, but she had to focus on the larger picture. And it was time to start Talbot along the path to being a Marine Raider. Once he was done, they'd expand the program to the rest of the marines he thought were suitable.

So much to do, so little time.

Kelsey found that her feet had taken her to her quarters. Talbot was in there, she knew. She set the door and her implants to "disturb only if something important is on fire" and slipped quietly inside.

Tomorrow's problems would still be there tomorrow. She needed to celebrate their successes today. Besides, once he started the surgeries, Talbot wouldn't feel much like making love. She needed him now and the rest of the universe would have to wait.

MAILING LIST

Want more? Grab any of Terry's other books below.

Want Terry to email you when he publishes a new book in any format or when one goes on sale? Go to TerryMixon.com/Mailing-List and sign up. Those are the only times he'll contact you. No spam.

Did you enjoy the book? Please leave a review on Amazon or Goodreads. It only takes a minute to dash off a few sentences and that kind of thing helps more than you can imagine.

You can always find the most up to date listing of Terry's titles on his Amazon Author Page.

The Empire of Bones Saga
Empire of Bones
Veil of Shadows
Command Decisions
Ghosts of Empire
Paying the Price
Reconnaissance in Force
Behind Enemy Lines
The Terra Gambit
Hidden Enemies

The Empire of Bones Saga Volume 1

The Humanity Unlimited Saga
Liberty Station
Freedom Express
Tree of Liberty

The Fractured Republic Saga
Storm Divers

The Scorched Earth Saga
Scorched Earth

The Vigilante Duology with Glynn Stewart
Heart of Vengeance
Oath of Vengeance

ABOUT TERRY

#1 Bestselling Military Science Fiction author Terry Mixon served as a non-commissioned officer in the United States Army 101st Airborne Division. He later worked alongside the flight controllers in the Mission Control Center at the NASA Johnson Space Center supporting the Space Shuttle, the International Space Station, and other human spaceflight projects.

He now writes full time while living in Texas with his lovely wife and a pounce of cats.

www.TerryMixon.com
Terry@terrymixon.com

http://www.facebook.com/TerryLMixon

https://www.amazon.com/Terry-Mixon/e/B00J15TJFM

Made in the USA
San Bernardino,
CA